Cocktails, Rock Tales & Betrayals

JULIE ARCHER

Copyright © 2016 Julie Archer

Jewel & Black Publications

All rights reserved.

ISBN: 0995600503
ISBN-13: 978-0995600508

Publisher's Note

This is a work of fiction. Names, characters, places and incidents are either the products of the author's imagination or are used fictitiously, and any resemblance to actual persons, living or dead, business establishments, events, or locales is entirely coincidental.

DEDICATION

For everyone that believed in me…

CHAPTER ONE

Even though the time was right, Caro Flynn was finding it hard to let go.

Tears pricked her eyes as she glanced around The Roca Bar for the last time, memories threatening to overwhelm her; the good, the bad, and the utterly heart-wrenching. It had, after all, been her home for the past five years since graduation.

But the moment had come; there was no turning back.

She knew that she would miss it dreadfully. Miss the friends she had made, Mariella in particular, who was her closest friend on the island. Miss the dramas and holiday romances - not always hers.

"You take good care of the place," she said to the new owners, a couple of ex-pats who had been regular visitors and had fancied retiring to run a bar, handing them the set of master keys that were never far from her side. A pang of bittersweetness overwhelmed her. "And look after Mariella too. Don't work her too hard; she isn't used to it."

She took one final look around the bar, so different now from when she had first walked in and started working there. The Roca Bar was a club in the Alcudia region of Mallorca, at best half-full on a good night but mostly pretty empty before Caro took it over. She surveyed all the changes that she had made to make it the success it was now. Her heart swelled with pride at what she had achieved.

But the decision had finally been made, after many hours of agonising and several changes of heart, to leave.

The opportunity to replicate what she had done with The Roca Bar back in North Ridge, where she had gone to university, had become too much of a lure.

Caro felt a brief twinge of guilt overtake the sadness as she left. While she hadn't exactly lied to Mariella about why she wasn't going clubbing with everyone after her leaving party, it wasn't quite time to call it a night. She wanted to spend her last few hours on the island alone.

Instead of heading back to the apartment she shared with Mariella, Caro headed off to Juju's. Juju's was a popular bar with locals and tourists alike, which often hosted open mic nights and karaoke. It was one of her favourite places and she loved spending time there listening to music and watching musicians perform. Set just off the main square in the centre of town, it had a cavernlike appearance, with stone walls, low tables made from old beer barrels, and a bar top hewn from local granite. Although there was a pretty big crowd at the bar, she was able to find herself a spot near the back of the room to watch the evening's entertainment with a large glass of the local Mortitx rosé wine.

There were a few people having a go at singing, with varying levels of success, which usually related to their level of drunkenness. A bleached-blonde girl, bursting out of a skintight lycra dress, was currently murdering something that sounded like Taylor Swift, although Caro couldn't be sure, such was the quality of the sound. After a few aborted attempts, the girl finally gave up, making way for a singer with an acoustic guitar, who caught Caro's attention despite the screech of feedback that reverberated through the room as he adjusted the microphone.

"Good evening," he said, "and thanks for taking the time to listen to me." His eyes fell on Caro, and although she was sitting at the back of the crowd, she could see him smile at her. Tapping his foot to count himself in, he started to sing.

Caro's eyes narrowed. His voice was soft, evocative, strong.

And familiar.

She couldn't put her finger on where, but she had heard it before.

She studied him. Long dark hair framed his face; a face with exquisite cheekbones that wouldn't have been out of place on a male model, although somewhat hidden by a week or so's worth of beard. And deeply intense, piercing blue-grey eyes, that she could easily get lost staring into, behind a pair of plain, black-framed glasses. He was dressed in skinny dark blue jeans and a simple, long-sleeved black t-shirt, blending in with the holidaymakers' style, but just different enough to make him stand out.

It was clear he knew how to command an audience. The female contingent appeared enthralled as he sang, and even the majority of men were nodding or singing as he ran through a few popular covers. Caro couldn't remember the last time that Juju's had witnessed someone so talented.

Searching the depths of her brain, she wondered again where she recognised him from.

After he finished his last song, he spoke again.

"Thanks for being a fantastic audience tonight. I wonder if you might indulge me and let me sing one last song, something I've written myself."

There was a general murmur of agreement. He'd been entertaining enough and, by the sounds of his guitar skills, wasn't about to play anything too offensive.

He started to play again, plucking the strings with more passion and confidence than he had done when doing the covers.

Caro watched, spellbound, as he became lost in his own world, not realising that she was actually holding her breath. She closed her eyes and let the sounds wash over her; his warm, chocolatey voice causing her body to melt.

All too soon it was over and he received rapturous applause. Caro's eyes flew open and she watched several members of the audience flock round him, congratulating him on the set and asking questions. Caro reluctantly turned her attention back to her drink, wanting to stay, yet knowing she ought to leave. She fiddled with the stem of her empty wine glass, looking at the crowd at the bar.

"Can I buy you another?"

She turned and stared directly into those intense, blue grey eyes.

And drowned.

He held out his hand. "I'm Nate."

Caro hesitated for a moment. One of the perils of being known around the island was that people tended to treat her differently; particularly musicians who had heard of her through the nights she ran at The Roca Bar, as they always wanted to know if she could get them a gig. Usually, she had to tell them to politely fuck off. But Nate appeared perfectly genuine, not to mention incredibly talented, and she didn't want to risk spoiling a good night.

"Olivia," she said, giving him the name of her best friend back in North Ridge. She was leaving early in the morning; she would never have to explain. "And yes, I'd love another glass of wine, thank you."

Nate and "Olivia" ended up talking late into the night, until the bar staff were tidying up around them. Three bottles of wine had disappeared, the ashtray on the table was overflowing, and the conversation had drifted along almost as freely as the alcohol. They talked about everything, but each managed to deflect anything personal with questions that sent the other off in a totally different direction or ended up in glasses being refilled or more cigarettes being lit. It felt perfectly natural when Nate reached for Caro's hand to study the infinity tattoo on the inside of her wrist, and stroked the skin there, before massaging her palm with his thumb.

After the bar staff politely asked them to leave, they walked hand in hand along the seafront, looking like any other couple on a romantic holiday.

Coming to a halt outside Hoposa Uyal, one of Puerto Pollensa's most popular hotels, Nate gestured to the building.

"This is me."

Caro nodded, not surprised that he would be staying somewhere like that. She wondered whether he had a roommate or hordes of friends that would be waiting for him to come back. She found herself hoping that he didn't.

They stood awkwardly outside the door. Caro wasn't sure whether she should make the first move, but wasn't ready for the evening to end.

Nate traced a finger along Caro's jawline, causing a tingle to course down her spine, pooling at her groin.

It had been the lightest of touches, but at that moment, she knew she wanted him. Taking the initiative, she reached into the pocket of his jeans and located his room key, dangling it in front of him.

"Your place?" she said, with a small smile.

He all but dragged her up the stairs to the second floor.

They crashed through the door to his room, not giving any thought to the occupants on either side, kissing wildly, hands everywhere; touching, stroking, caressing. Gently pushing him away, she kicked off her sandals and peeled off her white and black butterfly-patterned dress, revealing beautiful black lace lingerie and a voluptuous figure; full, creamy breasts, a tapering waist and curvy hips.

Sliding in behind her and discarding his glasses, Nate pulled her caramel-streaked hair free from its messy bun, tracing a line of kisses along her shoulder blade and up to the sweet spot behind her ear. She shivered involuntarily as his beard scratched her skin, feeling his guitar-calloused fingers stroking the tiny intertwined letters of 'C' and 'J' tattooed at the base of her neck, intertwined with thorns. She hoped he wouldn't ask what it meant.

She turned and pulled his t-shirt over his head, revealing his own set of inks, and she immediately realised why he had been wearing a long-sleeved shirt. Intricate designs covered his chest and ran down his arms, meaning that he would be judged before even opening his mouth. They intrigued her. She wondered what each of them meant to him, if they had their own significance like hers. Running her hands over his chest, she caught his nipple ring with the nail of her index finger and dropped her head, circling the sensitive skin around it with her tongue, feeling him getting harder against her. He unbuttoned his jeans as the two of them fell on the bed, quickly pulling on a condom before the moment was lost.

It was brief, it was dirty, but as the crashing orgasm they shared subsided, it appeared to unlock a release Caro hadn't realised she needed.

* * *

Caro woke abruptly some time later, momentarily confused by her surroundings. Where was she? As the room came into focus, she realised she was in a hotel. And that she wasn't alone.

Glancing over at Nate, who was snoring softly beside her, she remembered the glorious end to the previous evening. She gently traced the outline of one of the tattoos on his shoulder with her fingernail and watched him twitch, but not stir. Reaching into her bag for her mobile to check the time, she spotted numerous missed calls from Mariella. It was just after ten and she was due to fly out from Palma at one.

"Shit!" She grabbed her clothes and hurriedly pulled them on. She debated whether to leave Nate a note but couldn't find anything to write with. They hadn't swapped numbers and she couldn't see his phone to text herself his details.

Then she remembered that she'd lied about her name.

It was highly unlikely that she would ever see him again, so she quietly let herself out of the room, a smile creeping across her face.

That was certainly one way to remember her last night in Mallorca.

* * *

"Where the hell have you been? I've been out of my mind with worry, your last night on the island and I didn't know where you were..."

Mariella had already packed the last of Caro's things and was standing, arms crossed, in the centre of their living room. She reminded Caro of how her mother reacted to her nights out when she had been a teenager. Or at least she would have if she hadn't been wearing denim hot pants and a tiny crop top that was knotted under her breasts; not exactly the most maternal of outfits.

"And you're wearing last night's clothes. Who did you hook up with?" she said. "Was it Paulo?"

Caro was already stripping off her dress, heading into the bathroom for the quickest shower ever, and chose not to answer. "I'll tell you all about it later," she said. "I'll be ready to go in a few minutes."

She made the flight with moments to spare, after yet another tearful goodbye with Mariella. She'd had to call in a favour from one of her taxi driver friends to get her to the airport as quick as possible.

Being the last person on the plane was never a fun experience, and Caro slunk into her aisle seat, trying to be as invisible as possible, as the passengers surrounding her in business class threw poisonous glances her way. Even the cabin crew had been overtly frosty. The business man she was seated next to was already snoozing as the plane took off, and she was grateful for that. The last thing she needed was someone giving her more grief about why the plane was late. When the crew finally came round with the drinks trolley, Caro gladly accepted a glass of wine from the steward, despite the beginnings of a creeping hangover.

She couldn't stop thinking about Nate, how they had talked and talked. And connected. Had things been different, she would certainly have left him her number.

With a sigh, she put on her headphones and pulled a copy of *Roccia* from her bag and idly began flicking through the pages to pass the time. A short article in the news section about North Ridge caught her eye. She took a large sip of wine a read on, always interested to read about new local talent.

Recently signed to Numb Records, Alik Thorne and the rest of the Blood Stone Riot boys play their last gig at The Vegas in North Ridge next week before decamping to record their as yet untitled four-track EP at the renowned Newcomen Farm studios.

Set for release in the next few months, the band are also to film their first video to accompany the title track, "Bleed Like Cyanide," in addition to playing a number of low-key showcase gigs in preparation for their debut appearance at the Wilde Park Festival.

Caro almost spat out her wine in shock as she re-read the article and studied the picture that accompanied it more closely. There was a black and white photograph of a singer, caught by the camera snarling into the microphone. He was wildly attractive, with chiselled cheekbones, eyes flashing with passion, and bare-chested, showing an array of tattoos and a nipple ring.

She knew she had seen him before.

Knew that she had recognised his voice from somewhere.

In the magazine shot, he was clean-shaven and his hair was shorter, and he wasn't wearing glasses; looking totally different to the man she had left in bed that morning. But she certainly recognised the tattoos, having spent time up close and personal with them.

With him.

He had lied.

His name wasn't Nate.

Suddenly Caro was acutely aware of the fact that she had just slept with one of the hottest new properties in rock music.

Shit.

CHAPTER TWO

As Caro finally swept through the arrivals hall at Heathrow, almost two hours late because her plane had circled over the airport due to stacking, she wondered what her business partner, Nic Santino, had been doing to pass the time. She had gratefully accepted the offer from Nic to collect her, sparing her from senseless conversation with a taxi driver or waiting ages for the RailAir bus. Under most circumstances, she knew he'd be going stir crazy with boredom, but with the chaos of the club over recent weeks, she suspected he'd probably kicked back with another coffee and a copy of *GQ*. Or been ogling Antipodean tourists.

At least they would now be in the same country. Despite Skype, emails, and conference calls being the main staple of their relationship over the last couple of months, actually being in the same room when it came to choosing decor, soft furnishings, or light fittings was going to make such a difference. Particularly as they'd left quite a lot to the last minute. Such as recruiting staff.

She jostled with the mostly dark-suited men flowing through the door to the arrivals hall. Dressed all in white - linen trousers, a cotton camisole, and a pashmina thrown around her shoulders - she stood out beautifully, despite being totally inappropriately dressed for the weather she was coming back to. Her sun-streaked hair tumbled around her shoulders, held off her face by a pair of massive designer sunglasses. As usual, she was completely oblivious to the wistful glances of the men around her, contrasted with the glares of the wives and girlfriends wondering if their other half had been the lucky one to be seated next to the beauty.

What they didn't know was that she'd pretty much slept for the majority of the flight, giving in to the inevitable hangover brought on by her leaving party and realising the identity of her one-night stand.

Transferring the large oak leather Mulberry hobo from one shoulder to another, she craned her neck trying to see Nic.

Anyone witnessing their reunion would have assumed they were a couple, given that Caro practically leapt on Nic, wrapping her long legs around him and kissing him full on the mouth. With his tightly-muscled frame - a result of hours spent in the gym - long blond hair, and green eyes behind tortoiseshell-framed glasses, he wasn't short of admirers.

She could almost hear the collective sigh of relief from the waiting wives.

"Travelling light, I see," said Nic, indicating her small suitcase as he lowered her back towards the floor.

"A couple of t-shirts and a string bikini doesn't really take up a great deal of room," said Caro, laughing. "Although I definitely need to buy more clothes, it's freezing over here." She grabbed the sweater that Nic had slung round his shoulders and pulled it on, before wrapping the pashmina back around her body. "I'm getting some stuff shipped back once I know where I'm staying permanently."

Nic took her suitcase and marched off in the direction of the car park.

"You're in a rush, got a hot date or something?" she said. "Oh, no, wait, Olivia's said she'll be home by the time we get back."

When Caro had first heard about Nic dating Olivia, she had been both pleased and scared. Olivia Cole was Caro's oldest and best friend. They went way back to university days and had been firm friends since they were put into a group project in their first term of their media degree. The two of them ended up doing all the work, staying up late into the night to complete the mock up of a new music magazine, which had won them all distinctions. Olivia was now a freelance PR consultant, picking up a diverse portfolio of clients from an amazing propensity to network after a short, but successful agency-based career.

Caro and Nic had first met in Ibiza after Caro had graduated, and had embarked on a passionate, but tumultuous, affair. After numerous arguments, followed by fantastic make-up sex, they both realised that they worked better as friends and ultimately business partners. Several years later, they were still extremely close and cared about who the other got involved with.

Nic and Olivia getting together meant that they both knew things about Caro that she didn't necessarily want the other to know. Delighted as she was that they were together, she lived in fear of her deepest, darkest secrets coming out.

"She said she'd try to be back," Nic said. "But you know what she's like with work. And I don't want to get stuck in traffic. I thought you'd probably want a quiet night tonight, we can just get a take away and chill."

"I'm fine," Caro said. "I didn't have a late one last night, I'm not that tired. But it's okay for me to stay with you for a while until I'm settled?" They had touched on her living arrangements in the last week and Nic had offered her his spare room until she found somewhere else.

Nic nodded. "Sure, I know you'll get sorted soon."

Despite Caro's protestations that she wasn't tired, it took her all of about five minutes to fall asleep in the car, only opening her eyes when the engine was switched off.

"God, Nic, I'm so sorry, I didn't realise I'd dropped off. That must have been such a dull journey for you." Caro gave a catlike stretch, trying to muster the energy to get out of the car.

He laughed. "Don't worry, your snoring is still as delightful as ever."

They ambled round to Nic's flat. He still lived in the university district of North Ridge, which suited him well when he needed people to go to a gig or hang out in a club. But not so good when he had an early meeting with a solicitor and was kept up until all hours by banging drum-and-bass music.

While Caro installed herself in the spare room, her sparse amount of belongings exploding all over the bed as she looked for some warmer clothes to wear, Nic ordered Chinese food from the takeaway down the road.

Thirty minutes later, Caro had showered and the two of them were curled up on the sofa, boxes of noodles in their hands and a bottle of red on the go, music videos on the TV turned down low in the background.

Nic's phone beeped. He rolled his eyes as he read Olivia's text aloud to Caro, telling him she was working late and would be going back to her place that night. "She said to give her a ring though," he said. "Honestly, since she's started working for herself, I barely see her."

"Shows she made the right decision though, she's obviously getting some decent clients."

"Mmm," said Nic, as Caro scrabbled under a cushion for her phone. She switched it on to activate the UK network, making a mental note to get a new one. Almost immediately her phone chirruped into life with a message from Mariella saying how much she missed Caro already, and a couple of missed calls from Olivia.

Returning Olivia's call, Caro waited for her to answer.

"Caro!" Olivia squealed down the phone. "You're back! I can't wait to see you - you'll never believe who I've just scored a contract with..."

"I gather from Nic you're really in demand. Knowing you it could be anyone, just tell me!"

"Numb Records. They want me to work with Blood Stone Riot on their debut release."

Caro went cold. She hadn't expected to hear of Alik Thorne again - well, at least not so close to home. "Really? Blood Stone Riot? That's really cool, Olivia, congratulations." She hoped she didn't sound odd.

Nic looked up from his phone where he'd been checking email.

Caro arranged to have lunch with Olivia in Sarastro, a popular restaurant in the centre of North Ridge, the following day, before they ended their call.

"So Olivia's told you about Blood Stone Riot," Nic said. "And guess where they're going to be shooting part of their video? Yep, in our club." He beamed. "She thought it would be great for both of us; word should get round about The Indigo Lounge and when the video comes out we'll get more trade. They may even be up for playing opening night."

Caro nodded. She didn't want to think about Alik Thorne right now. Putting him firmly out of her mind, she turned her attention to the text that had arrived when she was on the phone to Olivia. The text was from Jonny Tyler, club promoter and Caro's on-off boyfriend.

"Jonny wants me to see a band with him tomorrow night." She avoided Nic's gaze, knowing what he thought of her relationship with the promoter. Although 'relationship' was probably too strong a word; 'friends with benefits' probably summed it up better. The easy, no strings, on again, off again that came with two people that knew each other intimately, but didn't want to make a commitment. Jonny had shown up in Mallorca on several occasions for a day or two. They had spent most of the time in bed or out at clubs and it suited them fine.

Caro knew Nic disapproved because he thought that she could do better.

But he didn't know about her most recent dalliance with the up and coming rock star. The up and coming rock star that was going to be around a lot.

Something that, right now, seemed best to keep to herself.

CHAPTER THREE

Having spent the last few years getting up around lunchtime and starting work mid-afternoon, it came as a bit of a shock to Caro to be up and in the office by ten o'clock. Nic had woken her shortly before eight and she'd struggled to remember where she was for the second morning running. After a quick cold shower, Caro selected an outfit from her meagre wardrobe. As she pulled on her jacket, she made a promise to herself that she would go shopping soon. She met Nic at the front door and they walked to the club together. It was Caro's first time actually seeing the club in the flesh - she'd seen plenty of pictures and floor plans over the past few weeks, but still felt excited.

The building itself was in a row of other bars and restaurants just outside of the main shopping hub of North Ridge, plain from the outside with big, black doors, which Caro had already decided should be painted indigo. Once inside, there was a large open space which they had decided would be akin to a reception area, with a cloakroom off it, before another set of doors which led into the main bar. This was dominated at the far end by a stage big enough to hold a decent sized band and all their equipment, but still small enough to have a slightly intimate feel to it. On the left hand side was a wide bar, with mirrors behind it to make the room look twice the size. Upstairs was the small and cosy balconied VIP lounge, as well as the facilities; Caro had insisted that the ladies be far more glamorous and spacious than all the other bars she frequented. There was a further flight of stairs led up to the top floor, which housed their office.

The office was open plan and took up the entire loft space. Caro and Nic each had a desk and there was a further table that held a lot of architect's plans and other paperwork, as well as a big, overstuffed, leather sofa. There was still quite a lot of work to be done and there were workmen, tools, dust, and general chaos everywhere.

Caro read through a pile of CVs from applicants for their bar manager job. "Urgh, can't people write a decent sentence anymore?" she complained, discarding the latest application.

"You look like you need this," said Nic, placing a large cup of black coffee in front of Caro.

She gratefully took a sip of the too-hot liquid before turning her attention to swatches of fabric that were her choices for the couches for the VIP area. "I'd forgotten what it's like to have a dearth of candidates. In The Roca Bar, you were tripping over people who wanted to work there."

"Wasn't that just because they didn't want to go home?"

Caro threw a balled-up piece of paper at Nic's head. "Ha, ha, you're funny. Where's the latest project plan anyway? I need to know when we have to interview."

Nic rooted around on the spare desk, finally unearthing the document he was looking for. He smoothed it down in front of Caro and she started checking dates against the calendar. As they counted the days and weeks off, there was a sudden realisation that the opening was a hell of a lot closer than either of them had anticipated, and panic started to set in. It had been increasingly difficult over the last couple of months to try to do everything remotely, despite access to the best technology enablers. Nic had been the one in situ taking all the meetings and making all the applications with the planners, the council, the builders, and the decorators. Caro had been the one doing a lot of the online snagging and getting things delivered to Nic, despite not always being able to see the products she was buying.

This had resulted in a random delivery of massive, bean bag-sized cushions, because Caro hadn't translated the measurements correctly. And while they thought there was some merit in the punters lounging around, it didn't really fit with the dynamic, rock-themed bar they were creating. Logic and sense took over and they started to make a list of everything that needed doing on a series of Post-It notes, sticking them up on the wall in some sort of order that led up to the opening. Staffing was definitely going to be an issue if they wanted to take on someone who had to give notice elsewhere, meaning that task suddenly moved up the priority list. They created piles of CVs for bar staff, security staff, cleaning staff, and general staff, with Caro taking overall responsibility for the task. She curled up on the sofa and started reading, creating piles of CVs for the people she wanted to interview and those they would reject. There was some semblance of order when her mobile rang.

"You're still free for lunch, right?" said Olivia, cutting right to the chase. "We have to catch up before tonight."

Caro looked over at Nic. "If we can agree on a shortlist for interviews, then I think Nic might let me out to play..."

"I'm guessing that's Olivia?" said Nic, as he looked up from the brewery price list he was studying.

Caro nodded. "Lunch...and maybe some shopping too? I need something to wear this evening. My wardrobe is more beach chic than city chic right now and I don't think a sarong is going to cut it somehow."

"You could always start a new trend. Look what it did for David Beckham," said Olivia.

"Somehow not quite in that league. I'll see you later."

* * *

Sarastro was heaving, as usual. As one of North Ridge's most popular restaurants, it attracted a wide range of clientele, from ladies who lunched and men on business, to students and couples and families. Even on a weekday lunchtime, it was almost impossible to get a table. Impossible unless you had been terribly organised, like Olivia, and had the foresight to book. Caro swept past the waiting line, straight to the maitre d, causing grumbles and dirty looks from the people who were queuing, as she advised him that she was meeting a friend.

The waiter reviewed the booking sheet, located Olivia's name and crossed off the details with a flourish. "Of course, madam, follow me."

He led her through to the back of the restaurant, where it was quieter and there was more space. Olivia was sitting at a table, studying a menu as she waited for Caro to arrive.

"Your guest, madam."

Olivia leapt up and threw her arms around Caro. "Oh my God, it's so good to have you back home! You've been gone for so long!"

In reality, it had probably only been about six weeks since they had last seen each other, during Olivia's last free trip to Mallorca. But her sentiment felt genuine.

Caro hugged Olivia back with equal enthusiasm. "And you look pretty hot." She held Olivia at arm's length and took in the smartly styled glossy dark brown hair, the tight navy cigarette pants, the stylishly-embroidered top and the perfectly made-up face. Working for herself obviously suited her.

"You don't look so bad yourself, considering you arrived back here last night and I doubt that you had an early one the night before."

As they sat down, Caro debated whether or not to tell Olivia what had happened with Alik Thorne. She was just about to say something when Olivia spoke.

"It's just crazy working with Edie Spencer-Newman and Alik Thorne. Talk about a power couple. I mean, I thought I was lucky to have landed the gig with Edie, but when she spoke to a couple of people and, I don't know, maybe greased a couple of palms or something, before I knew it, I was in Numb's offices talking to Parker Roberts about PR for Blood Stone Riot!" Olivia gestured to a waiter and ordered them a bottle of rosé. "One minute I'm talking about jewellery and lingerie and the next about black metal. It's mad!"

Caro was vaguely aware of Edie, but hearing that she was Alik Thorne's other half was news to her. He hadn't mentioned a girlfriend when they'd been together. Edie had been Olivia's first client and they had celebrated her winning the contract with way too much sangria the last time they'd been together. She had read something in a gossip mag about the vintage shop Edie was opening, but had dismissed it as nothing more than another pretty little rich girl dabbling in business.

"How much time do you spend with them?" asked Caro.

Olivia shrugged. "I've spent a lot of time in the shop or with Edie lately because it's not long until The Magpie's launch. I haven't met Blood Stone Riot properly yet, but I think Alik has been hanging out at the club with Nic."

Caro sighed. She thought it best not to mention her liaison to Olivia. She didn't want to put her friend in a difficult situation and it was likely that Alik wouldn't remember her anyway.

They spent the next few hours chatting, eating, and drinking as the lunchtime trade ebbed and flowed around them. Olivia explained that since landing the two lucrative contracts, she had been able to strike out on her own and it was now 'Olivia Cole, owner of The OC PR' rather than 'Olivia Cole, PR Manager for The View Consultancy.' Caro knew that Olivia's time at The View Consultancy had been hard. She had been constantly undermined by two old-school partners who thought that a young lady had no place in their boys' network, even though she regularly brought in high-profile clients and high-worth deals. It was, thought Caro, slightly risky working with just one couple, but she assured Olivia that she would get more clients - she always had in the past. Caro shared her excitement about returning to North Ridge and starting out with Nic. It felt like it was a new beginning for both of them.

They talked and talked until Caro noticed the time and suggested they get the bill.

Olivia paid and Caro didn't fail to notice the gold credit card that came out of the expensive leather wallet, clearly a result of her new found success. Caro didn't begrudge Olivia that. After all she had, for many years, been used and abused by the consultancies and agencies she had worked for, and should have been treated better; it made total sense that she should now be able to do her own thing.

"Now, I seem to remember you said something about needing a wardrobe makeover," said Olivia, tucking the card back into her purse. "Although you look fabulous, as always." Olivia ran her eyes over Caro's simple outfit of faded jeans, high-heeled boots, a crisp white, slightly-too-big shirt, and dark blue blazer. "But not 'rock chick' enough really, if we're going to a gig tonight."

The shopping trip turned into something more than just finding an outfit for that evening, and Caro returned to Nic's flat later with several bags full of clothes, shoes, and boots. As she emptied the contents onto the bed and looked around the sparse storage space, she wondered how practical it was for her to stay there long term. Not that Nic had given her any kind of deadline for finding her own place, but she didn't want to outstay her welcome or be a passenger for too long. Maybe tomorrow she'd turn her attention to house hunting.

Her phone vibrated with a text from Jonny Tyler.

Looking forward to seeing you tonight, babes, it's been a while & Blood Stone Riot are a good draw xx.

She stared at it for the longest time, her head reeling.

With a jolt she realised it wasn't just Jonny she was looking forward to seeing that night.

CHAPTER FOUR

A Tuesday night at The Vegas was usually pretty quiet and uneventful.

Except for this particular Tuesday night when the next big thing in rock music, or so rumour had it, were playing what was supposed to be a low-key gig. Word had got around and the club was heaving.

Blood Stone Riot.

With the ink barely dry on their recording contract, and billed by the popular music press as achingly hip, the band were destined to challenge the masses with their take on the rock genre. Hard-edged enough to satisfy fans of guitar solos and drums, cool and edgy enough to entice lovers of lyrics and well-worked melodies.

Alik Thorne; perfect frontman, the triple threat lead singer, guitarist, and song writer, with an ability to captivate and win over even the frostiest of audiences.

Nate McKenna; lead guitarist, effortlessly creating melodic riffs with a gritty quality that identified the Blood Stone Riot sound, drawing on the greats of rock to make himself the best he could possibly be.

Billy Walker; bass guitarist, providing the rhythmic and harmonic foundations of the songs, underpinning them with dirty, sleazy bass lines, bringing lead guitarist and drummer together.

Dev McLaughlin; drummer, occupying the space as the mad drummer, quiet in every other part of his life, except when he was behind his drum kit.

Strong friendships forged over the seven years or so since they had met as teenagers as well as an almost telepathic ability to know what the others were thinking onstage.

They were a formidable quartet.

* * *

Leaning against the bar, Alik casually observed the activity going on around him. Recently refreshed from the short break in Mallorca that he'd been told to take by Griffen Price, the band's tour manager, he was fired up by the prospect of the next few months of activity for the band. Griffen had seen him indulging a bit too much at one of Edie's parties and advised that he should get away and detox for a few days. Edie Spencer-Newman and her events were pretty legendary - at least for the gossip mags - and his girlfriend certainly wasn't backwards in sharing the recreational drugs that she was able to procure.

He and the rest of the band had been at the venue since six, sound-checking before the bar opened to the public and ensuring that their kit fitted into the somewhat compact stage area. Despite having played there a number of times before and already knowing exactly how the stage plan worked, Alik was a perfectionist and wanted everything to be just right.

He was psyched, gig-ready, and couldn't wait to get out there.

The audience usually loved him.

The audience that evening would also consist of his girlfriend, seeing him play live for the first time. It wasn't a scene that she was familiar with and he wasn't sure how she would fare in his world.

* * *

It had been about nine months since Caro had last been in The Vegas, but it felt like yesterday. It hadn't changed, and there was a comforting, easy, familiarity about it; the small, sweaty, upstairs that had a tiny stage and a simple long bar at the back of the room. It may have had a lick of paint and a few new band posters adorning the walls, but in the main, it remained as it had when Caro had been at university in North Ridge. For a long time, it had been the only venue in town that catered for live rock music, and The Indigo Lounge would immediately be a rival for it. If The Indigo Lounge was half as successful as The Vegas, Caro would be externally grateful.

Since meeting Olivia for lunch, she had managed to get her hair done and take a power nap before getting ready to go out. Nic and Olivia were meeting her there later, taking a rare opportunity to grab some dinner together first.

Jonny Tyler was waiting at the door for her, a grin on his face as he clocked her.

"Welcome back, babe," he said, gathering her into his arms and locking his lips on hers. "I've missed you."

Two girls walked past, shooting daggers at Caro. No doubt at least one of them would have slept with Jonny; his reputation preceded him. As a promoter, he was well known on the North Ridge music scene and extremely popular, not least for his ability to get into places for free. He always had a cheeky grin that went with his slightly dishevelled appearance, spiky blond hair that he was always raking a hand through, and excessive charm. The free-flowing compliments didn't hurt, either.

"Gotta love that welcome home," said Caro, as they made their way inside, hand in hand. The bar was already packed with punters. Her gaze immediately fell on Alik Thorne, standing casually by the bar. Steering Jonny away from Alik, she tried to ignore her mind screaming at her to go back in the other direction.

* * *

Edie Spencer-Newman shuddered as she sipped on her glass of slightly-too-warm Chardonnay. It had been years since she had drunk anything quite so distasteful, but The Vegas wasn't exactly a venue renowned for its wine list. The beer-and-shots bar definitely wasn't high on her list of venues to frequent. But when Alik had suggested that she see him play live, she hadn't exactly been able to say no. So far into their relationship she had managed to avoid places like this, making sure that she took Alik to dinner or met him in a wine bar she felt comfortable in, or inviting him to parties at friends' houses. She was eternally grateful that she had managed to persuade the team at *Pretty Rich Things* not to film her that evening. This definitely wasn't the way she wanted her glamorous life to be portrayed. The reality TV programme followed a cluster of both self-made and inherited wealthy young men and women who were trying to make their own way in the business world. In Edie's case, this was the opening of her own designer boutique, The Magpie. The little vintage boudoir-inspired shop had taken up a great deal of her time, as she sourced the chicest, most feminine, and, most of all, most expensive items that would appeal to her target market. Despite being pretty lazy when it came to work, she had thoroughly enjoyed scouring the internet and visiting suppliers to source the products and garments that would create the exclusive theme of the shop. Hanging out in seedy rock bars was not something that would resonate with her fans.

    She looked around - taking in the clientele - seeing mostly leather and tattoos, and held her Prada clutch more tightly. Not a designer label in sight, except for her Pucci-inspired print shift dress, which still made her stand out from the crowd despite it being one of the more subdued garments in her extensive wardrobe. However, it was a wardrobe that wasn't built for the rock scene. Perched uneasily on a bar stool, Edie wondered how much longer she would have to wait. Alik had just texted her to say he was backstage, which hopefully meant they would be starting soon.

"Hey, you didn't tell me you were coming tonight."

Like a beacon of light, Olivia Cole appeared beside her. She had been helping Edie with the PR for The Magpie and had become a firm friend over the last few months. Olivia's work had been amazing, already creating a buzz about the place, and anticipation was high.

Edie smiled. "Alik invited me, but I'm not sure this place is for me." She noticed Olivia was dressed similarly to her and was comforted by that fact. After all, Olivia was definitely more PR than rock, even though she would be working with Alik and the band. A couple of women walked past, heading towards the mosh pit close to the stage, clad head to toe in black, with matching pierced noses and heavily-studded ears. They cast a suspicious glance in Edie's direction.

"The lead singer is my boyfriend," Edie said, making sure they heard her.

One of them laughed. "Yeah, whatever, as if Alik Thorne would look at someone like you. I reckon he'll be seeing more of me later."

Edie watched in horror as the two women headed off towards the front. There was a flurry of activity as they heard a couple of guitars being tuned up

Olivia grabbed Edie's arm and pulled her closer towards the stage. "You'll be fine, their bark is usually worse than their bite."

All of a sudden, there was noise, in Edie's opinion anyway, and Alik appeared on the stage, bathed in a single spotlight.

"Good evening Vegas!" he roared. Edie thought it sounded as if he was pretending to play Las Vegas rather than North Ridge. "Thanks for coming down tonight. This is 'In It For The Craic'." She watched as he whirled across the stage, microphone in hand, with the guitar, bass, and drums crashing around him.

As the set progressed, Edie started to enjoy herself. Despite the fact that the music was so far away from being her sort of thing, she couldn't help but be enthralled by Alik and how he could hold the audience in the palm of his hand. She hadn't really known how talented he was, not to mention how popular the band were. She realised she would probably have to fend off all sorts of female attention for her man.

* * *

Much as she wanted to, Caro couldn't tear her eyes away from Alik.

The presence he had onstage in a larger environment than Juju's was overwhelming.

She watched him prowl across the stage, shirt undone, showing off his gorgeously-muscled chest and tattoos. She could remember his touch, the way his fingers caressed her skin, his lips on hers, the thrust of his cock inside her.

Glancing around at the rest of the crowd, she bet there were many women who were experiencing the same feelings. Or at least wished they were.

She felt Jonny's arms slip around her waist and momentarily felt a brush of unwarranted guilt. She and Jonny had never been exclusive, never claimed to be something that they weren't, just hooking up when it suited them both and they happened to be in the same place. She speculated whether her decision to move back to North Ridge had sent a different message to Jonny. One that said she was ready to settle down.

Maybe she was.

But maybe it wasn't with him.

* * *

Onstage, Alik took in the audience, his eyes scanning over the crowd in the club. Usually, he wasn't able to pinpoint anyone he recognised, but in amongst the people near the mixing desk he thought he spotted Olivia. With Jonny Tyler. In the last couple of days, his mind occasionally flitted to the night he'd spent with her, how simple their evening had been, talking, drinking, enjoying each other.

Particularly the enjoying each other part.

In the back of his mind, he knew he was comparing her to Edie. One night spent with someone who appeared to be so similar to him, versus his beautiful, elegant, monied girlfriend. They were a bit of a cliché, the rock star and the rich girl, and whilst he had initially enjoyed the novelty of them being so different, it was starting to wear off a little.

Shaking his head and focusing on the gig, he whirled across the stage, putting both women out of his mind.

* * *

Blood Stone Riot's short set was a success. The crowd was buoyant after they had finished, still bouncing around as the DJ played retro rock tracks to end the evening. The band had packed up and moved into the tiny VIP area, where Alik spotted Jonny Tyler again, this time chatting to Nic, accompanied by two women. As he approached them, he realised that he hadn't been hallucinating and that one of them was Olivia, although a very glammed-up, rock version of her.

In contrast to the flowing summer dress she had worn, she was now poured into a pair of tight black jeans, paired with an off the shoulder black chiffon top and skyscraper heels. Her make up was dark - smoky eyes and a matte lipstick - and her caramel-streaked hair was artfully styled as if she'd just tumbled out of bed.

He remembered that look on her too.

"Hi Alik," said Nic. "You know Jonny, obviously, and this is..."

"It's okay, Olivia and I have already met, said Alik. He felt a tiny stab of jealousy at Jonny's arm still around Olivia's shoulders.

"Er, no we haven't," said the other woman. "Not in person, anyway, although I have been sort of working for you for about a month. I'm Olivia."

Alik looked between the real Olivia and the pretend Olivia who, at least, had the decency to look suitably embarrassed. He looked at her. "Care to explain what's going on?"

The pretend Olivia looked Alik directly in the eye. "Maybe we could ask Nate the same question," she said.

"Nate?" Nic frowned at Alik. "When did you meet Caro?"

Any further explanation was cut short when Edie joined the group, air kissing Olivia and kissing Alik on the lips before linking her arm through his.

"What's going on? What did I miss?" she asked, oblivious to the tension hanging over the group. "You were amazing, babe."

Alik watched Caro's eyes narrow slightly at Edie's appearance. Interesting.

"I'm guessing that Caro is Caro Flynn, right?" said Alik. "The same Caro Flynn that's been running a pretty successful rock bar in Mallorca and is Nic Santino's business partner."

She nodded. "Then you can understand my reticence about telling a random musician in a bar my real name, *Nate*." She emphasised the name to make her point, keeping her tone cool.

"Then you can also understand why rock stars might not want to be completely truthful about who they are," said Alik, matching her tone. He leaned in close to her and whispered in her ear, "In case they end up with a kiss-and-tell girl. I guess I know now that the tat on the back of your neck is about you and Jonny."

The two of them held each other's gaze as they reached stalemate, an uncomfortable silence descending over the rest of the group.

It was Nic who broke the tension. "I'm not entirely sure what's going on here, but I definitely need a drink."

* * *

As the group dispersed, Olivia grabbed Caro's arm and steered her towards a quiet corner.

"You and Alik Thorne? How did that happen? And when?"

"It was just a one-night thing," said Caro. "My last night in Mallorca. He told me his name was Nate. I never thought I'd see him again. I guess we kind of played each other and it wasn't until the flight home that I realised who he really was."

"He obviously didn't mention that he was with Edie."

Caro looked over to the bar, where Alik was standing with Edie. She gave Edie a cursory once-over. The pretty silk shift dress and matching heels and bag reeked of money, and for a moment Caro wondered how on earth Edie and Alik got together. Alik, with his love of body art, festivals, and dark, dark music, seeing this King's Road princess - they just didn't make sense. She realised he was watching her. He raised his glass in her direction and then leaned over and whispered something in Edie's ear before nuzzling her neck. Caro didn't know how to react. In her head she had told herself it was a one-off, but seeing him again that evening, playing properly plugged-in with the rest of his band, had caused an involuntary ripple to course through her body.

She forced herself to look away.

"What are you doing to do?" Olivia asked.

"About what? Alik and Edie are clearly a couple and I'm with Jonny."

Olivia stifled a giggle. "Well, whatever happened on that one night seems to had more of an effect than anything, sorry, *anyone* has had on you in a long time."

Caro's romantic experiences had, in the last couple of years, been sporadic to say the least. Her focus had always been on her business and making that a success, leaving little room for anything else. That wasn't to say she had lived like a nun - far from it - however relationships hadn't always been top of her agenda.

Which was why hooking up with Jonny, which happened as and when, suited her just fine.

If only she could just ignore the fact that Alik Thorne couldn't take his eyes off her.

CHAPTER FIVE

Alik was sitting on the sofa in just a pair of boxers, his acoustic guitar cradled in his lap as he fiddled with some lyrics. Despite the late finish after the gig, he and Edie had gone on to an all-night bar to meet some of her friends for late drinks. By the time they had got back to his flat, he hadn't been able to sleep. He was still wired from the performance and bumping into Olivia - no, Caro. Not to mention the creative streak that was demanding to be listened to. The song was the one he had recently showcased at Juju's and was turning into something that definitely wasn't Blood Stone Riot material.

In fact, it almost felt like a love song. Or as much of a love song as Alik could write.

Fresh in his thoughts was that night with Caro. Having such a strong connection with someone after only a short time didn't usually happen to him. Prior to Edie, there had been a string of short-term, tour-type girlfriends who would be around for a few days or weeks and then be gone.

His mind turned to Edie, sleeping soundly in his bed, blissfully unaware that he was thinking of another woman.

He knew they had their differences and the things that they held dear were poles apart, but there had been a level of attraction that he couldn't fight. They had first met at a house party, somewhere in Notting Hill, hosted by a friend of a friend, and he had gone along with Billy, more to keep him company than anything else. They had got wrecked and he had seen this blonde vision who had captivated him the moment she walked into the room. They had flirted outrageously for the whole evening and ended up getting breakfast at a nearby greasy spoon the following morning before arranging to see each other again.

At the start, the couple were definitely hot property and it hadn't done Alik's reputation any harm to be seen in some of the bars and clubs that Edie frequented. It had been a whirlwind of parties and events and had brought Blood Stone Riot into the public eye a bit more, although he did sometimes wrestle with the mainstream publicity. Having Olivia on board to do the band's official PR was a definite plus. He'd witnessed the work she had been doing for Edie and The Magpie and if she could translate those results for the band, then it wouldn't be long before they would be headlining the Wilde Park Festival, rather than just being part of the bill.

Scribbling some more lyrics on the back of an envelope, he wondered what Caro was doing. Then he remembered that she'd been at the gig with Jonny Tyler and she had said they were together. Alik snorted, knowing that in Jonny's world "together" probably meant for that night. He couldn't believe that someone as headstrong and intelligent as Caro was being taken in by the promoter. And then he wondered why he should care so much.

He strummed the chords and quietly sang the words, trying to get the phrasing and flow of the song right, trying to capture the feeling of Juju's.

"Hey," said Edie, standing in the doorway of the living room, yawning. She was clad in a t-shirt of Alik's that was way too big for her delicate frame, although still very short, exposing her perfect legs. Her blonde hair was pulled back in a ponytail and with her face bare of make-up, she looked fresh and innocent. "When are you coming to bed?"

Alik glanced up at the clock and was surprised to see that it was after five in the morning. They had got back shortly after three and he'd said he wouldn't be long. Reluctantly, he put the guitar down on the sofa beside him.

He'd forgotten that the couldn't stay up and play guitar all night when he had a girlfriend.

Well, at least not when that girlfriend was Edie. She came over to the sofa and straddled him, the t-shirt slipping up to reveal her pert buttocks, clad in a pair of candy pink, lace trimmed scanty knickers.

"When you're in my bed, I shouldn't really have any excuse for not being there, should I?" he said.

Reaching around so he was cupping her arse, he got up off the sofa, Edie still in his arms, her legs finding their way around his body as he carried her off into the bedroom.

CHAPTER SIX

The morning after the gig at The Vegas, Blood Stone Riot attended a breakfast meeting to meet with their artist development manager at Numb Records. The band had travelled to London along with Griffen, to go through the plans for the next few months. The record company offices were in the West End, near Soho. The rich, glamorous, and beautiful were out in force.

Alik tried not to be impressed as they were shown to a top floor office with views over the city, but it was hard not to be. After all, they were just a small town band trying to make it big, like so many others before them. They trooped down a corridor adorned with silver and gold records, although the elusive platinum appeared absent. Billy and Nate headed directly for the table that had been laid out with bacon rolls and pastries.

"I could get used to this!" said Billy, loading a plate with savoury snacks and sweet treats before helping himself to a large mug of coffee, heaping in sugar and milk.

The others followed suit, settling down around the table and enjoying the food in a companionable silence, except for the occasional remark complaining about how early it was.

Alik was mainlining black coffee. The effects of a late night gig, limited sleep, and an untimely wake up call were starting to kick in. He hoped he wouldn't end up yawning at an inopportune moment or nodding off during the session. He was a little nervous about the meeting. He'd heard from a few other bands that had got to this point and had been asked to change what made them successful in the first place. There would be nothing worse than having to work with someone who was into hipster music and wanted them to be the next Coldplay. Because that was never going to happen. He wouldn't allow it.

He took a seat at one end of the table, drumming his fingers on the surface as he looked at the clock.

The door swung open and Parker Roberts entered.

Having not had any preconceptions of what he might be like, Alik was surprised to see a tall, skinny man in his early thirties, immaculately turned out in a Savile Row suit, with perfectly coiffured hair. He certainly wouldn't have looked out of place in the Square Mile. Immediately, Alik was suspicious. What did a guy like this know about what they did? This meet and greet was pointless, particularly as Parker hadn't even been at one of their gigs. Surely Griffen and Parker could just get together or exchange a few emails and get the same outcome. And at least get Parker to a gig. He guessed that the meeting was something to do with the label showing that they cared about their acts.

"Good to meet you, Parker," said Alik. "Although I didn't know we were signing with a city boy banker."

"And what makes you think that?" asked Parker.

Alik gestured to Parker's suit and made a face.

Parker raised his eyebrows in response. "Looks can be deceiving," he said. "Shall we start again?" He settled himself into the seat at the head of the table, opposite Alik, focusing directly on the singer. "The rough demos of your stuff are great and even better live, so it's a good thing we've already signed a deal with you, otherwise there would be competition!"

"You haven't even seen us live," said Alik.

Parker fixed him with a stare. "Then we need to rectify that." He looked over to Griffen. "Sort that out, yeah?"

Without further hesitation, he began talking through the plans for the band, gigs he'd lined up for them, warm ups to the Wilde Park Festival, ideas for their first video shoot - which included having Josh O'Brien direct it - merchandise, tour schedules. He threw out dates, venues, support slots, bands they could tour with. The information just kept coming and coming. Alik had a rough idea of how things worked, but he was more interested in the creative side. And finding out how many sales they made, of course.

As Parker continued explaining his role with the band and what he would do for them, Alik found himself warming to the guy. Not a lot, but enough to know that if he was going to spending a lot of time with Parker Roberts, he needed to know more about him.

Parker wound the session up and the others started to drift off. Alik approached him. He waited patiently, admiring the view, while Parker had a few words with Griffen. And then it was just the two of them.

"Ah, Mr. Thorne, the uber-talented guitar muso." Parker bowed his head.

"You got that right," Alik grinned. "Got any more meetings today? Thought we might head out for a drink."

"Nothing that can't be cancelled. Give me five minutes, I'll meet you in the lobby."

He was true to his word, and just over five minutes later joined Alik in reception. They walked less than a hundred and fifty yards down the road to The Blind Pig and Parker waltzed straight upstairs, clearly a regular. The interior was decorated with a vintage twist of antique mirrored ceilings, reclaimed wooden chairs, and a copper-topped bar. There was certainly nothing to rival it in North Ridge. Parker ordered them a couple of whisky-based cocktails and they took a table in the corner.

"I guess you're wondering why I'm the one looking after you," said Parker, straight out. He clearly was a sensible guy.

Alik nodded. "You don't exactly look like someone who has any knowledge or understanding of rock and metal, so yeah, I'm keen to know why you wanted to work with us. You look like you're more suited to the indie world or maybe some kind of bubblegum pop princess."

Parker took his iPhone from his pocket and tossed it across the table to Alik. "No code, check out the music. And if you're not convinced, maybe some of the pictures as well."

Alik did as he said, scrolling through bands he knew and admired, both old and classic; Five Finger Death Punch, Lamb of God, Pantera, Slipknot, Aerosmith, Guns 'n' Roses... the list went on. Checking that he wasn't just a fair weather fan or just had this pre-loaded in case he was asked about his music tastes, Alik fired a number of questions at Parker that he was able to answer with the speed of only a true fan. They bantered over obscure bands they had seen before they were famous, the best gigs they had been to and the bands they wished they had seen.

"Man, I wish I'd been at Milton Keynes for GnR in 1993," Alik said. "Great band, never saw them live."

"God, yes, Blind Melon, Soul Asylum, and The Cult. Of course, he's dead now, just like a number of his peers. God only knows how they're still alive."

They carried on talking and Alik realised this had probably been the most fun he'd had in a long while. If you didn't count the time he'd spent with Caro in Mallorca.

CHAPTER SEVEN

Builders and decorators mixed with film students and extras at The Indigo Lounge on the morning of Blood Stone Riot's video shoot. Nic had generously offered Alik and the band the use of the club to film some of the scenes for 'Bleed Like Cyanide,' the lead track on the EP, that they hoped to release as a single. Parker Roberts had drafted in Josh O'Brien, an up and coming director, to shoot the video as he had done successfully for a couple of other emerging bands in the genre. It was something of a coup, as he was in high demand, but he liked the challenge of working with new bands and pushing the boundaries, where established groups were more nervous about doing anything different. It was another master stroke that was really helping Olivia's PR campaign. She and Parker had been working pretty hard to make sure the band had the best possible press.

Josh was in dialogue with one of the cameramen; he was a thin, wiry chap and wore wire-rimmed glasses that he kept pushing back on his nose, as they slipped off with annoying regularity. Blood Stone Riot wanted to compete and make an impact and getting Josh involved was certainly one way of doing that. The director was currently standing on the dance floor, consulting his script and barking orders at the runners who were putting props on the stage.

Caro and Olivia were on the VIP balcony, surveying the activity going on beneath them, cups of coffee in hand.

"Such a good idea of Nic's, particularly if we can get the single out to coincide with the opening," said Olivia, resting her elbows on the edge of the balcony.

"Mmm, so good to have the club over run with egos just when we're trying to get everything finished."

Olivia flashed her a sidelong glance. "By ego, do you mean Alik?"

Caro grunted. Since their run in at The Vegas, Alik had become a permanent fixture in the club and had been working with Josh on the script for the video. The pair had hit it off instantly and were frequently found bent over Josh's laptop, pointing at ideas and inspiration. Or laughing at pointless clips of jocks falling over and hurting themselves, *Jackass*-style. It was like working with children. On a couple of occasions Edie had popped in, totally ignoring Caro's presence and chatting with the boys, often excluding her from the conversation. It was a bit like being back at college and not being included by the cool kids. Caro's response had been to see a lot more of Jonny, inviting him to the club and planning promotions with him. There had been a few times when Caro and Alik had been alone and the night in Mallorca hung in the air between them, the elephant in the room.

But they didn't speak of it.

* * *

"Are you sure about this, Alik?" Josh asked, surveying the scene in front of him.

A huge wooden cross dominated the centre of the stage and behind it, the walls had been dressed in swathes of black and red velvet, with various implements of torture, including handcuffs, whips, shackles and chains.

"You know we wrote it like this," Alik replied. He caught sight of Caro walking across the floor towards them.

"Love what you've done with the place, maybe we should leave it like this after you've finished," she said to Josh, with a smile.

"What and have people think you're an S&M club?" he replied.

She smirked. "Might bring a few extra punters in. Maybe we should consider a bondage night. I'll suggest it to Nic. Talking of which, I really should get back to him otherwise he'll think I'm skiving. Again." She wandered off in the direction of the office.

Alik responded by flirting outrageously with the make-up artist who was preparing him for the shoot, making risqué suggestions to her until Josh came over and rescued the woman.

"Ignore him, I think he's just over excited about making a video with me," said Josh, without a trace of irony.

The woman giggled and left to work on the extras who were getting ready backstage.

"Thanks, Josh, now you make me sound like a child." Alik rolled his eyes at the director.

"A child, huh?" Josh smiled. "Remember, I've seen the storyboards you suggested for this piece and I don't think there's much of a PG rating going on. Are you sure we're not playing out your sexual fantasies on screen?"

Alik grinned. "Who said anything about fantasy?"

"Shall we get on with it then?"

Alik peeled off his shirt and vaulted onto the stage, followed by Josh and one of the runners, and moved towards the cross before turning his back to it and raising his arms in the air.

"Are you sure about this?" asked Josh.

"Just do it."

Josh shrugged and nodded to the runner. A couple of minutes later, Alik was lashed to the cross in a Jesus Christ post, unable to move. He flexed his arms, testing the strength of the rope, but was totally powerless.

"Right, who wants to oil him up?" Josh looked around for the make-up artist, but couldn't see her. The remainder of the volunteers in the room were all male and looked at the floor or shuffled around trying to look busy doing other things.

"I'll do it."

The sound of Caro's voice grabbed Alik's attention, it's husky undertones an immediate turn on.

"I said I'll do it," she said.

Alik watched her catch the bottle of baby oil that Josh threw at her and make her way onto the stage. He shifted uneasily, wondering what she was going to do.

Her eyes locked on his. Violet on blue.

And that spark was there again.

He frowned slightly. She raised her eyebrows in response. She stopped inches in front of him.

"Where would you like me to start?"

"Where you want to." His heart started to beat a little faster.

Alik watched as Caro opened the bottle and tipped a little of the oil into her hand. She placed the bottle on the floor and straightened up, rubbing her hands together. Staring him directly in the eye, she placed her palms on his chest. His breathing became shallower as she began stroking the oil over his pecs, the tips of her fingers brushing over his erect nipples, playing the the sensitive area around his nipple ring, moving slowly along his biceps, to his wrists, down his back until finally she caressed his stomach.

Her touch was light, slow, erotic.

Alik wanted her to stop and carry on all at once. His senses were working overtime. Her hands slipped around his waist, her fingers dipping in and out of the band of his jeans, and he was now acutely aware of the audience they had.

She met his gaze again.

Laughing to herself, she withdrew and stepped back.

"Prick tease," he said, hissing and straining against the rope that bound him. "Untie me."

"I don't think so, Alik, after all, isn't that the idea behind this video?" she said. "The defenceless victim in the power of the women surrounding him, totally unable to resist the charms of his tormentors, 'poison creeping, flesh eating, cut too deep you can fucking bleed, bleed like cyanide...'" She lowered her tone as she leaned in closer to him again, using the lyrics of the song to illustrate her point.

Her voice was low and hypnotic, but Alik tried not to fall under its spell. Her touch had him incredibly aroused and he was fleetingly pleased that she still stood directly in front of him as his erection bulged against the fly of his jeans. He could smell her perfume, the fresh, clean scent he identified with her, and it was driving him crazy.

"Dammit, woman, let me go," said Alik, struggling to get some give on the rope.

Caro smiled and shook her heard. "Josh, I think he's ready now." She tossed the bottle of oil back to the director and walked away.

Alik glared at her as she left the stage. The female extras joined him, directed by Josh as to where to stand and what to do. He could still feel Caro's touch burning his skin.

The camera rolled, and his desperation was fitting in perfectly with what he had scripted, but each touch from the extras drove him insane. As a result, they kept having to stop and re-start the filming, as he kept flinching.

The exquisite torture he was experiencing was translating well to the screen, and after a while Josh called a halt to proceedings.

"That's fantastic, ladies, I think we have it just about right," he said. "I wasn't sure at first, but Alik, you nailed it."

The immediate thought that flashed through Alik's head was how much he'd like to nail Caro right now. He wriggled impatiently as he was finally cut free from the cross.

"Where is she?"
"Who?" asked Josh
"Your very tactile assistant."

"I think she went back up to the VIP bar with Olivia."

Alik bounded up the stairs, taking them two at a time. He spotted Caro immediately, her back to him as she talked to Olivia.

"What sort of fucked up power game were you playing down there?" he said, grabbing her arm and whisking her round to face him.

Caro shrugged, pulling herself free from his grasp. "No game, just thought you'd appreciate getting in the mood for the shoot."

"Yeah, right." Alik flexed his aching arms, the adrenaline still pumping through his oiled body.

Alik stared at her, remembering what she felt like. What it was like to touch her. And what that touch could do. She stared back at him, blissfully unaware of the thoughts going on in his head. Thoughts that were driving him to distraction. And before he could say something he regretted, he stormed off.

CHAPTER EIGHT

Edie and Olivia were sitting outside Sarastro, taking advantage of the late afternoon sunshine and unusually balmy temperature. A bottle of Sancerre sat in the cooler in the centre of the table, although it wouldn't be long before they would need a refill. Edie was explaining that *Pretty Rich Things* were planning to do an episode featuring just her and the opening of The Magpie. The Magpie was Edie's brainchild, a tiny space nestled just moments from the heart of North Ridge's shopping district, rubbing shoulders with the larger department stores and designer brands, as well as the Chi Chi one-off stores. It was a shabby chic, vintage-style store with lots of sleek, expensive items that would appeal to a certain type of shopper, as well as being aspirational. The additional exposure from the show, she hoped, would ensure that it hit its target market. And being able to use the Spencer-Newman name was also a bonus. The family had made its money through buying and selling wine at the right time, and their cellar was legendary.

"I thought it might be good if we can get them out and about with me while I'm sourcing products in the lead up to the opening as well. What do you think?"

Olivia nodded and Edie allowed herself a small smile. It had actually been the idea of the show's story editor to tag along while Edie was basically shopping. But Olivia didn't need to know that right now. Edie was already looking forward to the extra publicity that should be generated. She took a mouthful of wine, keeping an eye out for the waiter so they could get another bottle, and picked at the bowl of olives on the table.

"When do they want to do that?" Olivia opened up her diary. "I've managed to persuade Belle Cassidy at *Aspire* magazine to do a feature on The Magpie's opening and she wants to meet you first to work out some initial copy with her. Your schedule is pretty hectic over the next few weeks. We can move a few things because I know how important *PRT* is to you." She scribbled something on her notepad, before crossing out something else.

A teenage couple walked by; the boy was wearing a Blood Stone Riot t-shirt. Edie turned the stem of her wine glass around in her fingers.

"Olivia, this might be nothing and I know she's your best friend, but has Caro said anything to you about Alik?"

"What do you mean?" Olivia frowned.

"I thought they seemed touchy feely with each other after the show at The Vegas and he was whispering in her ear. I know he's been hanging out at the club with her as well."

"And based on that, you think that he's sleeping with her? Edie, she's hardly been back in the country five minutes, so I think it's highly unlikely that she would have managed to hook up with your boyfriend, had some secret fling and then broadcast the details to me. Nic would have said something to me if he thought anything was going on." Olivia shook her head and changed the subject, talking about some of the online bloggers she thought they ought to work with and needed Edie's approval on.

Edie's eyes narrowed. "I mean, I know she was at The Vegas with that Jonny Tyler, but he's hardly boyfriend material, is he? I'm sure I've seen him with a different girl every time I've bumped into him."

Olivia reached for her wineglass. "If you're that worried about it, why don't you talk to her at Billy's party this evening?"

CHAPTER NINE

The party at Billy Walker's proved to be something of a revelation - not least because of the impressive house that he lived in. The house was a rambling barn conversion in Stratfield, a quiet and exclusive country village on the outskirts of North Ridge. Rumour had it that his parents had bought it for him to keep him and the rest of the band away from the neighbours. A strategy that seemed to work, as the band spent a lot of their time there, rehearsing before gigs and generally hanging out. It was evident that the Walker family had money, although it appeared to be something that Billy didn't openly flaunt.

Caro had received a text invite from Alik, which she was surprised about given how the video shoot had ended. He hadn't been to the club since, and she found herself missing his presence. He had asked her to come along and meet some of the other North Ridge bands as potentials to play at The Indigo Lounge in the future.

All extremely polite and professional.

Unsure of the true motives behind the invite, Caro had asked Jonny to come along as the perfect foil. The pair of them had arrived fashionably late, moving through the rooms on the spacious ground floor; kitchen, living room, dining room, TV room, and music room, until they came to the well-equipped games room where most of the party seemed to be congregated. Jonny stopped along the way, introducing Caro to various people until their names started swimming into each other and she couldn't remember who she'd met and who she hadn't, or what they did and which band they were in.

A full-sized pool table dominated the centre of the room, and in opposite corners were flat screen TVs, one attached to a PlayStation and the other to an Xbox. Another TV streamed *Kerrang*, where music videos played as background noise, when someone hadn't picked up a guitar and started playing, themselves.

A quick glance around the assembled people there told her that it was very much a North Ridge music scene event. From the people Jonny had introduced her to, there were members of Dagger Drawn, Go!, Forrest Fraser, and ThrashGun, and of course Blood Stone Riot. These bands usually played on the same bills together or supported each other on out of town gigs, making it a proper scene. There was plenty of support for those that went on to make it big, and currently it was Blood Stone Riot that occupied that slot.

Alik was holding court by the bar that ran along the whole of one wall with pretty much any drink one could imagine. He broke away from his audience to greet Caro and Jonny.

"Hey guys, thanks for coming along tonight. Just the usual jam session for the North Ridge musos." He grinned. Caro could tell he'd already had several drinks. "You want a beer?" He wore dark grey jeans, teamed with a lighter grey tight t-shirt that clung to his chest, outlining his nipple ring.

"Sure," said Jonny. "Caro?"

"Bloody Mary, please."

"Good choice, beer can be so gassy, can't it?" Edie Spencer-Newman's tones cut into the conversation. "Jonny, Caro, how lovely to see you." She leaned forward and air kissed Caro on both cheeks. "Alik, why don't you get the drinks?"

Edie's socialite air felt somewhat disjointed in the current environment, clashing with the hard-working, if slightly dirty vibe of the rest of the party. Olivia had briefed Caro on what to expect when spending any length of time with Edie, so she felt prepared.

Edie took Caro's elbow and steered her to a couch on one side of the room, slightly away from the rest of the party, where the two of them sat down. "Thanks for coming this evening, I know that Alik thought it was important to clear the air between the two of you. I gather there was some kind of misunderstanding at the video shoot the other day."

Caro didn't know how to respond. She wondered how much Alik had actually told her, and whether he had fessed up about their encounter in Mallorca. "It was nothing important. I'm sure working together like that will get us both the publicity we need."

Edie beamed. "I know, Olivia is such a good PR rep, isn't she? And such a good friend. We've become so close since we've been working together."

Caro frowned. She hadn't realised that the two of them had become best buddies, but what did she expect when she had been away for so long? She didn't have a monopoly on Olivia's friendship.

Edie continued to regale her with the amazing things that Olivia had done; setting up various bits of press and engaging with the right outlets to get the best publicity possible for The Magpie. Caro listened politely. She knew Olivia was good at her job, and it sounded as if she was just doing it. Edie changed the subject and started talking about Alik and the band.

"There are the girls, of course," Edie said. "Silly little groupies who think that with their interest in rock music they can steal my boyfriend because they know more about Metallica or Iron Maiden or whatever than I do. But they don't know how solid Alik and I are. And it would be silly to try and break us up, because I could quite easily ruin them if I wanted to."

It sounded like a warning.

Alik brought over the drinks. "There you go, ladies," he said, handing them their drinks before returning to the bar where Jonny was.

Draining her Bloody Mary, Caro politely excused herself to get another. She was going to need it.

* * *

Edie watched Caro walk over to the bar. Her friend Araminta, Minty for short, came and plonked herself on the stool Caro had just vacated. Minty was lovely, but a little bit dim sometimes and didn't always get what was going on.

"Who's that?" Minty asked, sipping on some violent orange concoction, festooned with fruit and umbrellas, that Billy had made for her.

"That's Caro Flynn," replied Edie, her eyes fixated on Caro at the bar with Jonny. She would be keeping a close eye on her.

* * *

Alik leaned down over the pool table to pot a ball, a cigarette dangling from his lips. He saw Caro and Jonny at the bar, wrapped in a heated embrace. Billy was watching him from the other side of the pool table, a grin forming on his face.

"Mate, you want to go and get some practice in?" he asked as Alik sank the black, winning yet another game.

"May as well." Alik dropped the cue on the table. "Seeing as I've whipped your sorry ass again."

They moved away from the rest of the party and into Billy's study. They would often disappear off together to play guitar when they got bored during parties, trading riffs from their own songs and other tunes they used to play in their first covers band. On more than one occasion, a new song had emanated from these sessions. Alik was playing with the chords from the Mallorcan-inspired song. Billy was listening in, putting down a bass line that complemented the softer sound of the number.

Lost in the music, they didn't hear the study door open or see a tall, skinny bald man dressed in an impeccably-cut charcoal suit enter. "Evening gents, I was told you might be in here."

"Alright, Leo," said Billy, putting his bass back on its stand. "I've been waiting for you to get here, what have you got?"

Leo Kendrick was Billy's dealer. He was a familiar face on the North Ridge music scene and had a fierce reputation, particularly if you couldn't pay your debts.

"I'm not sure I should be selling to you at the moment, Billy, you're running up a bit of a bill," Leo said, examining his knuckles.

Alik pretended to be immersed in what he was doing. He didn't mind the occasional indulgence, but hearing that Billy was using more regularly was a concern. The bassist had a hedonistic streak that could easily get out of hand. Alik had found himself cleaning up after Billy on more than one occasion.

"Come on, Leo, you know I'm good for it."

Leo glanced around the room. As well as a Rickenbacker and an Epiphone bass, there were also a couple of Fender guitars and a slightly damaged Tanglewood acoustic. The dealer nodded. "Yes, I understand you are on the up at the moment, so I could probably make an exception. But remember, I always make sure my debts are settled. One way or another."

He reached into the inside pocket of his jacket and pulled out a small package, passing it to Billy. "Will this suffice? I know what you rock stars can be like..." He gave a smile.

Billy returned the smile. "I think that might just work."

As the dealer left the room, Billy set about chopping the cocaine into big, fat lines, offering a rolled up twenty pound note to Alik to join him.

Alik shook his head. "Keeping a clear head, mate. Not touched anything stronger than alcohol since before Mallorca." He watched as Billy snorted the remains of the line, vaguely aware of someone else coming into the study.

Billy sniffed loudly and focused on the newcomer. "Hey, babe, you want some?" he asked, as Caro's face came into view.

"Probably not her scene," came Edie's voice from behind Caro. "But if you're offering..."

CHAPTER TEN

Remembering Edie's earlier warning, Caro backed out of the study feeling the need to sober up. Mainlining vodka during the course of the evening hadn't been the best of plans. She discovered a stash of San Pellegrino in the back of the massive American-style fridge and was just extracting a bottle when she heard something smash on the tiled floor behind her.

"Shit!" a female voice said, tinged with a hint of an Aussie accent. "I shouldn't have had that last shot."

"Are you okay?" asked Caro, turning round to see a tall auburn-haired woman bent over shards of broken glass.

She helped the woman up and took over sweeping up the glass.

"Thanks," the woman said. "I'm such an idiot, Nate says I should come with a warning. I'm Poppy by the way, Nate's fiancée."

Caro vaguely remembered Edie mentioning something about another woman who was part of the band's entourage, but Edie had seemed to dismiss her as not being important. "I'm Caro, I'm here with..."

Poppy cut her off. "Oh, I know who you are. Alik doesn't talk about much else these days, unless Edie's around of course."

Caro dropped the unbroken glass onto the tiles.

"Okay, so maybe I'm not the only one who needs a caution attached to them." Poppy bent down and shoved the remaining pieces into a tea towel before putting them in the bin. She opened the fridge again and pulled out two beers, passing one to Caro before hoisting herself onto the worktop. She patted the space next to her. "Come join me."

The gesture reminded Caro of her friendship with Mariella; easy and uncomplicated. It transpired that the Australian girl was lonely. She and Nate were due to get married in a matter of weeks and her best friend from back home had just emailed to say she wasn't going to be able to make it.

"I mean, she didn't even call," Poppy said. "And every time I've tried to get hold of her, it's her answering service. I know she's not dead, I checked; she's still on Facebook and everything. I've got heaps to do for the wedding and I've barely started."

"You want some help?" The words came out of Caro's mouth before she'd even had time to think.

"You'd help? But you don't know me!" Poppy's green eyes grew wide. She jumped off the worktop and threw her arms around Caro. "That's amazing!"

"She is a pretty amazing person." Olivia entered the kitchen, a glass of wine in her hand. She jumped up and sat next to Caro.

Caro kissed her cheek. "Takes one to know one, hon," she said. "Have you met Poppy before? She's Nate's fiancée."

Olivia shook her head. "Not yet, but I can't say that Nate hasn't mentioned you a hundred times. When's the wedding?"

The three women started talking about Poppy's nuptials, The Indigo Lounge opening and Olivia's latest trials and tribulations with Edie before the conversation turned to men.

Poppy poured Olivia another glass of wine and found more beer in the fridge, passing one to Caro. "I know Alik was looking forward to you being here," she said.

"Really?" asked Caro. She cast a glance around the kitchen. She'd been careful not to mention Alik while talking to Poppy, not yet knowing where her loyalties lay. For all she knew, Poppy and Edie were best friends, and Edie was to be the maid of honour at the wedding.

"Yes, really," said Poppy.

Olivia gave Caro a meaningful look. One that said 'are you sure that you only slept with him the once in Mallorca?' "But Caro's been seeing Jonny Tyler since she came back, haven't you?"

Caro nodded. As she did so, she thought she spotted Jonny in the hallway looking more than friendly with one of the women she had recently interviewed for a job in The Indigo Lounge. Just as she was about to go and confront him, Nate appeared followed by Alik. Caro did her best to act casual.

"What have you been up to?" asked Nate.

"Oh, you know, just talking about boys and make-up," said Caro, laughing.

"I can't believe I haven't met Caro before," said Poppy. "She's amazing. And she's offered to help with the wedding."

"Thank God for that!" said Nate. "I mean that, Caro. She needs a lot of help. We need to head off now though, babe."

Poppy kissed Caro on both cheeks and gave Olivia a quick hug before she and Nate left. Caro swirled the remains of her beer around, conscious that Olivia was sitting next to her and Alik was ferreting about in the fridge.

Olivia slid off the counter. "I need to find out where Nic's got to." She leaned in close to Caro's ear. "Don't do anything I wouldn't do," she said. And then she was gone.

Alik shut the fridge door with a bang and turned to Caro. Their eyes met.

"I was just going to find Jonny," she said. She placed her bottle on the side and headed towards the door.

"Wait," Alik said. "I want to talk to you."

Slowly, Caro faced him. He extended a hand and pulled her to him, leaning back against the kitchen counter.

"What about? What I saw earlier?"

"No, what happened between us." He stroked her knuckles and caressed her palm.

She pulled away. "Alik, don't. It was nothing, we're both with other people."

He laughed. "You think I don't know Jonny's reputation? I hardly think the two of you will be settling down any time soon. Do you know what he's doing now?"

Caro realised that Jonny had probably been doing more than just chatting to the woman she thought she had seen him with a couple of minutes ago. "I don't," she said. "But you're still with Edie and she pretty much said she would ruin me if I went anywhere near you. I'm not about to be painted as the scarlet woman on the strength of a quick shag. We had a one-night stand, Alik. I don't even know you."

Alik flinched. "But all that time we spent talking before that... We get each other, Caro, we have so many things in common, not just the music stuff. Edie and I don't have any of that."

"That's not how she sees it." Caro extricated her hand from his.

It took every ounce of her willpower not to turn back.

CHAPTER ELEVEN

The day of The Magpie opening finally arrived. Edie woke early, much to Alik's dismay, and flitted around his flat, unable to settle, until he finally asked her to leave.

She had been at the shop since eight, directing her minions in setting up the products and finding space for the drinks and canapés that would be arriving later that afternoon. She had even drafted Olivia in to help out, although strictly speaking it wasn't a PR task, but it was difficult to say 'no' to Edie. The camera crew from *Pretty Rich Things* were trying not to get in the way, but there wasn't a whole lot of room for them and everyone's nerves were getting frayed.

"No, I don't think the diamante earrings should go next to the skull scarves, you're mixing jewellery and accessories!" she said to one hapless helper. "And we really need to leave space for people to put their glasses down."

Not to mention leave some space for people to move around, she mused. It was going to be difficult to fit everyone in the shop. Olivia had kept the guest list deliberately light - or elite, depending on your point of view - picking select editors from the glossies and identifying a few online bloggers who would give honest opinions. Of course, she hadn't managed to stop Edie inviting all her friends and acquaintances.

"Where do you want these?" one of the waiters asked, brandishing a platter of bite-sized pastries.

"Erm..." Edie looked around, desperately trying to find a spot big enough for the dish.

"I could always eat some?" Olivia's voice was a welcome relief.

"Thank God you're here," Edie said. "I think I'm having a slight panic attack."

Olivia took the plate from the waiter and somehow managed to clear an area big enough to accommodate it on the cash desk. The cash desk itself was a beautiful duck egg blue vintage dressing table that had been fashioned into a vessel that now housed a till and card machine, along with various sizes and colours of tissue paper and ribbon, ready to wrap the products in, waiting to be placed in the matching duck egg blue stiff paper carrier bags with a silhouette of a magpie on it in one corner.

Edie had put a lot of thought into the design of the shop, as well as sourcing much of the stock. She had surprised Olivia, and even herself, with her talent for design and planning, not to mention having an eye for a trinket or piece of clothing that would engage and beguile a buyer into wanting it. Beautiful things for beautiful people.

The products weren't simply stacked on the shelves - bookcases, shelving units, and dressers had been sourced from a variety of second hand, antique, and vintage outlets, stripped and painted to match or complement the cash desk - they were artfully arranged. Everything looked like it belonged together and she had created areas with a theme around either a product or a concept. And in between the larger items of furniture, there were smaller racks dotted about that held clothes; sleek slips of silk and sheathes of cashmere and pure lamb's wool, each with a similar colour palette, creating a rainbow effect as one looked around the room.

"You'll be fine," Olivia said. "Now what else can I do to help?"

A couple of hours later, everything was ready. Edie was resplendent in a clinging patterned dress and skyscraper heels, in almost the exact same shade of blue as her shop's colour scheme. She stood on the steps to the mezzanine level, surveying her empire, and as she cast a glance over every area, a smile crossed her face.

She noticed some activity outside and briskly clapped her hands to get everyone's attention, making sure that the camera was focused on her.

"We have a few moments before people start to come in and I want to make sure that everyone knows their roles, so listen up."

After Edie's rallying speech, which took three takes before the production team was happy, Olivia opened the doors. It wasn't long before the little shop was rammed with women ooh-ing and aah-ing over the merchandise, sipping lavish cocktails, and partaking of the delicious tiny canapés and pastries, while husbands and partners waved the credit cards and flashed the cash. The waiting staff weaved effortlessly through the crowds, handing out flutes of champagne, crostini, and petit fours.

Edie was holding court by the cash desk, observing the journalists and bloggers and watching them whisper to each other. Alik was by her side, looking as if he'd rather be anywhere else than where he was, and studying his phone intently. Out of the corner of her eye, Edie noticed Caro enter the store. Alone. Edie frowned. She didn't realise that Caro had been on the guest list. Edie got the attention of one of the waiters and made a beeline for her with two glasses of champagne.

"Ah, Caro, glad you could make it," said Edie, passing her a flute and clinking her glass with Caro's. "How are things coming along with your little bar?" she asked, with a false smile.

"It's going well, thanks for asking." Caro responded politely, her smile matching Edie's. "Olivia seems to have done a great job in getting the right kind of people here tonight. I see a lot of serious editors browsing."

Edie raised her eyebrows, thinking to herself that Caro probably had no chance of recognising the important people in the fashion business. But then, she reasoned, she probably wouldn't know the main players in Alik's world either. "Yes, Olivia has done so much for me. And for Alik too, of course. Blood Stone Riot are definitely profiting from her skills."

"Of course, so many talents," said Caro. "Now if you'll excuse me, I'm going to take a look around and see if there are any little trinkets of interest." She melted into the crowd.

Edie watched her go, her eyes narrowing as she sipped her drink. She still wasn't sure if Caro was someone to be trusted.

CHAPTER TWELVE

Caro's hunt for her own place was bumped up the priority list by Nic after his discovery of a stark-bollock-naked Jonny Tyler striding across the landing one morning as he went for a five o'clock piss. Caro had laughed and accused him of being jealous. But Nic had been adamant; he didn't want Olivia to come face to face with that when she was staying over, which she was doing more frequently.

After trawling websites and checking out a few of the local estate agents, Caro had narrowed down her selection to six properties around North Ridge and the surrounding area. With a surprisingly practical head on, she had managed to get them all with the same agent and had arranged to see them all on the same day.

Olivia had been nominated to go with her so Nic could keep things on track at The Indigo Lounge.

Just before she was about to leave, Caro's phone rang.

"I'm really sorry, Caro, but I have to sort something out for Edie. One of the printers we use has just pulled out and we have to find a replacement."

"Surely Edie can spare you for a few hours?" said Caro. She heard Edie shouting out to Olivia in the background.

"I'm sorry," Olivia said. "Call me and let me know where we're having the housewarming party."

Caro sighed, glancing over to where Nic was chatting quietly with Alik. They hadn't really spoken since Billy's party; Caro tried to avoid him.

"Olivia can't come with me today," she said. She sounded like a pouting child who had been told that she couldn't go out to play with her best friend. "I'm a bit nervous of going on my own. One random estate agent and me, who knows what might happen?"

Nic looked up. "Can't Jonny go with you?"

"He's in Manchester. He was promoting a club night."

"I could come with you?" said Alik.

"You?"

"Why not? I'm just hanging out here today; nothing planned. No issues if you don't want me to come." He resumed looking at the copy of *Roccia* balanced on his knee.

The thought of spending some one on one time with Alik, albeit in the company of an estate agent, was an attractive proposition. Although their recent encounters had been pretty tense, to say the least. Perhaps it might be different in the cold light of day, with no alcohol involved, doing something normal. And she really didn't want to go on her own.

"Okay," she said. "That would be great, thank you."

* * *

Nic loaned them his car for the day. They headed out to Kingbridge Drive first, which was one of the most exclusive and coveted areas of North Ridge. There were two apartments available in a converted pottery, which formed part of a larger gated development.

Waiting at the front door of the building was a young man in his early twenties, clutching a leather folder to his chest. He was wearing an ill-fitting suit and an outrageous floral tie, which clashed horribly with his striped shirt. His jaw dropped when he saw Alik get out of the car.

"Crikey, Alik Thorne!" he said. "You were the last person I expected to see on a house viewing!" He stuck out his hand, which Alik duly shook. "Blood Stone Riot are amazing. It's so great to have a local band making it in the business, one of our own so to speak. Where are you guys playing next?"

Caro watched as the estate agent went on firing questions and comments at Alik without giving him chance to reply. After a couple of minutes, she cleared her throat.

"Um, Marco, shall we go and see the flats? After all, we've got a lot to see today."

"Gosh, sure, sorry, Ms Flynn."

She caught Alik's eye and he winked at her.

As the three of them walked into the building, Marco gave them a short history lesson on the property, telling them how the Grade II-listed building had been several things over the years, including a paper mill, a bakery, and even a brewery. Caro thought he was trying to impress Alik, as he hadn't been this forthcoming over the phone with her. The building had been developed in the past few years to create a number of beautiful apartments, surrounded by a development of town houses, built to be in keeping with the original property. The two apartments were pretty much identical, presented to a very high standard, with distinctive oak flooring, exposed beams and columns, plus under-floor heating and lovely views over the Ridgeway Canal. They were both very nice properties, but Caro felt that there was something a bit clinical about them. She didn't get the feeling that anyone really 'lived' there - more that it was an address to have as a status symbol - and they felt cold and unwelcoming. She didn't share her thoughts aloud, but nodded and made non-committal sounds when asked her opinion by Marco. Alik had been quite enthusiastic, opening wardrobes to find out how much space there was, and trying to find the bin in the cupboards in the kitchen.

"You're playing your cards very close to your chest," he whispered, when Marco left them alone for a few minutes. "Is it because there's only one en suite?"

Caro laughed. "You're not shopping with Edie. I couldn't care less about en suites, but I do feel like I'm in an office or a doctor's surgery." She gestured to the white walls and stainless steel surfaces in the room.

Alik nodded. "I know what you mean, it feels like you'd always have to put on an act to make sure you fitted in with the surroundings. You couldn't relax." He met her eyes and she realised that what he'd just said didn't just apply to the house they were standing in.

The next two properties Marco showed her were a waste of time. One only had a single bedroom, and the other was in a part of town that could best be described as 'questionable.' Alik confessed that even he was watching his back as they went into the house, and that he would worry about Caro being there. Caro was touched by his concern.

The penultimate property was close to the centre of town, again with an outlook over the Ridgeway Canal. It was a recently-built three-storey townhouse. Entering on the middle floor, there was a small study-slash-third bedroom as you walked through the door, leading through into a spacious living room with a balcony, just big enough to stand on. Downstairs was a long, open-plan kitchen diner, with a tiny piece of garden that backed directly onto the water. Upstairs there was one good-sized double room, a family bathroom, and a master bedroom suite that housed an enormous king-sized bed, a walk-in wardrobe, and a large en suite with a huge rainfall shower head. As it was still in show home mode, everything was immaculately presented. Alik teased her that the shower was big enough for two and they should test it out.

Caro walked up and down the stairs and around the rooms. She didn't get the same empty feeling she had in the flats at Kingsbridge Drive. There were neighbours close by. It was near The Indigo Lounge. It would be perfect. Alik steered her upstairs to take another look at the master suite, making her uncomfortable about being in a bedroom with him again.

"I can tell you like this place,'" he said.

She grinned. "Is it that obvious? I have to have it."

"You can't tell Marco that, you have to make him wait," said Alik, his tone loaded with meaning. "You can't come across as too easy."

Caro stuck her tongue out at him, wishing she could simply push him down on the bed and have her wicked way with him. All thoughts of that were soon crushed; Alik's phone rang and he waved it at her, showing her that Edie was calling him. He disappeared down the stairs and out the front door, leaving her to find Marco, who was waiting eagerly in the living room.

"I'm not sure," she said. "There are a few compromises here and we've still got another place to see."

After they had seen the final house - a perfectly acceptable flat in a perfectly acceptable estate, but nothing like the townhouse that Caro so desperately wanted - they went their separate ways. Marco went back to his office with a promise of VIP access to the next Blood Stone Riot gig, and Caro and Alik went to get a late lunch. They found a quiet pub on the outskirts of Stratfield and ordered a couple of sandwiches, beer for Alik, and wine for Caro, before settling side by side into a corner table.

Caro spread the particulars of the six properties they had seen on the table in front of them, shuffling them and ranking them in order, even though it was patently obvious which was her top choice.

"Thank you for coming with me today," she said, sipping on the slightly too-sweet rosé. "I really do appreciate it. If I'd have been on my own, I think I would probably already be moving in."

Alik shrugged. "Marco seems pretty harmless, but I would have worried about you. Glad I could have been of assistance. And that townhouse is pretty amazing. When's the housewarming?" He grinned.

Caro picked up her phone and dialled the estate agent's number. "Hi, can I speak to Marco please? There was a pause while she was put through. She put in an offer some thirty thousand pounds below the asking price, reminding Marco that she was a cash buyer, had nothing to sell and could move quickly.

"Jesus, remind me to ask you to do my negotiating with Parker," said Alik as she hung up. "What did Marco say?"

Caro popped a piece of tomato in her mouth and chewed on it before answering. "Not much, he's going to talk to the developers and get back to me. Now, we wait."

They spent a companionable hour or so chatting about the bar and the band as they ate, briefly touching on Olivia's working relationship with Edie. Caro was on tenterhooks, checking her phone every few minutes making sure it had enough power and signal. She had texted Nic and Olivia to say she thought she had found something, but would let them know as soon as she heard.

Finally, Marco's number appeared on her screen and she leapt to answer it. Channelling her inner calm, she spoke. "Hello, Marco... Uh huh, yes I see... Well that's interesting... And when will they be able to do that?" She paused, her expression impassive, listening to the estate agent carefully. "Okay, thanks, Marco, I'll be in touch again soon." And she ended the call.

"And? Christ, Caro, the suspense is killing me!"

Caro broke into a wide smile. "It's mine, they'll let me know when I can move in, but basically it's a done deal."

"That's brilliant!" He enveloped her in a massive hug and kissed her cheek.

He was so close to her. She breathed in his scent, briefly closing her eyes and imagining how they could celebrate properly. If they were together, of course.

CHAPTER THIRTEEN

The Phoenix was one of those old-school rock pubs. The type that, even after a face-lift, had a slightly sticky, patterned carpet with suspicious stains, and the scent of un-emptied ashtrays, long after the smoking ban had been introduced. On the main road between North Ridge and Stratfield, it attracted a loyal crowd who supported local, and not so local, bands. Blood Stone Riot were one of those bands, one that usually drew quite a big crowd, and that evening was no exception as they did another warm-up gig on Parker's list for the Wilde Park Festival.

Caro's invite had come from Poppy, which was a great opportunity to get to know her better. After Billy's party, Caro had initially been reluctant, but relented in the end. It was just another gig after all, what could possibly go wrong?

"I'm so pleased you came," said Poppy, pouring Caro a glass of wine. "I couldn't bear spending another evening with Edie looking down her nose at me. Plus, I wanted to say thank you for agreeing to help me."

Caro nodded. "No problem. We really do need to arrange a time for a proper chat about everything."

They chatted while the band were setting up; Poppy telling Caro about how she had been working at a fashion jewellery and accessories retailer, spending her nights out with friends and in bars watching bands - not dissimilar to Caro - when she had stumbled across Blood Stone Riot. It had been a couple of years since she and Nate had first started seeing each other properly, and Nate had proposed six months ago. After that, Poppy had thrown in her job and basically followed the band around. She did odd bits and pieces for them, like booking hotels and vans, but since they had signed with Numb Records, there wasn't so much for her to do anymore.

"Not that I mind really," said Poppy. "I can't think of anything worse than having a nine to five office job these days."

Caro laughed in agreement as Alik signalled that the band were ready to start. About halfway through their set, the power went off, leaving them strumming ineffectively on electric guitars, with Dev's drums still at full volume.

"It's okay, we've got a generator!' called the bar manager, scurrying off with a torch to investigate the problem.

After a few minutes, some emergency lighting came on, bathing the bar in a subdued, hazy light. The crowd started murmuring about what a let down it had been and how could a band like this play a couple of songs and then leave them in the lurch. Hearing the potential disquiet, Alik went to the band's van and found his acoustic guitar, returning as quickly as he could.

"Now I know it's not what you were expecting, but I can't do justice to the usual Blood Stone stuff without them being fully plugged in, so let me play something else. This is a work in progress, called 'The Girl From The Blue.'"

Caro stopped mid-conversation. She recognised the music and certain lyrics also seemed familiar. With a jolt, she recognised it as the song Alik had sung the night they met in Mallorca. Something he said he'd been working on at the time. And as he played on, she heard changes he'd made, adding references to her.

"I'm sorry, Poppy, can I just listen to this for a minute?" she said, turning her full attention to the stage.

"Nate said this was about you," Poppy said, softly. "Apparently he won't sing it in front of the whole band, just

Nate. And no-one else knows what it's about; they just think it's Alik playing around with stuff."

The softer edges to the song certainly didn't fit in with the rest of Blood Stone Riot's repertoire, but somehow, that evening, it seemed appropriate. Caro closed her eyes, remembering his touch. Jesus, being around him was hard.

All too soon, the song was over.

"Thank you," he said, as a round of applause rang out. He passed the guitar over to Nate. "Time for a few covers, mate?"

Nate started playing the chords to 'Vermillion Pt. 2' and seconds later, Alik's voice kicked in, several tones lower than usual. Caro found it unusually hypnotic, again almost spellbound by the effect he had on her.

"That was some performance. And quite romantic," said Poppy, breaking Caro's reverie. Poppy handed her a large glass of wine that she downed about half of in one mouthful.

"I'm just hoping Edie won't get the reference."

"Hoping I won't get what reference?"

Edie appeared beside them. "I somehow managed to miss most of Alik's acoustic performance as I got cornered in the ladies by some girl asking me whether she could sell her jewellery in The Magpie." Edie shuddered. "As if I'd give space to cheap tat like that."

Caro breathed an imperceptible sigh of relief. She hadn't heard the song.

"Much nicer song than the usual stuff the band play though," Edie said. "horrible racket really. Although I'd never actually say that to Alik. I don't really like seeing him perform."

"How can you say that?" asked Caro. "He's an amazing performer. Has such an effect on his audience, a real connection." She couldn't explain any more without giving herself away, but hearing Edie talk like that about him made her blood boil.

"What would you know about connections? You've seen him play twice."

Caro pulled herself together and decided to take the professional approach. "Blood Stone Riot are a great band, and with the right promotion and backing they'll go a long way. You'll need to get used to following Alik all over the country, maybe even all over the world, and seeing him make that connection with hundreds of audiences."

Edie wrinkled her nose. "Mmm, I don't think I'm the same type of groupie as you. As if I'd hang around waiting for him to finish a set. I'd expect him to be waiting for me."

"But Edie," Poppy said, "if it's the man you love, you'd do that. Look at me and Nate, we're happy and I've been to hundreds of gigs to see him play."

"Well, if that's the life you want, then your expectations can't be that high, can they?" Edie said. "Why don't you just concentrate on your little ideas and leave me to mine?" She melted into the crowd, leaving Caro and Poppy open-mouthed behind her.

Poppy turned to Caro. "This is getting complicated, hon, what are you going to do?"

Caro stood firm. "They're together. There's nothing I can do."

"But you want to, right?"

Caro thought for a moment. "Yes, I want to."

CHAPTER FOURTEEN

The invite Edie extended to Caro for a weekend at her West Country retreat came totally out of the blue. After all, Edie had made it patently clear that she and Alik were solid and there was nothing that could come between them. And God help anyone or anything that did.

Recently purchased, and beautifully renovated by the Spencer-Newman family, Gramercy Lodge was an historic Tudor Gothic-style house with glorious views over the Westbourne Deane creek and the wooded hills that ran over the adjoining villages. Westbourne Deane was nestled in the South Devon countryside, and was popular for those living a city lifestyle, with second homes in the country. With eight bedrooms, all en suite, a grand dining room and a ground floor ballroom-esque space with a massive, back-lit inglenook fireplace, the house was the perfect quiet weekend haven.

It was also an amazing party house.

"I think she's trying to make an effort," said Olivia, as the two of them travelled down to the south west by train. It was late on the Friday night, and both of them had been working. They were sitting in First Class, surrounded by magazines, several mini bottles of wine, and the remnants of some M&S sushi. "After all, you weren't exactly on great terms the last time you were together."

"Yeah, I can see that, but what are we going to talk about this whole weekend? Shoes?" Caro sipped her wine slowly, trying to eke it out until the trolley came round again.

"Alik?"

"Ha, ha, very funny."

"What's going on with you two anyway?"

Caro shrugged. "Nothing. I'm with Jonny."

"He's a good distraction, but doesn't that complicate how you really feel about Alik?" Olivia hit the nail on the head.

Caro didn't have the chance to answer as the train manager announced that Westbourne was the next station. The two of them frantically gathered their belongings together.

They got off the train and headed towards the taxi rank, to be met by a driver bearing a card with Olivia's name on it.

"Trust Edie to send a car," said Olivia. "Totally her style."

Caro rolled her eyes. She wondered how much of a real friendship Olivia and Edie shared. Or was Edie was just being nice to Olivia as 'one of the staff?'

They drove down the snaking lanes. The small market town of Westbourne disappeared as rolling hills and fields came into view, and they headed towards the estuary side town of Westbourne Deane.

The car swung into a particularly steep and winding driveway, weaving around to Gramercy Lodge.

"It looks like something you'd find in a horror film from the seventies," said Olivia, as they got out of the car.

Caro didn't say anything, concerned about the horrors that might await her inside.

"I thought I heard a car." Edie appeared at the front door, dressed casually in a Juicy Couture playsuit and Ugg boots. Her blonde hair was piled up in a glossy bun, and she held cocktail glass in one hand. "I'll have your bags taken up to your room while we go and get drinks with the others."

She led the way into a lavish drawing room, dominated by the impressive fireplace, where three other almost identical blondes were sitting sipping lurid coloured drinks.

"Caro, this is Minty, Mischa and Karine; friends of mine from London," said Edie, though she didn't point out who was who. "They've been helping out with ideas for the shop."

"Hi, Caro," the girls said, in unison. "Lovely to meet you."

Edie poured two more of the brightly-coloured cocktails and gestured for them to sit down. "We're having dinner here this evening, then we're booked into The Maybeech Spa for a day of pampering tomorrow before the boys arrive, and dinner at Gallacher's tomorrow evening. We can just chill out here on Sunday until Caro and Olivia head back."

Caro had to restrain herself from downing her drink in one as she heard the plans for the weekend. She certainly didn't object to a bit of pampering and relaxation, but she preferred to do it on her own terms, and the thought of spending an entire day trapped inside a spa with women she barely knew didn't exactly fill her with joy.

"Ooo, you didn't say the boys were coming," said one of the girls. "Who did you invite?"

"Patrick, Jamie, Simon, Tommo..." Edie reeled off a list of names before pausing and looking directly at Caro. "And Alik."

Caro turned to Olivia and hissed under her breath. "Did you know Alik would be coming?"

Olivia shook her head. "Edie just said it was a girls' weekend. You know; spa, pampering, dinner, that sort of thing. She didn't mention anything else."

The ridiculously sweet drink burned a path down Caro's throat as she drained her glass. "Sounds great, Edie, thanks for inviting me."

CHAPTER FIFTEEN

Edie wriggled her freshly-painted toes as she settled down on the lounger beside the pool. The Maybeech Spa was on the outskirts of Westbourne Deane and catered mostly for ladies who lunched and those who were extremely well off. Edie thought she had already seen a couple of Russian oligarch's wives in the mud spa and there was always a supermodel or actress or two in residence, pretending to need time off for exhaustion or some other such ailment. She had often been there with Minty, Mischa, and Karine. She had suspected that Olivia would enjoy it, and hoped against hope that Caro would loathe it. She didn't see it fitting in with the rock chick lifestyle that Caro seemed to live. Slipping off her robe, she adjusted the tie of her tiny Melissa Odabash halter neck striped bikini and briefly checked the back of her thighs for any trace of cellulite. Thankfully, still none.

It was Minty who joined her first. She was slightly overweight and there was definite evidence of cellulite. She sank onto the lounger next to Edie in a simple, but flattering, black one-piece.

"What treatment are you having next? I've just had a Champagne and Strawberry Float Away. They use this really yummy-smelling body scrub and then there's a dry floatation thingy. I feel quite light headed."

Edie stifled a smile; that was Minty's usual state of mind. "I've just had my nails done, so nothing that might ruin them. I'll probably go for a facial and a scalp massage or something. And get my hair done for tonight." She glanced around to see if there was anyone else from their group around. "How are the others getting on?"

"I think Mischa and Karine are playing tennis, but I haven't seen Olivia and Caro. I keep forgetting that Olivia works for you, she's so lovely."

Edie tended to forget that too. In the time they had been working together, Olivia had become more of a friend than anything, particularly supporting her with The Magpie, and not just the PR work. This weekend had been partly to thank her for doing that. But also to see if there was anything going on with Caro and Alik. Alik had texted her an hour or so ago to say that he was on his way down and the boys had been instructed to keep him occupied until she returned. She had already had her skin buffed to shiny perfection, everything had been waxed, she had a suitcase full of Agent Provocateur lingerie, quarter-cup bras and crotchless panties, and she had a number of things in mind to remind him of why he was with her. Just thinking about what she wanted to do was making her hot. She waved to one of the pool attendants and asked him to bring her a glass of freshly-squeezed mango juice. Minty opted for the same. Edie knew she would have preferred a hot chocolate, but was keeping up appearances in her company.

Caro and Olivia walked through from the changing room and into the pool area. Minty waved at them, pulling up a couple of loungers so they could join her and Edie. Both of them looked fresh-faced and glowing from recent treatments, and Edie tried to contain her jealousy as Caro discarded her robe to reveal a sky blue Heidi Klein bikini that flattered her curvier figure.

"This place is amazing," said Olivia. "I can't believe I had so many knots in my neck that needed working out!"

Edie laughed. "I guess I've just been working you too hard. Good thing the launch is over now, although I'll still need your support as the orders start coming in."

"Of course, I had no intention of looking for anything else. You and Alik are definitely keeping me busy enough," said Olivia.

The main reason Edie had hired Olivia was to get The Magpie out into the marketplace, but there was also the follow-up activity that came with a growing brand. With the Blood Stone Riot work starting to grow, Edie suspected that Olivia would start to be pulled in many directions. She had heard from Alik that Parker Roberts was becoming more and more demanding by the day.

"You'll only move on when I'm ready," said Edie, lightly.

"Hang on a minute, Edie," Caro said. "What gives you the right to talk to Olivia like that?"

"While she's working for me, I'd rather she didn't work for anyone else. And if I found out she was, then I could easily put the word out and have her blacklisted in the industry."

Caro sucked in her breath. "I thought you said she was your friend? If that's your idea of friendship…"

"I can fight my own battles, Caro," said Olivia.

Edie examined her freshly-painted nails. "No doubt as supportive a friend as she will be to you in making sure The Indigo Lounge is successful."

Caro laughed. "I'm not paying her to do that. Olivia hasn't been involved in the PR for us at all; I've been able to manage that myself."

"And clearly you have the support of Jonny Tyler," Edie said.

"You know nothing of my relationship with Jonny. I suggest you concentrate on your own affairs instead."

Edie's head snapped up. "What do you mean by that? What have you heard about Alik?"

Caro didn't respond.

Minty put a hand on Edie's arm. "Don't worry, Edie, she's probably just jealous."

Olivia gathered her things together. "I think I'm going to head back to the house now. I need a break before dinner."

Edie offered to go with her but Olivia refused.

As Olivia walked out of the pool area, Edie raised her glass towards Caro.

CHAPTER SIXTEEN

Edie's family had been coming to Gallacher's since before Edie had been born, and the staff were always very accommodating and attentive. Despite it being an extremely busy Saturday night in early season, the group had a prime table in the upstairs restaurant and two waiting staff allocated to them alone.

Gallacher's was the kind of family-run establishment that had been at the core of Westbourne Deane life for as long as most residents cared to remember. Established in the late fifties by Bernie and Joan Gallacher, it served dishes containing good quality, locally-sourced produce at affordable prices. Almost fifty years later, not much had changed, except perhaps the decor.

Caro found herself seated between Tommo and Minty, with Olivia and Jamie opposite. Edie was holding court at the head of the table, Alik at her side. It was all Caro could do to stop staring at him. He looked as delightfully out of place as she did. He wore a plain dark grey t-shirt that was cut just low enough to glimpse the tattoos on his chest, whereas the other men wore polos and shirts from Jack Wills or Henri Lloyd and crisp shorts or chinos. In contrast to the other men, who were drinking pints of dark ale and playing drinking games, he nursed a glass of whisky.

Edie had ordered a selection of starters for everyone, showcasing some of the restaurant's specialities including whitebait, warm brie with a whole head of roasted garlic and homemade chutney, as well as scallops with chorizo and a pea puree. Beer was replaced by wine. The plates were passed around so everyone could take a sample. Caro locked eyes with Alik, but immediately looked away, regret washing over her.

It would have comforted her if she had known he felt the same way.

* * *

After the starter plates had been cleared, Alik excused himself from the table and headed downstairs to escape outside for a cigarette. He was already bored of Edie and Karine's shallow shopping talk. He wished that any of the band were there with him to distract him. Or even to have more of a conversation with Caro.

The fact that Caro appeared deep in discussion with Tommo instead was starting to irritate him. The beginning of jealousy, tinged with guilt.

He leaned against the doorway of the gift shop next to Gallacher's and lit a cigarette, sheltering from the light drizzle that had just started to fall.

It didn't come as a total surprise when Caro joined him a few minutes later. She took the cigarette from between his fingers and drew deeply on it. Their eyes met, but neither of them spoke as they shared it, taking turns to pass it between them, lingering slightly longer than was necessary as their fingers lightly brushed against each other.

It was Alik who finished the cigarette, dropping the end on the floor and snuffing it out with the heel of his boot. "You and Tommo seem to be getting on well," he said. "What do you think Jonny would say about that?"

"As everyone keeps reminding me, Jonny's reputation doesn't lend itself to monogamy, so I doubt he'd mind too much," she said.

"Maybe that's not the point."

Instinctively, Alik grabbed her hand and pulled her into the neighbouring alleyway, where no-one could see them. With one hand entwined in her hair, he pulled Caro towards him, his lips crushing hers, tongue gently probing into her mouth, before becoming more urgent and insistent. He felt her respond to his touch, tasting smoke and whisky. Edie's face swam into his head and he reminded himself this shouldn't be happening. Despite how totally right it felt. Caro pulled back, breathing heavily.

"We should head back in," he said. "People will be wondering where we are." The effort it took to pull himself away from Caro was immense. "Caro... I..."

"Alik..."

"I haven't been able to stop thinking about you," he said. "Since I saw you in The Vegas a couple of days after we... you know... and then again at Billy's party. And now..."

He watched her take a steadying breath.

They stood there, the rain growing harder, neither of them prepared to leave first. Alik gently pushed Caro back in the direction of the restaurant.

"Go. I'll be back in shortly."

* * *

Caro returned to the restaurant, stopping in the ladies on the way, which is where she had said she was going in the first place.

Olivia was in there, checking her make-up. Immediately, Caro felt guilty.

"Where have you been?" Olivia asked. "You've been ages and you're all wet."

"I wasn't feeling well," said Caro. "I needed to get some air." She ran some cold water over her wrists, trying to make her excuse look genuine.

"You do look a bit flushed," Olivia said. "Maybe it was something you ate?"

"I'm sure I'll be fine, maybe I just need some water."

They exited the toilets, as Alik was just coming back up the stairs, equally as wet as Caro was. He nodded at Olivia and Caro and let them go ahead first.

"There you are, Caro," said Edie. "We were wondering where you were." Her eyes narrowed as Alik came in behind them.

"I wasn't feeling well, so I headed outside for some air," said Caro. "It's raining," she finished lamely.

Alik took a sip of whisky, staring down at the table, unable to make eye contact with either Edie or Caro.

The somewhat awkward atmosphere hanging over the table was temporarily interrupted by the arrival of the main course.

"You'll feel better if you eat something," said Olivia, as the waitress placed a fillet steak in front of Caro.

Caro reached for her wineglass instead and downed what was left, before turning back to Tommo and resuming the conversation they'd been having before she'd left the table.

* * *

The rest of the meal passed without incident. Alik deliberately avoided looking at Caro or talking directly to her. There was plenty of alcohol being consumed and the chatter got louder. Edie was practically sitting on Alik's lap and everyone seemed to be getting on like a house on fire the more they drank. A selection of desserts had been passed round, along with pots of coffee and digestifs, and it was only when the head waiter came over to tell them, gently, that it was an hour past closing time, that they realised how late it was.

The larger group walked back to the house and separated into smaller ones: Edie and Minty, arm in arm, leading the way, with Olivia, Mischa, and Karine close behind, followed by Alik, Tommo, and Caro dawdling at the back. Alik was apprehensive about being in such close proximity to Caro again after their liaison outside the restaurant and made sure that Tommo was between them.

Tommo was asking him about life on the road and how he dealt with the hordes of women that undoubtedly threw themselves at him after each gig.

"It's hardly hordes," said Alik. "You learn to distinguish between the ones who want to bed you for being famous," he made finger-quotes to illustrate the last word, "and those who are genuinely interested in you."

"Which category does Edie fall into?" asked Caro.

"Probably the former, knowing her," said Tommo, laughing. "You're not her usual type."

"Opposites can attract," said Alik. "Although you can find instant attraction with someone you only spend a few hours with." He looked across at Caro as he spoke.

CHAPTER SEVENTEEN

By the time they arrived back at Gramercy Lodge, the ballroom-come-games room had been totally transformed. Groups of candles had been strategically placed around the room and the lights were turned down low, creating a rosy glow and sultry atmosphere. There was also the unmistakeable scent of cannabis penetrating the room.

Edie curled up on one of the sofas and gestured for Alik to join her. Tommo and Caro helped themselves to the shots that were laid out on the sideboard before grabbing a couple of cushions and sitting on the floor directly opposite the sofa.

"We're playing truth or dare," Edie announced to the group, snuggling in to Alik's body and positioning herself between his legs. "Where's the strangest place you've had sex?" she asked Caro.

"You're really asking me that question?" Caro said. "What are we, fifteen?"

Edie pouted. "I once had sex in the back of a limousine."

"Was it your prom night?" asked Caro. "I imagine that's probably when you first did it, am I right?"

Edie sat up straighter. She didn't want to let Caro get to her. She had to show that she could compete with Caro, that she wasn't bothered about being less experienced or worldly-wise.

"Caro, have you ever kissed another woman?" she asked.

She watched as Caro shifted awkwardly, taking a sip of her tequila. Finally, she answered, shaking her head.

"I'm afraid I'll have to take a dare on that one."

Alik almost choked on his drink. Gently, Edie placed a hand on his thigh, insinuating her fingers higher up his leg until she reached his crotch. She could feel the increased tightness of his jeans as she inched her hand closer.

Edie fluttered her eyelashes. "Gosh, I wasn't expecting that," she said. "In keeping with the line of questioning, I dare you to kiss..." Her eyes moved around the room, briefly falling on Olivia. "Me!"

Caro started to protest, but Edie knew she wouldn't back down. She slid off the couch and crawled over to Caro. Pushing Caro's caramel hair away from her face, Edie ran a fingernail around her lips and knelt in front of her. She leaned in and kissed Caro full on the mouth, closing her eyes as she did so. Bolstered by drink, Edie put her hand around the back of Caro's neck and slid her tongue into her mouth.

A sly glance at Alik watching them told her that he was certainly enjoying the spectacle. And the fact that the other guys were wriggling around in their seats told her that the effect was pretty universal.

Finally, Edie drew breath, sitting back on her heels and biting her lip, a smile flitting across her face. She stood up gracefully. "If you'll excuse me for a moment." And she exited the room.

She didn't have to wait long until Alik joined her.

"What the hell was that all about?" he said.

Edie dropped her eyes to his crotch, still half erect. "What do you mean? Did you enjoy watching me getting it on with someone that you want to do the same with? Or maybe you'd like us both at the same time?" Her tone was honey, but she wasn't going to be messed around.

"Don't be silly," he said, softly. "I only want to be with you. Caro means nothing to me."

But Edie wondered who he was trying to convince - her or himself.

CHAPTER EIGHTEEN

Since the, frankly awful, weekend at Gramercy Lodge, Edie had made more of an effort with Alik, even taking some time to go and visit him and the band at rehearsals. And just before they'd finished the previous day, she had asked Nate if he and Poppy were around for dinner and had promptly booked a table in Sarastro.

But, of course, they were running late.

Edie had been trying on different outfits and wondering what to wear; she knew she needed to impress.

Twenty minutes after they should have been there, they finally arrived at the restaurant.

"I am so sorry we're late!" exclaimed Edie, leaning down to kiss Poppy on both cheeks. "You know what the traffic can be like getting into town." She sank down a little breathlessly into her chair.

Alik sat down next to her, opposite Nate. "Alright, mate?" he said. "Have you been waiting long?"

Nate reached for his beer. "We were a bit early. Poppy wanted to go to the shops." He gestured to the colony of carrier bags clustered around the table leg. "Apparently she wants to get a few things for her weekend break."

"A girl can never have too many bikinis, right, Edie?" said Poppy.

Edie glanced down at the H&M, Zara, and Mango bags. "You can get a lot for your money there, can't you?" She waved to get the waiter's attention. "Personally, I find they fall apart after one or two wears."

The waiter came over and Edie took her time in choosing some wine, forcing the others to wait. Again.

Finally settling on an expensive South African Pinotage, she turned her attention to the menu.

"I bet you boys will be having steak, won't you? Build you up for the festival. Nate, I really liked what you were doing at rehearsals the other day, you seem so energetic. I bet it takes a lot of stamina to run around the stage like that for such a long time." Edie smiled.

Nate nodded in response. "Thanks Edie, yeah, you do need to be pretty fit. Which reminds me, Alik, we need to hit the gym again."

Alik groaned. "Can't I exercise in another way? Like in the bedroom?" He winked at Edie and placed a hand on her thigh, before squeezing it.

"I was thinking of the steak, or maybe a burger," said Poppy, running her finger over the menu.

Edie's head snapped up. "Really? This close to the wedding? You're not on a diet or a detox by now?"

Poppy laughed. "Um, hardly." She waved her empty glass. "I need filling up!"

"But every bride needs to lose weight before her wedding day."

"Not this one."

Edie cast her gaze over Poppy's figure. "Oh... right..."

An uneasy silence descended over the table, before Nate broke it, changing the subject.

"Tell me about The Magpie, Edie. What made you decide to open it?"

Poppy muttered something under her breath about her needing the attention, but Edie chose to ignore it. Instead she regaled Nate with the story of how she had come up with the idea and how *Pretty Rich Things* had picked up on it and decided to feature her. She explained that it was a little intrusive having people follow her around with a camera, but it hadn't interfered with her life too much.

"And the publicity for both me and Alik has been brilliant."

"Yeah, I always wanted to be in *Apsire* magazine," said Alik, rolling his eyes.

"You can't deny that we've had a bit more interest in Blood Stone Riot since." Nate said. He gratefully accepted the beer that the waiter brought over. "Although some of the offers of gigs have been quite interesting. What was that person who wanted us to do their birthday party? Some twelve year old with a billionaire father?"

Edie smiled. "But why wouldn't you do that? Surely it would make you money?"

They paused as the waiter came over to take their orders: steak for Nate and Alik, and a burger for Poppy. Edie chose the seafood salad, making a comment about watching her weight and glancing at Poppy.

"Good choices all round," the waiter said. "We'll get them out to you as soon as possible."

Once he had gone, Edie asked Nate about how he and Alik had met and how they'd started the band. Truthfully, she was bored, as Alik had told her about a million times how things had come about. But it was definitely time for her to show that she was there to stay. It certainly wouldn't hurt to get to know the band a little better, although Dev barely spoke to anyone outside of the band, and Billy wasn't exactly the type she could have a long conversation with, beyond what his favourite sex position was. She'd have to engineer some kind of party and invite them all, along with her real friends. She couldn't bear to go to too many more gigs in horrible little clubs with horrible little people. Nate was definitely nice enough, but Poppy... Edie was glad that she hadn't invited her along to Gramercy Lodge as well as Caro.

When the food arrived, she noticed that Poppy didn't eat a great deal, and just pushed her food around her plate. Maybe Edie's words had sunk in after all. They ate in relative silence, commenting on how good the steaks were, ordering more drinks, and mentioning the upcoming warm up gigs for the festival. Edie decided not to order dessert, instead switching to sparkling water. She said she needed a clear head for work in the morning and watched as Poppy ordered another huge glass of wine. Nate and Alik headed over to the bar, leaving the girls alone. Edie reached into her bag for her phone to pass the time until they came back. She could feel Poppy's eyes on her. They hadn't really had a great deal to do with each other in the past, even though Poppy had been around a lot longer than she had. She put her phone down on the table as Alik and Nate came back.

"Any plans for your hen night yet?" she asked, with a smile. "I know a few spas I could put you in touch with if you were interested. I think they have some cheap package deals if you can get enough people to go along."

"Not made any decisions on that, have you?" said Nate. "Unfortunately, most of her friends are in Australia so it's unlikely to be a big do."

"Chrissy and Lara are definitely coming," said Poppy. "They're just as keen as you are to know what the plan is, Edie. Although I don't actually remember inviting you."

Edie gave a tinkly laugh. "Sorry for assuming, but I thought that as another band girlfriend, I'd be one of the first on the list. We have to stick together after all."

"I know what I'd like to stick..." said Poppy, before Nate hissed something in her ear.

Edie checked her watch. "Gosh, is that the time, we should really be heading off. I've got a load of deliveries tomorrow that I can't miss. Exciting new stock; you should come and take a look, Poppy, see if there's anything for the wedding." She paused. "I could probably offer a small discount if it wasn't on one of the popular sellers."

Nate put a hand on Poppy's arm and answered on her behalf. "Thanks, Edie, we may just do that." He stood up and embraced Alik in a man hug. "We'll catch up again soon, mate," he said. "Maybe just us the next time though," he added, quietly.

Edie gathered her bag and coat together and made a show of air kissing Poppy on both cheeks as she said goodbye, leaving the couple at the table. She smiled at Alik. "I thought that went rather well. Nate is so lovely. Such a good friend of ours."

Alik hesitated for a moment before speaking. "You're right, he is. Poppy is great too, you should give her a chance."

"What do you mean? I'm sure I'll get to know her a lot better by the time the hen night comes round."

"If she invites you, Edie. And I think right now, that's a big if."

CHAPTER NINETEEN

Caro was buried under supplier invoices, CVs, attempts at rotas, posters, and cocktail menu proofs for approval, and all manner of other chaos when Poppy stopped by the club the following morning.

"I'm so glad you're here!" said Poppy. "I had an awful time last night."

Caro looked at the paper mountain on her desk and then at Poppy. Work needed her attention, but apparently the bride-to-be did as well. "What happened?"

Poppy briefly described the double date that she and Nate had been on with Edie and Alik. "I mean, seriously, what does Alik see in her?"

Caro thought about Alik's confession outside Gallacher's, but decided Poppy didn't need to know that. "Having spent time with both of them, I'm curious about that myself." She went on to tell Poppy about the awful weekend at Gramercy Lodge. "I don't know who she was trying to impress, me or Alik."

Poppy shuddered. "What are you doing this weekend?"

Caro gestured to the bomb site that was her desk before answering. "Um, probably working."

"You can't! Pack a bikini and a pair of sunglasses; we're going away."

Caro laughed. "Poppy, be serious. I can't just drop everything. I've just been away with Olivia. Nic will kill me if I disappear again."

"Please?" said Poppy. "I promise it will be better than last weekend." She made puppy dog eyes.

Caro gave in. "I'll talk to Nic."

Which is why, that Friday, at some godawful hour of the morning when it was still dark and in her old life she would probably just be going to bed rather than just waking up, Caro was waiting outside Nic's flat for Poppy to arrive. A weekend bag was at her feet. As expected, Nic hadn't been pleased that she was taking off for the second weekend running. Caro reasoned that they wouldn't make any progress anyway as all the people they needed to contact weren't working and it would give him an opportunity to spend quality time with Olivia. When she mentioned Olivia, he reluctantly agreed.

A people carrier pulled up and the driver got out and opened the door for her. Clambering into the back seat, she was surprised to see that as well as Nate, Alik was also in the car. She started looking around for Edie.

"It's just the four of us," said Poppy. "I wanted to say thank you for agreeing to be my maid of honour."

"Hey, when did I do that? I only remember offering to help you out." Caro laughed. "You could just have bought me a drink, you didn't need to take me on holiday."

They sped along the motorway, mercifully free of traffic at that time of day, and made good time in getting to the airport. After check-in, they made their way through security and into duty free. Poppy and Caro made a beeline for the perfume outlet, while Nate and Alik went to find a pub - even at that time of the morning, they could be persuaded to have a beer.

"You didn't say anything about Alik coming along," Caro said, as they browsed.

Poppy grinned. "Alik is Nate's best man and we thought we could do some wedding planning. If I had mentioned something, you'd definitely have said no. Am I right?"

Caro smiled and sprayed some Prada perfume on her wrist. "Jesus, that's awful, if you were trying to repel men then that ought to do it."

Poppy gave her a sidelong glance. "Are you trying to repel men? Or one man in particular?"

Caro sighed. "Poppy, you know it's complicated. Alik's in a relationship with Edie and I'm...seeing Jonny." She picked her words carefully and hoped Poppy could understand the underlying meaning of how she categorised her own liaison with Jonny. "If things were different..." Shaking that thought from her mind, she headed over to the DKNY counter.

When the girls finally caught up with Nate and Alik in The London Bar, the boys had already sunk a couple of pints.

"Another round?" said Nate.

Caro checked the time. "We should really be heading to the boarding gate now." She looked up at the departure board and saw that they were calling their flight to Rhodes. "The sooner we get there, the sooner we can all start drinking."

"What do you mean, start?" said Nate.

* * *

By the time they had landed, got their luggage, and completed the hour and a quarter transfer to the villa, none of them wanted to do anything else except stretch out by the pool and relax.

Situated on the coastal road between Lardos and Pefkos, their villa was in a prime location, ten minutes from the beach and around a half an hour walk to the nearest bars, shops, tavernas, and restaurants. The three-bedroom villa was well-equipped, with air conditioning and wifi, an enclosed lawned garden containing an inviting pool, and a covered pergola with seating for alfresco dining. Poppy and

Nate bagged the massive downstairs bedroom, with tiled floors, a huge king-sized bed, and light and airy en suite with a huge shower. Alik and Caro took a room each upstairs at either end of the house. Alik graciously let Caro have the larger bedroom with the en suite and balcony.

They made plans to chill out for the afternoon, before heading into Pefkos for dinner that evening. Alik and Nate clearly had no interest in lazing by the pool and decided to check out the nearby beach, leaving Caro and Poppy stretched out under the massive umbrella that protected them from the strongest rays of the sun. Tall glasses of freshly-squeezed, chilled orange juice stood on the table between them as they debated whether or not to add alcohol to the mix. With the heat, they both decided it might be better to keep a clear head.

Caro had a notebook and pen balanced on her thighs, having decided that this would be a good opportunity to start making plans for Poppy's hen night. "Right then, missy, who's coming, where are we going and what do you want to do?"

"Aren't you meant to organise it all as maid of honour and then all I have to do is turn up?" asked Poppy, taking a large sip of her juice. Why did things always taste so much nicer in the sunshine?

"I could, but then where's the fun in that? Plus, I have no idea of your friends, so would invite Olivia and that would be it!"

Poppy laughed. "Yes, you're probably right." She reeled off a list of about twenty people, then stopped. "God, how big do I want this thing? At this rate the hen night will be bigger than the wedding!"

"Do you know what Nate's doing for the stag?"

"Apparently it involves guitars, surprise surprise. And he mentioned something about speed boats. He's having it on the same weekend."

Caro reached for her phone and did a quick internet search, to find a website that had heaps of hen night ideas. "Okay, listen to this..." She read out a list of ideas, ranging from relatively sedate activities such as afternoon tea, chocolate making, and karaoke, to things like cheerleading, belly-dancing, and go-karting. "What on earth happens in foreplay lessons?" she said, scrolling down the page.

"Oh God, do I really want to know?"

"Apparently it's the perfect naughty girly hen night and will give us the chance to learn the sexy foreplay techniques that will have him on his knees, not to mention being cheeky hen night fun with some great techniques for the wedding night!" said Caro, trying not to laugh as she read out the description.

Poppy rolled her eyes. "Maybe if I was about seventeen and naive, but somehow I think we might be past all that."

"Come on, give me some clues here otherwise it will be tea at the Ritz and a matinee at The Globe." Caro tossed the phone over to Poppy to look through the list of activities. She stood up and stretched, before sitting on the edge of the pool and dangling her legs in the water. The temperature was pleasantly cool and refreshing in contrast to the air and it was very tempting to just dive in.

"How about a burlesque night?" Poppy said. "They do lessons and then you get VIP seats at one of the evening shows."

Caro turned round. "Really? You think people would be interested in doing that?"

"More importantly, it's what I'd like to do, so who cares about other people?" Poppy reread the description to Caro. "Come on; drinking, dancing, dinner, what's not to like? And we can pretty much stay at the same place for the whole day, no faffing about with taxis or anything except to get back to the hotel."

"Sounds like you've already got it sorted, my work here is done! You do need to give me a clue on the guest list though." Caro got up and moved back to her sun lounger. She took the phone back from Poppy and reread the details, making some notes and taking down the numbers to call. She yawned. It had been an early start and the heat was making her sleepy. She settled down on the mattress and closed her eyes.

She came round to the feeling of strong hands running gently over her back. She didn't know how long she had been sleeping. Caro turned her head to see a bare chested Alik rubbing after sun cream into her skin, running his fingertips over the 'C&J' tattoo on the back of her neck.

"You were getting burned," he said, softly. "How long have you been lying here?"

"No idea." She settled back down again, enjoying the feel of his touch as he gently massaged the lotion in. Out of the corner of her eye, she saw Poppy wink at her and turn away. Suddenly she felt extremely self-conscious about the situation, being so scantily dressed and having Alik behave so intimately with her. His hands moved up to her neck and shoulders, pushing her hair to one side, and she found herself becoming aroused as his fingers worked around the knots in her neck. Alik placed a tiny kiss between her shoulder blades as he finished and Caro shivered involuntarily. She watched as he dove cleanly into the pool and began stroking up and down, his arms cutting powerfully through the water.

She wondered whether he was doing that to cool off.
Just like she felt she needed to.

CHAPTER TWENTY

Caro got dressed for dinner, and suddenly realised that she was wearing the same white and black butterfly-patterned dress that she had been wearing in Mallorca when she and Alik first met. She rifled through the rest of the clothes she had brought with her, but there wasn't a sensible alternative and it was too late to get something else. Hoping that she wasn't sending him the wrong message, she slipped her feet into the same silver jewelled sandals. She looked at herself in the mirror, after applying some light make up, and decided to pull her caramel-coloured hair up into a half ponytail, streaked tendrils falling around her face. Caro pulled on an oversized cardigan, in an attempt to mask the similarity, threw a few things in a small clutch bag, and decreed herself ready.

Alik was the only one in the living room when she came downstairs. A bottle of chilled rosé was open on the coffee table. He held out a glass to her, which she took gratefully and took a large sip before setting it down on a side table.

His eyes ran over her outfit. "Nice dress."

He remembered.

Reaching into his pocket, he pulled out a tissue-wrapped package. "I saw this when Nate and I were out earlier and it reminded me of you." He handed it to Caro.

"You didn't need to get me a present," she said, tucking her bag under one arm so she could open the parcel. Inside was a beautiful leather and turquoise beaded wrap-around bracelet, interspersed with silver. It complemented her current outfit and worked with her image.

He knew her well.

She struggled to fasten it. Alik took it from her.

"Here, let me help." He wrapped the leather around her wrist a couple of times, tying it with ease. As he did so, his thumb traced a line on the inside of her wrist over her infinity tattoo. She shivered as her groin tightened in response to his touch and she drew away sharply, reaching for her wine glass.

"Thank you, it's gorgeous," she said.

Alik clinked his own glass with hers.

Caro drained her drink. "Shall we go?"

* * *

They took a leisurely walk to Terpsis, a lively restaurant in the centre of town. They were shown to a table in one corner, with stunning views over the sea. Their waiter appeared with menus and began regaling them with stories about how the restaurant's name came about, explaining that Terpsichore was one of the nine Muses in Greek mythology and ruled over dance and choral song. She was a goddess that ruled over the arts and inspired all artists; especially poets, philosophers, and musicians. Nate and Alik laughed, stating that was the reason why they had chosen the restaurant - two musicians with their muses. They listened intently as the waiter went on to describe the menu - slow-cooked Greek dishes in traditional clay pots - and the chef's preference for recreating family recipes using the finest local ingredients, including basil, mint, bay leaves, rosemary, and oregano from the kitchen garden, as well as meat from nearby farms. The most popular dishes were chicken breast stuffed with feta cheese, fresh tomato, and fresh mint, and pork fillet in a sauce of plums, honey, and wine, not to mention the traditional baklavas. Leaving it up to the waiter to decide on their dishes, they turned their attention to trying some of the best in Greek wine. With Greece being one of the oldest wine-producing regions in the world, they were pleasantly surprised to find that there were some delicious options to choose from. After some deliberating and tasting, they chose a couple of reds. They talked incessantly throughout the meal; about the band, the club, the wedding. Alik avoided mentioning Edie, and Caro didn't speak about Jonny. It was almost as if they were a foursome enjoying a holiday together. Which, in some ways, they were.

It was close to midnight when they finally left. They walked back to their villa along the beach. Caro tried to not get too close to Alik, or to think of how much the night reminded her of Mallorca.

* * *

The villa looked beautiful at night; twinkling fairy lights in the trees reflecting in the pool, creating splashes of sparkly light. The temperature was still balmy enough for them to sit out by the pool, and when they got back it seemed the only sensible thing to do was to have another drink. Nate had discovered a bottle of port in one of the kitchen cupboards - so dusty it was hard to tell how long it had been there - and took four glasses out onto the terrace. Pouring generous measures into the tumblers, he sat down on one of the couches and Poppy snuggled in next to him. Alik and Caro sat on the sofa opposite them, Caro with her legs tucked under her at one end and Alik at the other. There was some distance between them.

"Gosh, it's so lovely out here," said Caro, feeling delightfully full after a lovely meal, not to mention the copious amounts of wine. "I almost feel like I've relaxed."

"About time too," said Poppy. "You work far too hard."

"Yeah, it's not as if I'm opening a club or anything."

Nate took a long sip of his port and swirled the remaining liquid around the glass. "Have you got a live act lined up for the opening?" he asked, glancing over at Alik.

Caro shook her head. "Not yet, Jonny has suggested a few people, but I haven't had chance to contact them yet."

"There's always Blood Stone Riot..." said Alik.

"I'm not sure we could afford you."

Alik laughed. "Come on, I'm sure we would be able to work out mate's rates or something."

"Or you could play for free?"

The two of them continued to banter back and forth, each of them coming up with the pros and cons of the band playing at the opening. After a few minutes, Poppy nudged her fiancé. She took Nate's hand and the two of them quietly slipped back into the villa, unnoticed by Alik and Caro.

It was several minutes later that Alik realised Caro was practically sitting on his lap. Over the course of their conversation, the distance between them had lessened and they had managed to meet in the centre of the couch, their bodies gently touching. Caro still had her legs pulled up underneath her and Alik was resting a hand on her thigh. It was comfortable, relaxed. And felt right.

Alik turned towards Caro, his eyes on hers. He lifted a hand to her face, his fingertips tracing a soft line down her jaw, his thumb gently running along her bottom lip. He leaned in as if to kiss her, but she pulled back.

Alik sank back against the cushions, defeated. "There's something I need to get off my chest, Caro. We have this undeniable chemistry and you must know by now that I care about you. Most girls love a guy they can live a great life with, make each other laugh..."

Caro wasn't most girls, though and she cut in. "I love your company and we do have the best times, but what you're pining after with me just isn't going to happen. It can't happen."

"I've told you several times that I want to be with you. I want to be the person that makes you smile and that makes you happy."

"You do make me smile and you do make me happy," said Caro. "But all I can offer you right now is my friendship."

Alik sighed. "I know, but it's not quite the same. Stuff's just going to have to change."

"Like your relationship with Edie?"

He paused. "If our friendship changes, which it will, that means I won't get to see you as often as I'd like to..."

"I know." Caro took a final sip of her drink and stood up. "That's pretty horrible for me too, but I can't be that selfish and I'm not going to tell you that I want your company and you should leave your girlfriend because that's not fair to either of us. To any of us." She placed the empty glass on the table. "Goodnight, Alik, I'll see you in the morning."

Alik watched her retreating figure as she walked into the villa. He went to put his own glass on the table, but misjudged where the edge was and watched as the tumbler shattered into pieces. Like his friendship with Caro just had.

CHAPTER TWENTY-ONE

Caro and Poppy were stretched out on one of the large, canopied, four-poster sun loungers by the side of the pool, sipping mimosas in the vain hope that the sharp, citrus grapefruit juice would cut through their immense hangovers. Both of them were wearing huge shades that covered their eyes from the blazing close-to-midday sun. They had only just got up and were enjoying a relaxing start to the day.

"I can't wait any longer," Poppy said, throwing her magazine to one side and taking a huge swig of her drink. "What happened last night?"

Caro pulled her sunglasses down her nose and stared at Poppy over their rim. "What do you mean?" she asked.

"You and Alik, what else?" Poppy said, launching a cushion in Caro's direction.

Caro ducked and the cushion flew over her shoulder.

"You two were up late," Poppy said.

Caro chose to keep her in suspense a little longer, sipping some more of her mimosa as she decided how to reply to Poppy's question. "We were talking and..."

"And...?"

"Nothing happened. Well, we almost kissed, but I stopped it."

Poppy squealed. "I knew it! But, Jesus, Caro, why'd you stop? It's not as if you don't already know him better than that."

"Because he's with Edie."

Poppy pulled a face. "But you're much nicer and much better for him than her."

"Obviously, but I'm not in the market of shagging some bloke when he's got a girlfriend. I don't particularly want to be painted as the scarlet woman who split them up. I can imagine the media would have a field day with that."

Poppy sighed. "Alik's a big boy, no pun intended and I haven't personally seen the goods. I'm sure he didn't invite you out here to 'almost kiss.' Besides which, aren't you forgetting what happened in Mallorca? A certain one-nighter?"

"I didn't know who he was then!"

"Not sure that's any excuse, hon." Poppy shook her head. "You still shagged someone with a girlfriend."

Caro sighed. The conversation with Alik the previous evening had been playing on her mind, and she had barely been able to sleep for thinking about him. Much as she wanted him, what she had said to Poppy was true - she wouldn't go there until he was single. There would be no playing second fiddle to anyone and she certainly wasn't prepared to be sneaking around.

She'd been there, done that, got the scars, literally, to prove it. But she wasn't about to share that part of her life with Poppy.

* * *

The night that Josep Leon walked into The Roca Bar was the night that Caro's life changed. But she didn't know that at the time.

Before Caro started working there, The Roca Bar was at best half-full on a good night, but mostly pretty empty. Caro had sweet-talked the manager into giving her a few shifts when she had first arrived on the island, even though there didn't appear to be that many punters. When Caro and Mariella started working shifts together, there seemed to be more people in the bar. Particularly men.

Caro and Mariella swiftly became firm friends, both having escaped a somewhat dreary existence in their own countries - Mariella hailed from Norway - after university to travel and experience the Spanish life. It hadn't been long before they had moved into a shabby, one-bedroom apartment near to the beach.

They became a familiar pairing around the town, usually partying together on the nights they weren't working and spending their days at the beach. They made for a striking couple; Mariella with her Scandinavian parentage - blonde, sharp good looks, and glacial eyes - and Caro with her darker-haired, rock-chick-slash-boho appearance. They certainly weren't short when it came to admirers.

In his mid-forties, Josep Leon was impeccably dressed in a beautifully-cut suit that was at odds with the usual attire of the holidaymakers. He had dark hair that was streaked with silver and twinkly, mischievous, eyes, and was by far the best-looking man in the bar. Even if he had the worst attitude.

"Cerveza," he demanded, taking a seat at the bar.

"Cerveza, por favor," replied Caro, pouring his drink anyway. "Manners always get you further in this bar, even if it is quiet."

He grunted in response. "And why is it so quiet?"

Caro looked around at the bar, watching people nursing their drinks, sometimes chatting to the people beside them. There was the odd stag or hen party that popped in, never staying for longer than one drink before moving on to somewhere more lively.

"There's nothing going on," she said. "There's nothing to do; no music, no TVs for MTV or sport or anything. Nothing to keep the punters in for more than one drink. Sure, there's plenty of drinks to choose from, but if you can't get anyone to stay to buy them, there's no profit to be made."

Mariella, who had come to meet Caro after her shift, gestured at her to stop talking. Caro ignored her.

"You've got it all worked out, haven't you?" Josep said.

"Just a few ideas that I've seen work elsewhere." Caro shrugged and went about tidying up a few glasses that had been left on the bar.

"What would you do to improve this place then?"

"Why do you care? You've just come in for a drink."

"A drink in the bar that I own."

Mariella cut in smoothly. "Caro, this is Josep Leon, he owns The Roca Bar."

Caro couldn't believe she'd put her foot in it. Telling the owner of the bar that it wasn't working and he should make changes would probably get her the sack. As she examined the man in front of her, she noticed that he didn't look cross. In fact, totally the opposite. He looked happier now than when he'd first walked in.

"I like your ideas." He smiled at her, his eyes twinkling. "I have a small amount of money that I could use to improve this place, a tiny amount." His Spanish accent became more pronounced as he became more animated. "Tell me why I should get you to spend it."

Caro looked at Mariella, who shook her head. Caro briefly outlined what she thought would make the difference, talking about live music, promotions, deals and other events that might keep people in the bar longer.

Josep reached into his pocket and drew out his wallet. He passed over some euro to cover his beer and then handed a roll of notes to Caro. "This is it. Do what you need to."

"I can't accept your money, you don't even know me."

"Not yet, I don't, but I will."

He was true to his word. Over the next few weeks, Josep made regular visits to the bar to check up on progress as Caro steadily made changes and introduced the things she had discussed in their first meeting. The more time he spent here, the closer he and Caro became. After his fourth visit, he asked her out to dinner. Flattered that someone other than a spotty, virginal teenager on a lads' holiday was taking an interest, she accepted. And each time after that, she accepted, until they were going out almost every night of the week. As they spent more and more time together, the dynamic of their relationship changed, from business to something more personal. It came as no surprise that, finally, they slept together.

Mariella couldn't believe it, finding Josep snoring loudly in their living room, having spent the night on the foldout sofa bed that Caro had commandeered when she had moved in.

"You can't let this go on," she said, pulling Caro into the tiny kitchen. "He's married."

"Separated," said Caro. "He told me himself."

"If he's that separated, tell me why he was out last night with his wife." Mariella pushed a newspaper at Caro, which had a shot of Josep and his wife, attending a gala dinner in aid of a local charity.

Caro had discovered by now that Josep was something important in the town, simply by the amount of people he spoke to or had contact with during the course of their dates. And then she realised that all of their meetings had been in other places, far away from The Roca Bar. He had told her that he and his wife were still legally married, although had agreed to go their separate ways. The article in the paper seemed to point to the contrary. She hated being deceived, but enjoyed the time that she spent with the older man. She ignored it until one night, after a long dinner that led to them making love on a secluded beach, Caro tackled the situation head on.

"Why did you lie to me?" she asked. "About Consuela?"

They were lying on a blanket, huddled up beneath a second, the air still warm and sticky. Josep shifted uncomfortably.

"I didn't lie, specifically... I just didn't tell you everything."

"The two of you have been carrying on like nothing happened, even though you said you weren't together. Are you ashamed of being with me?"

Josep stroked her hair. "Never."

"But not open enough to leave your wife."

He shifted into a sitting position, rubbing his chest. "Caro, I can't have this conversation with you now. I need to get home."

"Home to your wife."

"Just home." Josep hauled himself up off the sand and pulled on his clothes, before walking up to his car.

He never made it home.

He suffered a massive heart attack, which caused him to lose control of the car and veer off the road into a ditch.

He died instantly.

In the aftermath of his death, his affair with Caro came out, and she discovered he had left her The Roca Bar in his will. There was an acrimonious battle with Consuela, who demanded that it should be given back to her, to compensate for Josep's infidelity. Caro refused to give in to her and instead she ploughed every bit of energy she had into The Roca Bar, making it the most successful it had ever been. Creating a legacy to the man who had given her a start in the business.

She also distanced herself from relationships, preferring instead to stick to the occasional one-night stand or meaningless hook up. She was wary of getting close to anyone again. Particularly if that man was already involved with someone else.

CHAPTER TWENTY-TWO

Alik had been a little reluctant to go to Minty's Charity Ball, but Edie had been more than persuasive, saying it would be good for his image, not to mention getting him some mainstream press coverage. She had also informed him that the cameras from *Pretty Rich Things* would be there, although way after it was too late for him to back out. After finding out that Parker Roberts was also going to be there, he agreed to go. Despite his protestations, Edie had forced him into a tuxedo that covered almost every tattoo he had. She was convinced he looked like some kind of movie star, but he felt like a total fraud. He disliked going to events without the rest of the band, particularly ones like this. He had no idea how he was going to get through the evening.

They arrived at The Cartier Hotel in the limousine that Edie had booked and got out of the car to a blinding flash of cameras and paparazzi. Edie was used to this type of attention as she twisted and turned for the cameras, making sure they got her best side and the full effect of her dress; a dark red fitted number from Amanda Wakeley. Alik let her preen, trying to stay out of the limelight, but she grabbed his hand and pulled her close to him.

"Smile," she said. "At least make it look like you want to be here with me."

He forced a smile as they walked up the short red carpet to the entrance. Once inside, the smile slid from his face as he saw what awaited them. The ballroom had been decorated with various coloured ribbons, denoting the different types of cancer, and while Alik had every faith in the fund-raising efforts of the evening, the decor was making his eyes hurt. It looked as if someone had thrown up rainbows. Around the edge of the room were various tables with the lots for the evening. Ranging from yacht trips, spa days, race days, polo tickets, rugby boxes... There wasn't one thing that Alik would contemplate bidding on, even if he could afford it.

Minty bounced up to the pair, proffering them raffle tickets for some of the more inexpensive prizes such as dinner or opera tickets. "Hello you two, can I interest you in some of these? They are twenty-five pounds for one or one hundred pounds for five. Or you can put some bids on the auction lots."

Alik coughed. One hundred pounds would almost cover the entire audience's drinks in the some of the bars the band had played in recently. And Minty wanted that much on the off chance that you might just get to see Madame Butterfly. Edie nudged him in the ribs.

"Of course, Minty," she said. "Alik, we'll take five. I'm not so bothered about these prizes, but it's all for a good cause, isn't it?" She stared at him until he got his wallet out and peeled off some notes to give to Minty. Edie tucked the tickets into her tiny Chanel clutch bag, which probably cost more than the tickets in any case, and kissed Minty on both cheeks. "It looks like tonight will be really successful, well done."

Minty beamed. Alik thought Edie was being patronising, although seeing how the other girl basked in Edie's praise was interesting. She clearly thought the world of Edie and any positive words were coveted.

"I think we'll go and take a look at some of the lots. I could quite fancy the yacht trip to Cannes."

Edie pulled Alik away and they meandered around the room, moving from table to table. Each lot had pictures or videos describing it, with envelopes so that interested parties could make sealed bids before the ten o'clock deadline. There would then be a period of reviewing the bids made and winners would be announced before midnight. With around thirty lots to distribute, Alik was already thinking about how dull that would be.

"I need a smoke," he said, as they stopped at a stand auctioning race days at Goodwood. Edie had already bid on pretty much everything and he couldn't face listening to yet another weak-chinned hooray talking at him. "I'll meet you at the bar in a bit."

Escaping outside through the back door, he was pleased to see Parker Roberts already on the patio puffing away at a cigarette. The artist development manager was alone. Hearing someone else in his space, he turned, saw Alik, and offered him his pack of Malboro.

"Ah, good to see someone else who needs a breather. Although not too many of these, Mr Thorne, I don't want to have to cancel gigs because of throat problems."

Alik laughed, accepting the cigarette, and bending over slightly as Parker flicked an engraved Zippo. "Good to see you too. I didn't think this would be your scene either though?"

Parker shook his head. "Not mine, no. The lovely Lexi insisted that I accompany her here this evening, much as I expect Edie did with you?"

"Lexi?"

"Lexi Bloom."

Alik's eyebrows shot up. Lexi Bloom was the indie actress of the moment and an overall press magnet. It transpired that Parker had been seeing her on and off for a few months, initially attracted by her seeming disregard for the limelight and mainstream events. Lexi had also recently appeared in an episode of *Pretty Rich Things,* seen shopping at The Magpie. Edie hadn't stopped talking about it for weeks. He exhaled a stream of smoke.

"Never thought she would be your type," Alik said at last.

"Nor Edie yours," said Parker. "I thought you'd be hooked up with a rock chick."

Caro's face immediately entered Alik's head. He hadn't been in contact with her since their very frank conversation at the villa in Greece, and what had been a burgeoning relationship now appeared dead. He contemplated whether or not to tell Parker about her. Did he really need to burden him with his love life?

Parker waved to a waiter and ordered them some whisky.

"Let's sit out here and chat for a while," he said. "I'm sure Lexi and Edie can manage without us."

A bottle of Laphroaig and two immaculately-cut crystal tumblers arrived on a silver tray within minutes, and the two men settled down at one of the heavy oak garden tables.

It felt strange having such a personal conversation with someone that he'd only met a couple of times before, and someone who was effectively his boss, but Alik found it easy to open up to Parker. He told him about what had happened in Mallorca and what had almost happened several times since they'd been back.

"I was with her at the weekend," he said. "Poppy wanted to thank Caro for agreeing to be her maid of honour and it just happened. We... Well, I told her what I wanted and she turned me down. Told me that all we could be is friends."

Parker took a long sip of the whisky. "That's pretty messed up. But what about Edie?"

"That's the thing, she doesn't know I was with Caro in Greece."

* * *

Edie had stepped out on the patio to get some fresh air. All the entertaining and being nice to people took its toll after a while. There had been plenty of interest in The Magpie and she had made a couple of contacts who could really help her to expand in the online markets. Now she wanted Alik. She knew that he probably felt a little uncomfortable at events like this, but he'd have to start getting used to it. He hadn't come back to find her as he said he would so she'd had to go to him. Spotting him sitting chatting with Parker, she headed across the terrace, her heels gently clacking on the stone. Neither of the men heard or saw her coming. As she approached, she heard Alik talking.

"That's the thing, she doesn't know I was with Caro in Greece."

Edie stumbled on a slightly loose paving slab and gasped. Both men spun round and Alik leaped up from the table.

"Are you okay?" he asked.

Should she confront him about Caro now? What else had gone on while they had been away? Was he going to break up with her?

"Owwww!" she cried, instead, collapsing in a heap on the concrete. "My ankle! I think I sprained it as I fell."

As expected, Alik came to her aid, gently stroking her back and feeling her ankle. "It doesn't appear too bad, but perhaps we should head home? I'm sure Minty will keep you posted on any prizes you win."

Edie fluttered her eyes at him, eyes that were damp with crocodile tears. "Yes, I think going home would be a good idea. See you again, Parker."

CHAPTER TWENTY-THREE

Alik was on edge. He wasn't usually that nervous before a gig, but he knew that Parker was going to be there and he respected what he thought of them, particularly this close to the Wilde Park Festival set. He had suggested that Parker came along to see them before the festival when they'd talked at the auction a couple of nights ago. They were at The Vegas again, somewhere that felt comfortable and where they knew that the crowd would be into them. The plan was to run through the set they would play at the festival, making sure it was as tight as it could be. In the tiny, cramped backstage area, Billy and Nate were tuning up their guitars, while Dev was air drumming. Alik waved the setlist at them.

"You know what we're doing, right?"

"You worry too much," replied Billy, looking up from replacing one of his strings. "Plus you made sure that the setlist is taped to practically every amp or mic stand. We're not going to forget."

"I just want to make sure everything goes smoothly. You know Parker's coming tonight?"

The others nodded. It wasn't as if Alik hadn't mentioned it about a hundred times. He wondered whether he was going over the top. He wanted to make a good impression and make Parker realise that Blood Stone Riot were a good investment. He took a sip of water from the bottle on top of one of the drum cases. There was nothing wrong with the adrenalin that was running through his body; he needed to channel that energy in a show. Before it spilled out anywhere else.

Finally, the bar manager indicated that they should go on.

Strutting onto the stage, Alik grabbed the microphone. "Good evening, Vegas!" he yelled. "We're Blood Stone Riot and this is 'Bleed Like Cyanide!'"

The crowd erupted. Alik whirled across the stage, energised by their response. He flitted between Nate and Billy, alternately singing with them and holding the mic out to the crowd. He knew he was being a bit optimistic, but luckily it was an audience that knew them well and could, at least, sing back some of the chorus. Nate and Billy played their parts, swapping sides on the stage, singing harmonies together in the same mic and including Dev in their antics. Alik spotted Parker standing near the front to one side of the stage and raised a fist in acknowledgement. He was pleased to see that Parker responded with a grin. They blistered through the short, six-song set, finishing up with 'In It For The Craic,' another fan favourite.

"Thank you! You've been an incredible audience tonight!" cried Alik as the cheers died down. "We've been Blood Stone Riot and we'll see you at the Wilde Park Festival next weekend!"

The band left the stage, applause and whistles ringing in their ears. Alik still got an overwhelming feeling of pride whenever he got a reaction like that, no matter how many times it happened. Someone had enjoyed something he had poured his heart and energy into. He had bared his soul out there. And they had liked it.

Parker approached the band. "Guys, that was immense. I admit, I've never seen you play live before, just heard clips from social media and that was a mistake. I can honestly say that you put everything into that performance. If you pull it off at the same level at the festival, they'll definitely be asking you back for a main stage appearance." He slapped Nate on the back. "Good job, mate, if I could only play guitar like you."

Nate laughed. "Thanks, Parker, means a lot. After all, you'll be making a lot of money out of us if things go well, right?"

"We can but hope." Parker gestured for Alik to join him in a quieter area. "In all seriousness, Alik, that's one strong band up there. It all works. The four of you are a force to be reckoned with. You keep it up and we'll have GnR begging you for a support slot. Look, I've got to shoot off, Lexi's expecting me at some drinks party, but keep in touch, we'll speak soon." And then he was gone.

Alik felt as if he were in another world as he stripped off his sweat soaked t-shirt and freshened up. He went back into the main body of the club, buoyed by Parker's comments.

Edie was waiting for him by the bar. "You were amazing," she said, standing on tiptoe to kiss his cheek. "Everyone at the festival is going to love you."

Alik laughed. "God, I hope so! We've worked so hard for this. I dreamed about playing that festival since I first went there when I was fourteen and standing ankle deep in mud. Although I'm hoping for better weather."

"Urgh, mud." Edie made a face. "It's not going to rain, is it?"

"You need to be prepared for every eventuality, anything could happen." Alik looked around the crowded bar. "Let's get out of here." He grabbed Edie's hand and took her through the backstage area, where the band were packing up. They exited through the back door into an alleyway. Still high from the excitement of the gig, Alik pulled her towards him and kissed her, his lips crushing hers. She moulded her body into his, kissing him back hard. He laced his fingers through her hair, feeling himself getting hard. If he wasn't careful, he'd seriously embarrass himself in the back alley of a club, something that hadn't happened to him since he was a teenager.

"Let's go back to my place," whispered Edie. "It's closer." She broke away from him and stepped into the road, hailing a passing taxi.

Thankfully, it didn't take them long to get back to Kingsbridge Drive and Alik pushed a twenty pound note at the driver without waiting for any change. They climbed the stairs to the first floor, too eager to wait for the lift, and crashed through the front door, heading straight for the bedroom, both of them shedding clothes on the way. Falling onto the bed together, Alik rolled Edie onto her back, looking her straight in the eye as he slid gently into her. Her eyes were closed in rapture as he thrust inside her, her nails scratching at his back. The energy of the evening coursed through him as he brought them both to shattering orgasm. He collapsed on the bed beside Edie, breathing heavily. She turned to look at him, her pupils dilated.

"If that was just a warm up, I can't wait to see the main event!"

CHAPTER TWENTY-FOUR

Wilde Park Festival always delivered in relation to its name.

Set in the Midlands, it had previously been a racing circuit until the money in Formula 1 became too rich and forced it out of business. When the promoters of the festival came to the venue's rescue a few years ago, it was the start of a great relationship. The 90,000 rock fans that made an annual three-day pilgrimage to the sprawling site enjoyed bands playing across five stages, a myriad of stalls selling an eclectic mix of products, and every kind of food you could think of.

And this year, Blood Stone Riot got to play.

Having attended the festival as fans in previous years, they were understandably ecstatic when Parker Roberts had announced several months ago that he had managed to secure them a slot - albeit an early Saturday afternoon slot in one of the smaller tents.

Their touring entourage consisted of Griffen and the band, Edie, Poppy, Caro, and a last minute addition in Olivia. Parker had decreed that Olivia needed to be there to manage any PR and interview requests, as new and up and coming bands were always popular with the online radio stations and other social media-driven channels.

They had travelled up on the Thursday night in relative luxury. Edie had taken one look at the mini-bus that Alik had shown her and flatly refused to travel in the shabby-looking vehicle, declaring it a death trap. Subsequently, she had generously offered to provide a more suitable mode of transport and arranged for a twenty-seater, air-conditioned coach with an on-board toilet, more than adequate for the two and a half hour journey up the motorway.

They arrived in good spirits and parked around the back of the hotel, just in case there were any fans waiting for them. As soon as they got off the coach, Griffen left to answer a call from Parker, leaving Olivia in charge of checking them in.

"I'm a PR rep, not your bloody PA," she said. However, when she managed to get them upgraded at no extra costs, there were murmurs as to whether she should consider a PA role instead.

* * *

After unpacking, they decamped to the penthouse bar, which had been cordoned off for the exclusive use of artists and their associates, as well as those guests who were staying in executive suites. It was much quieter than the main bar downstairs near reception.

Caro was sitting with Poppy, nursing a large gin and tonic, every so often casting a glance in Alik's direction. "I don't know why I came with you guys," she said. "Things have been a bit odd with Alik."

Poppy reached for her mojito and sucked up a generous amount before responding. "Nate says he hasn't been himself either. Apparently he went to some charity ball the other night with Edie, all dressed up, and ended up in the gossip pages of *Aspire*."

Caro made a face. "Bet that went down well!"

"Even Parker was there. Did you know he was dating Lexi Bloom?"

"Who?"

Poppy shook her head. "Just the most famous actress on the block at the moment... Oh wait, you wouldn't notice if it doesn't come accompanied by music."

"And that's why I came here," Caro said. "I'm here for the music. If Blood Stone Riot weren't playing I'd still be here, although perhaps not in the same element of luxury. I came for the headliners, the bands making a start on the smaller stages, the atmosphere, the sense of belonging."

"Why is Edie here, then?"

* * *

Edie was thinking exactly the same thing. Since the minute they stepped on the bus, Alik had withdrawn, barely saying two words to her. She sat alone in the bar until a couple of women who recognised her from *Pretty Rich Things* started asking her about The Magpie.

"You should definitely come into the boutique," said Edie, pulling one of her cards out of her bag.

The two women started cooing over the duck egg blue card, comparing it to Tiffany branding and asking where she sourced her products from.

"Barcelona should really be an option, but I'm all about giving opportunities to up and coming suppliers," she said. "I've been working with a number of art schools, getting final year students to produce pieces for me to sell. There are some really talented people around. Plus, the prices I have to pay are a lot cheaper than if I were using established suppliers." Olivia had said it would be a great marketing angle and would easily secure more articles in various publications, which meant more publicity. And she had been right.

"Ooo, do you have a website?"

"It's in production at the moment," Edie said. In truth, all she had registered so far was the name and got someone to design a pretty front page telling people the site was under development. She knew that she ought to do something about it now that the shop was up and running. Olivia said she should really be making the most of her online presence and once this festival was over, Edie would have her full attention again. "Let me show you some of the things I've got coming in," she said, reaching for her phone to show them pictures of her stock.

The two women continued to coo over the items and pointed out at least a dozen that they wanted to purchase. Perhaps coming along on this festival jaunt hadn't been a bad thing at all.

CHAPTER TWENTY-FIVE

The following morning, Edie was anything but happy.

"I didn't bring any other boots," she said to Alik. "I wasn't expecting to be outside the whole time."

"Be grateful it's not raining," said Alik. "At least your heels won't sink in the mud."

Edie pouted. She had dressed in what she thought was appropriate attire for a festival, based on what she had seen others wearing in magazines at V and Glastonbury, so she was sporting denim short shorts, a scoop-neck t-shirt with a nondescript imaginary band logo on it, a fake fur gilet, and spike-heeled ankle boots. She had plaited some of her blonde hair and then drawn it into a half-ponytail, accessorising the look with a few flowered hair pins.

She hoped that Alik didn't think she was trying too hard. She wanted to make an effort for him, to show that she was part of his fully plugged-in rock and metal world.

They met up with the others downstairs. Edie cast her eyes over their outfits. Caro and Poppy appeared to be a bit more in-keeping with the rock scene; a lot of black, skulls, and crosses and, more importantly, flat boots. Both of them had waterproof jackets tied around their waists and cross-body bags, and lanyards hanging around their necks with stage times and band info on.

"You've clearly done this before," said Edie, though she thought that they both looked horrendous and would definitely be appearing in the 'Worst Dressed' lists. If *The Goss* even bothered to show up at an event like this.

"You could say that," said Poppy. "Guess we're a bit more accustomed to this scene."

A couple of hours later, Edie was standing on her own by the bar, wishing she could sit down.

Her stupid feet in her stupid, impractical, heels were killing her, and she was convinced that Poppy and Caro were laughing at her. Caro, especially. She had just discovered that she had no service on her mobile and she couldn't even text Minty to pass the time.

In fact, the whole idea to come along on this trip had been stupid.

"Whatcha doing?"

Edie turned to her left to see Billy Walker had settled himself next to her. She had always been a bit wary of him, with his long hair and scary tattoos alongside a belligerent and sometimes slightly misogynistic attitude. They had barely spoken for any length of time before, despite their occasional shared indulgences, and to have him in such close proximity made her a little uncomfortable.

She shrugged, unsure of what to say.

"Fancy a drink?" He flagged down the barman and ordered two tequila shots - one of the benefits of being in the VIP area was a wider choice of beverage available. He downed his in one and challenged Edie to do the same.

Edie shrugged again and sank the shot, shuddering delicately as the liquor burned a path down her throat. Billy laughed at her.

"Didn't think you'd be the sort of bird who'd be able to do that," he said. "Thought you might be a bit too posh."

"You'd be surprised. When you've been out with as many bankers as I have, you know how to hold your drink."

"Bankers? Yeah, reckon they'd probably put us to shame. Known a few merchant bankers as well."

Edie frowned. How on earth would Billy know people who worked in financial services? Then she understood his rhyming slang reference and laughed. "And there are probably a few over there at the moment." She nodded in the direction of the press.

Billy ordered them another couple of shots. "He's in his element there, isn't he?" He gestured towards Alik with his glass. "Always gotta be the one in the limelight."

Secretly, Edie thought that was true. But she felt the need to defend him. "Come on, Billy, he's just passionate about what he does."

"And who he does it with?" Billy ran his empty shot glass down Edie's bare arm, fixing her with an intense stare. "Surely he can't be that passionate all the time."

Suddenly she felt her whole body leap to attention. The way Billy was looking at her, the underlying meaning of his words, the seeming disloyalty to Alik, his best friend and bandmate. She shook her head. Of course he wasn't coming on to her. He was just passing some time before the set started. Wasn't he?

"Been good talking to you, Edie. Should do it more often."

With that, he was gone just as suddenly as he'd appeared, leaving Edie to ponder what had just happened.

* * *

Alik was starting to get edgy, and was grateful when Olivia finally shooed away the last of the journalists just before two o'clock, leaving the band about an hour before they needed to be onstage. He was keen to get out there and play, and the interminable stream of questioning was becoming repetitive and dull. It became apparent that the rest of the band were feeling the same, particularly when Nate emptied the best part of a bottle of mineral water over him for no apparent reason.

"Right! That's it!" Alik grabbed his plastic pint glass and filled it with ice, throwing it at Dev.

Within seconds, it had descended into total chaos, with everyone laughing and chasing around and drenching each other with water, beer, ice, anything they could get their hands on. The warm, early summer sunshine meant that everything dried within minutes - not least because they weren't exactly the best shots either. Alik noticed that even Edie had joined in, leaping out and getting Billy full in the face with a whole pint. The bassist shook his head, droplets of water splashing over her. He grabbed a cup from Dev and threw the contents straight at her chest. Alik watched as she angrily shook her head and stalked off, leaving the others to play.

He saw Caro step away from the group to take a breather at the bar. After a couple of beats, he went to join her.

"Hey," he said. "You okay? You've been pretty quiet."

They hadn't really spoken since Caro had blown him off in Greece. He had avoided the club and she had avoided any of their gigs.

"It's nothing. I realised how much we still have to do to get the club open and I've gone gallivanting off leaving Nic to it. Again. I feel guilty, I guess."

Alik assumed, correctly, that the recent trips to away hadn't impressed Nic all that much, as Caro had only been back in the country a few weeks.

"You're entitled to a break," he said.

"Mmm, I guess."

They both leaned back against the bar, watching the rest of the band, and Poppy and Olivia chasing around.

"Edie's not exactly enjoying herself, is she?"

"Perhaps not her scene, no." Alik had been amazed when Edie had decided that she was going to come along. He hadn't expected it to be a place that would be in her comfort zone. "Thought it was a bit odd myself, but she insisted. Although maybe I should have supervised her packing."

Caro laughed. Alik watched her relax slightly and, not for the first time, he wished he could spend more time with her.

CHAPTER TWENTY-SIX

The VIP area was practically deserted when Edie got there. With the headlining bands not due on for another couple of hours and the acts that had already played enjoying the rest of the festival, there was barely anyone milling around the cabins, with the exception of a few security guards and backstage hands.

The portacabin allocated to Blood Stone Riot was empty. Edie let herself in to sort out her hair and make-up after the silliness of the water fight. She checked her reflection in the mirror. Not too much damage, or at least nothing that couldn't be fixed by an appointment with her hairdresser and a facial at The Maybeech Spa when she joined Alik at Newcomen Farm after the festival. She pulled a tiny brush through her hair, fluffing it up again, and pouted, wondering whether she could be bothered to find her phone for a quick selfie.

A noise behind her made her stop. She turned to see Billy Walker in the doorway, his eyes blatantly roaming over her body. Her t-shirt was now totally see-through and was clinging wetly to her lacy bra.

"Can I help you?" she asked.

"That depends on what you're offering," he replied. He entered the cabin and closed the door, leaning against it and trapping her inside with him.

She thought back to their earlier flirting. She knew his reputation - he was the one in the band who always had groupies, never had a serious girlfriend, just liked a quick shag. And now, here he was, wanting her.

"What if I'm not offering anything?" she said. "You know I have a boyfriend."

"Yeah, a boyfriend who takes away some girl he barely knows to a romantic Greek villa instead of his beautiful, sexy, gorgeous, girlfriend." With every word, Billy stepped closer to Edie until he was standing right in front of her.

He reached out and cupped his hand around the back of her neck, pulling her towards him until their faces were inches apart. She could smell beer and cigarettes on his breath, but she wanted him as much as he wanted her. He leant in, crushing her lips with his, almost devouring her, his tongue probing, intense, their bodies pressing together with need. Billy's other hand delved between Edie's legs, finding a way under her denim shorts, and slipping two fingers into her wetness. She bucked against him, biting his lip as she helped him find her clitoris so she could reach the release she so desperately wanted from him. He was rock hard against her and she could tell he was big, which aroused her even more. She needed him inside her. Pulling away momentarily, Edie peeled off her t-shirt and bra - her small breasts swollen, nipples standing pertly to attention - before pulling down her shorts. She left on her heeled boots. Billy wrestled his jeans and boxers off, before pushing Edie down onto the couch. The cheap, rough fabric grazed her delicate skin. As he positioned himself above her, Edie glanced at the size of his cock and was delighted to see just how erect he was. He paused before slamming into her, pumping hard. She writhed and bucked with his rhythm, feeling the delicious girth of him, her legs spread wide to accommodate him. The rising orgasm threatened to overwhelm her, but it was too soon. She wanted this to go on, wanted him to bury his cock right inside her. Billy thrust one final time and with a grunt, he came hard. Realising that she was still on the edge, he pulled out, replacing his cock with his fingers again, his thumb teasing and stroking her into final submission. It was just as one of his fingers started to probe her anus that she climaxed, a shuddering, dirty orgasm that exhausted her.

They were silent for a few moments, before Billy stood up.

"I like what you've got to offer," he said, breathing hard. "I never knew you'd be so filthy; the Chelsea girl coming with a finger up her arse after being fucked butt naked except for kinky boots in a portacabin. I like your style, sweetheart. Bet you never did that with Thorne, did you?"

CHAPTER TWENTY-SEVEN

"Where the hell have you been?" said Alik, as Billy joined the rest of the band in the wings of the stage mere seconds before they were due on.

Billy gave a knowing smile. "Gotta love a pre-gig shag," he said. "And she was filth, mate, pure filth." His eyes strayed to Edie, who was standing next to Olivia at the side of the stage, fiddling with her phone, studiously trying to ignore him.

Alik glared at him. "I don't care how amazing she was in the sack, disappearing five minutes before we do a gig this big isn't acceptable."

Alik stalked onto the stage and made his way to the mic stand, front and centre, surveying the audience in the small tent. This was the first time he'd been on the other side at a festival, having spent many years of his youth attending the event and hoping against hope that one day he would be able to play there. A headlining slot would be nice, but he knew that they had to start somewhere.

And a mid-afternoon slot on Saturday was about the best there was for a band such as Blood Stone Riot right now.

He looked to the side of the stage, where Edie was, and smiled at her. She waved back half-heartedly, looking less than interested. He thought back to the support she had given him at the warm up gig at The Vegas and was grateful that she was there with him. In the pit in front of him, he caught sight of Caro and Poppy, who had chosen to get the full experience from in the audience, rather than the VIP treatment. It was one of the things that attracted him to Caro.

Although for someone who was opening a rock club, he wouldn't have expected anything less.

"Good afternoon!" he yelled, catching the attention of the crowd. "Let's do this!" And he whirled across the stage as the opening bars of 'Bleed Like Cyanide' kicked in.

* * *

Despite having not really paid much attention to anyone other than Alik when she had seen the band play before, Edie was transfixed by Billy. She had been focused on Alik and how he commanded the audience and captured them in the palm of his hand. But now, after being with Billy, she couldn't stop staring at him. The concentration he had as he played the intense basslines, the way he moved as he cradled the guitar in his hands, the way he flung his head back in total abandon as the music played. There was an intensity about him, the same as when they'd had sex, total focus on what he wanted right at that moment. And she had been what he wanted. Her gaze wandered to Alik and she realised that he didn't have the same effect on her anymore.

"Are you okay?" Olivia asked. "You seem distracted."

Edie shook her head. "Sorry, no...um, I'm not feeling all that well to be honest, I think I should just head back to the hotel for a bit. I can feel a migraine coming on." She put a hand to her forehead for effect.

Olivia gave her a hug. "Probably too much beer in this heat and not enough water, easily done. Feel better, hon."

Having escaped from the cloying atmosphere of the tent, Edie practically skipped towards the exit. She needed some time to think about what had happened that afternoon and what that meant for her and Alik.

* * *

Out of the corner of his eye, Alik could see Caro and Poppy near the front of the mosh pit, a couple of beered-up lads dancing around them. He carried on singing, trying to focus anywhere other than where they were standing. As the set progressed, he saw the men link hands, trapping Caro between their bodies. Poppy was trying to pull them off her, but wasn't having any success.

Alik tried to signal to security to intervene. But as far as they were concerned, as long as no-one had passed out or was being crushed, then they were probably just having a good time. As the band started playing their final song, one of the men had his arms around Caro and was grabbing her arse, which was the final straw for Alik. He threw the microphone into the wings and launched off the stage in the direction of the man. Nate, Billy, and Dev frantically looked at each other, but carried on playing, Nate half-heartedly carrying on the vocals. The rest of the audience in the tent had already turned their attention to the fight that was now going on just in front of the stage. Alik wrestled the guy off of Caro and threw him on the ground. He was just about to wade in with a few punches when the security guards finally acted.

"Now you react," he said, as they held him back. The man cowered on the floor in front of him. "I guess the set's finished, guys," he yelled out to the audience as he was frog-marched backstage, leaving the melee behind.

Caro followed them, Poppy and Olivia hot on her heels.

"Where's Griffen?" Caro asked. "He'll go ballistic when he finds out."

"I don't know," replied Olivia. "He was watching the set, then disappeared when he got a call. He's been waiting to hear something from Parker about the EP release date. I'll try and get hold of him. Poppy can you let the rest of the band know what's going on? Caro, stay with Alik." The two of them hurried off, leaving Caro trailing behind the heavies.

Alik had been taken to a holding area in the VIP backstage area, where a couple of security guards stood watch over him. Normally they didn't get much trouble from the bands, usually they dealt with dealers or over amorous groupies, so the security guards weren't quite sure how to react.

"This is ridiculous," Alik said. "He was the one in the wrong."

The two meathead guards were clearly waiting for someone more senior to come along. Caro had tried talking to them to explain what had happened and that Alik had only been trying to protect her. But they weren't listening to any of it.

Finally, a burly, shaven-headed man appeared. His bright orange armband told them that he was the Head of Security. He drew himself up to his full height. "Right, what's going on here then? We've had a report of assault."

Alik was about to launch into what had happened, but Caro stopped him.

"It was hardly assault, sir," she began, trying to charm the man. "Alik didn't even touch him, well, apart from getting him to let go of me."

"That's not what the gentleman says, miss."

"Gentleman?" Caro snorted. "I suppose he didn't tell you about groping me either?"

"Er, no..."

"Then perhaps you should reconsider the report."

The man turned his back and contacted someone on his radio. There was a crackly exchange, which neither Alik nor Caro could hear. "Wait here," he said. "I'll be back." He gestured for one of the two guards to follow him and they could hear them talking outside.

Caro went to Alik, gently pulling his shirt around him. The garment had been torn during the altercation and despite the earlier sunshine, the afternoon was chilling down somewhat.

"I'm sorry," he said, resting his head on her shoulder.

"Hey, you were only trying to protect me, don't be sorry about that."

"God, I hate this," he said. His emotions were all over the place; pride and happiness in playing at the festival mixed with jealousy at seeing some random guy being all over Caro, and confusion over how he felt about Edie. He needed to get out of there. He closed his eyes, imagining that he and Caro were anywhere else but there, in any other situation but this.

The moment was broken by the return of the security head

"You can go," he said. "We've spoken to the gentleman concerned and he's decided not to take it any further. But you're banned from the festival site for the rest of the weekend. All of the security personnel have been briefed and have your details, so any attempt to enter the site will be stopped. You're extremely lucky."

Alik felt anything but lucky. He just wanted to get out of there.

* * *

Edie was sprawled on the bed, wrapped in one of the hotel bathrobes, a champagne flute in her hand, with an accompanying bottle on ice on the bedside table. She was still pink and flushed from her earlier liaison with Billy. Okay, and a sneaky session of self love in the shower remembering it.

"Where the hell were you?" said Caro as she and Alik burst into the room.

"I, er, came back a bit early..." She stumbled over her words, trying to avoid eye contact with both of them. "I wasn't feeling too well."

Caro's eyes swept over her "Well, I hope you're feeling better," she said, before turning to Alik. "Job done, you're back safely without beating anyone else up, so you're her problem now. Although I wouldn't want to be in your shoes when Griffen and Parker find out. You might want to figure out what you're going to say to them." She headed towards the door. "I'm going to find Olivia and Poppy."

She slammed the door behind her. Alik sank down on the edge of the bed, pushing the heels of his hands into his eye sockets. Edie knelt behind him, gently massaging his shoulders.

"I'm sorry I left," she said. "What happened?"

She listened intently as Alik explained.

"That's awful!" she said. "It sounds like they're blaming you when it was clearly the other man's fault."

He laughed hollowly. "Yeah, but it's a bigger story if they lay the blame at my door." He stood up, stripping off his shirt, jeans and boxers. "I need a shower. Can you order up some room service? And maybe several beers?"

Edie did as he asked. As she put the phone down on reception, her mobile vibrated with a message from a number she didn't recognise. It read: *Had fun today, very unexpected. Fancy round two? xB*

CHAPTER TWENTY-EIGHT

"Blood Stone Riot's debut appearance at the Wilde Park Festival ended in disgrace last night as lead singer Alik Thorne was banned from the final day of the event. Thorne had an altercation with a fan towards the end of the band's set and had to be restrained by security..."

Alik buried his head under the pillow to drown out the sound of the music channel's TV presenter. What was supposed to be a landmark for the band was being remembered for all the wrong reasons.

He turned the TV off and emerged from his cocoon. Edie appeared to be engrossed in a marathon texting session with someone, judging by the amount of pinging and typing going on.

Alik reached out and ran his fingers down her arm. "Do you want to help me forget about yesterday?"

"And how could I do that?" she said.

He took the phone from her grasp and discarded it on the bedside table. He pulled her on top of him, his hands roaming over her, caressing her buttocks as she knelt over him, reaching for one of her small breasts and taking it into his mouth. A brief reminder of Caro's full, voluptuous figure entered his thoughts, but he tried to banish it. He had to stay focused for the upcoming time in the studio and he couldn't have any distractions. And Edie was being distracting enough as she writhed against him, contracting around him and making him come a lot quicker than he had wanted to. He shouldn't complain about a quickie, even if he had wanted a more leisurely start to the day. She slid out of the bed and headed towards the bathroom.

"Hey," Alik called after her. "You're in a rush, got a hot date or something?"

"I'm meeting Poppy and the girls for breakfast and then we're going to head over to the festival site to see a few of the bands," she replied over her shoulder.

"And you didn't think I might want to come along?"

"I thought you weren't allowed?"

Alik groaned in defeat. He didn't want to risk going anywhere near the site in case it jeopardised them playing there in future. He had to be a good boy and stay at the hotel.

* * *

A couple of hours later, Alik found himself in the hotel gym. After Edie had gone, he ordered up a room service breakfast and feasted on a full English, with black pudding and hash browns and several mugs of excessively strong, sugary tea. Then instantly regretted it. Working out wasn't top of his list of things to do, but to keep in shape for gigging, he needed to get some kind of exercise. Particularly after some of his recent excesses.

As he pounded the treadmill, his head whirled with a myriad of thoughts culminating in the euphoria of playing their first major festival and the crushing disappointment at how it ended. Parker often told him off for being way too passionate.

He almost didn't notice that Nate had entered the gym until the guitarist tried to turn up the machine.

"Jesus!" He stumbled before landing in a heap on the floor.

Nate laughed. "Sorry, mate, you looked so engrossed in whatever is on your mind that your legs just seemed to be on auto pilot."

Alik picked himself up and sank down on the seat of one of the other torture machines. Nate followed suit.

"I'm sorry about yesterday, Nate. I just saw that guy all over Caro and..." said Alik, towelling his face.

"It wasn't how I envisaged our first festival gig would pan out, but I do understand why you did it. If they'd have been trying it on with Poppy, I'd have done the same. Next time, try and ignore it, mate."

"How come you're not with Poppy this morning?" Alik asked, changing the subject.

Nate made a face. "Why on earth would I want to go shopping with the girls? She's gone into Derby with them, apparently to join civilisation for a few hours. I think after yesterday they were looking for some normality."

"I thought they were going to see some bands. Edie was going with them."

"I can definitely see her going shopping, but back to the festival?"

Alik's expression wavered momentarily. Why had Edie lied about what she was doing? Surely his behaviour hadn't freaked her out that much. He wouldn't have minded if she had said she was going back to North Ridge, he would almost have expected that. Maybe she was heading home and just didn't want to tell him. He'd check their room later. Putting his suspicions to one side, he changed the subject.

He and Nate began discussing the plans for their upcoming studio break and what they needed to achieve. Parker had given them some specific targets, which was something they weren't used to. If they wanted the EP to come out on schedule, then they definitely need a plan, and one they had to stick to. Release dates and deadlines were important.

People came in to use the equipment, but the pair were oblivious as they sketched out a few ideas for new tracks, Nate putting the thoughts into his phone. It wasn't until Alik's calf muscles started to cramp up that they stopped.

"I need to warm down properly, mate," he said. "I think I'm going to get a swim."

"I'm going to find Billy and head over for a couple of bands," Nate said. "I'll get some video for you if you want?"

Alik shook his head. "Don't make me even more depressed about this than I already am. I'll catch you later for a couple of beers."

Out of the corner of his eye, he thought he saw Caro enter the pool, but dismissed it. She was probably with the girls, too.

* * *

Caro had turned down Poppy's suggestion of a shopping trip to get a massage at the hotel spa. As the masseuse worked her magic on the knots in Caro's back, she started to relax. Until she hit the cluster in the centre of her shoulder blades and Caro almost hit the ceiling. Damn, this woman was good. After about an hour, during which she alternated between blissful relaxation and uncomfortable tension, she started to feel better. And a lot looser. She hadn't quite realised just how stressed and tight she was. Although most people around her probably would have done. Giving the woman a hefty tip, she headed towards the swimming pool to further unwind. Pulling her caramel hair up into a messy ponytail, she slipped into a pair of houndstooth checked bikini bottoms and a simple black tankini top. After all, it wasn't as if there was much sunshine to get a tan with.

Sliding effortlessly into the water, she started to swim, a slow, lazy breast stroke. The peace was shattered by someone diving straight over her head, cleanly into the water, and surfacing almost immediately in front of her.

"What the..." she began, aggrieved at being disturbed. "What are you doing here?"

Alik faced her. "I thought you were out with Poppy."

Caro shook her head. "Couldn't face it. Needed some time to myself this morning after yesterday."

"I hear you. I've been working out."

They circled each other, treading water. Their bodies were getting closer, drawn together by the gentle swell of the pool. Caro was acutely aware of their lack of clothing and their proximity to each other. Alik reached past her to steady himself against the wall, his fingertips brushing her shoulder. The gentle fluttering of his skin on hers brought a shiver to her spine, despite the humidity of the pool room. He moved toward her, placing his arm the other side of her, effectively trapping her between the side of the pool and his body. She couldn't breathe, the effort of treading water, trying to ignore the feelings that were dancing around her head, plus the way her treacherous body was responding. She closed her eyes and when she opened them seconds later, Alik's face was directly in front of her, their noses almost touching, a mixture of lust and longing reflected in those beautiful blue-grey eyes of his.

It wouldn't take much...

Suddenly Alik sprang away from her. She focused and saw Edie sashaying towards them.

"Funny how you two are together again," said Edie. "One would almost wonder who Alik's girlfriend actually was."

Alik hauled himself out of the water and Caro watched the water cascading off his muscular, tattooed arms. Arms that had, until moments ago, almost encircled her. Taking a steadying breath, she addressed Edie. "One would, considering that you were nowhere to be seen yesterday when Alik needed you."

"And you just happened to be there to step in." Edie peered down at her in the water. "Conveniently."

Caro shook her head, ignoring what her heart was telling her. "I'm not having this conversation with you Edie. Given that the festival isn't your scene and Alik can't go back there today, maybe your time would be better spent together as a couple. I can highly recommend the masseuse." And she swam away from them.

CHAPTER TWENTY-NINE

Alik had been delighted when Edie had pulled a few strings with the owners and arranged for Blood Stone Riot to record at Newcomen Farm Studios. Sometimes it really did pay to have friends in high places.

Newcomen Farm, once a working farm, had been converted in the late nineties into a stunning recording studio with luxurious accommodation onsite. Nestled in the beautiful South West countryside, not far from Westbourne Deane, it had played host to the creation of more than one seminal album. Frequented by established and up-and-coming artists alike, it consisted of a rambling house with seven ensuite bedrooms, a games room, a home cinema, a swimming pool and jacuzzi, as well as a large, welcoming, kitchen and dining room. The house itself was run by Mike and Mary James, a local couple hired by the owner to try and keep the bands in check and ensure that their every need was catered to. Well, almost every need. They had their own annex in one of the many outbuildings to escape to if things got too debauched in the main house.

Which, on more than one occasion, they had.

The recording studio was housed in what had once been a set of stables; a long outbuilding leading off from the home cinema. Set up with state of the art recording equipment, Blood Stone Riot were excited to get started on the creation of their first real EP. Parker had secured the services of Dion Robson; a producer who had worked with a number of the major players, but preferred to be involved in breaking new bands. The majority of bands he worked with then went on to critical acclaim or commercial success, sometimes both, and Blood Stone Riot were hoping to get at least one of those things from their first EP.

The band were taking a lunch break, sitting around the long antique oak table in the massive kitchen of the main house. They tucked into soup, hot crusty baguettes, and salad, all homemade by Mary. Billy had been chatting quietly to someone on his mobile for the past five minutes, his hand cupping the speaker so no-one could hear what he was saying, while the others ate.

Alik watched Mary bustling around, refilling their glasses and ensuring that none of them had empty plates for very long. She had confided to him that she thought that these boys were lovely, always complimenting her on her meals, and one of them even volunteered to wash up. It showed how appearances could be deceiving.

"You're an amazing cook, Mary," said Nate, as she whisked another freshly-baked quiche from the oven and put it on the table. "If I stay here too long, I'm going to end up the size of a house!"

"Thanks, love." She beamed. "Not all the bands that come here eat as much as you do though, so much waste. They don't seem to have any appetites... probably too many drugs."

Alik almost choked on his piece of quiche at Mary's matter-of-fact delivery. "Well, I'm sure we can help finish this lot off." He cast a nervous glance in Billy's direction.

Billy finished his call and turned to Alik. "Leo's going to deliver tonight. Well, one of his connections down here is."

After Mary's comment, Alik couldn't believe Billy was being so open about it. "What the hell are you thinking?" he said. "Edie's done us a massive favour in getting us into this place and you're prepared to risk it with a drugs bust?"

"It's not as if your Chelsea girl hasn't dabbled in a bit of champagne and charlie is it? How do you think Leo knew where this place was?" Billy smirked.

Alik fell silent. He knew what went on at Edie's parties, and it wasn't always about the Bollinger and the Tattinger.

He wanted studio time to be clean; he was much more creative when he was sober. He would need to stay strong and not bow to Billy's persuasion tactics. He wondered whether it was a mistake to have invited the girls along, but Edie had been adamant that they wouldn't get in the way after all, there was an amazing designer outlet nearby as well as a spa; they would have plenty to do whilst the band were in the studio. Sometimes Alik wondered if Edie realised that being in a band wasn't exactly a nine to five job and if it took them ten hours to get a decent take or if creativity struck at two in the morning, he'd need to do something about it.

But he was also extremely grateful to her for getting them into Newcomen Farm, after all it wasn't every day they opened their doors to a new band with such a small track record.

* * *

Several hours later, Alik wondered whether it had all been a horrible mistake. Dion had been working them hard all day, making them play 'The Imperial Kill' over and over again, determined that it would be perfect. By the end each member of the band loathed the track. Even the production guys were beginning to get bored, having heard the same thing so many times.

They needed a break.

Alik noticed that Billy had already snuck out to meet Leo's connection as soon as they had finished the final session of the day and was definitely ready for an evening off. As the weather was decidedly inclement, the original plan for a barbecue had been discarded in favour of giving Mary the night off, ordering in pizza, and spending the night by the indoor pool.

The atmosphere in the pool house was distinctly steamy and heady, being several degrees warmer than outside. Ripe for a good evening.

Edie and Poppy had arrived earlier that afternoon and had already been in the sauna by the time the others came down to the pool. They were lying side by side on the loungers, large cocktails in between them as they chatted quietly.

Edie sat up as Alik and the others entered the pool house. "Hey, babe, had a good session?"

"He's been a slave driver," Billy said. "Doesn't know when to stop."

"I just want it to be right," Alik said. "We don't want to look sloppy, and Dion agrees that we're doing a great job so far."

"But you don't have to work any more today, do you?" Edie pouted. "I wanted to have some fun this evening."

"No, we're all done for tonight. Well, except Dev, he wants to try out some new beats for one of the songs." Alik gestured to the drummer, who had settled himself in one corner, headphones on, in his own little world, tapping away on an iPad.

Edie smiled back at him, taking a large sip of her cocktail as he sat on the lounger next to her.

Nate dive-bombed into the pool and was starting to splash Poppy with water. "Come on in, the water's lovely. You know you want to."

Poppy laughed and lifted her lithe frame from the lounger, twisting her long hair into a ponytail, before diving cleanly into the pool, surfacing with what looked like Nate's shorts in her hand. "And you didn't even notice!" She crowed.

Nate started chasing her around the pool, water splashing everywhere, as he tried to get his shorts back to cover his modesty.

Alik watched them messing around, not imagining for one second that Edie would take part is such silliness. He wished that Caro was there, because he was sure she would. Stealthily, Billy lifted Edie up and gently threw her into the pool. She grabbed him by the ankle and he toppled in after her. Alik watched as the two of them raced up and down, each challenging the other to do sillier or more extreme strokes or seeing who could go the longest underwater. Nate found a Hello Kitty ball lying behind one of the loungers and the four of them began an energetic game of water volleyball. As the game began to get more competitive, Alik noticed that Billy was lifting Edie up to enable her to reach some of the shots, his hands firmly around her waist, moulded to her hips or lingering too close to her breasts.

And he didn't like it.

The ball rolled to his feet after a particularly enthusiastic over hit by Poppy. He picked it up and slammed it back towards Billy, where it hit him squarely on the head. Hard.

"What the fuck..." spluttered Billy.

"I should be saying the same to you, mate. What do you think you're doing?"

Edie, Nate, and Poppy started treading water, quietly watching what was going on.

"What do you mean?"

"I mean, why have you got your hands all over my girlfriend?"

"Mate, we're just messing around..."

"Alik, it's fine," Edie said. "It's not as if he was trying anything on. We were just playing a game."

"See, it's not like Edie wasn't enjoying it," Billy said. "Like she said, we were playing a game."

Alik looked at the pair, Edie staring at him with her clear blue eyes and Billy imploring him to believe what he was saying. His thoughts turned briefly to Caro and their stolen moments, which put him in the exact same position, and he doubted that Edie would be as understanding. "Whatever," he said finally, diving into the pool himself to try and clear his head.

CHAPTER THIRTY

The next day Alik holed up in the study just after breakfast with Josh O'Brien. The director had arrived at Newcomen Farm late the previous evening with a missive from Parker Roberts for Alik's ears only, stating that some of the original video footage for 'Bleed Like Cyanide' needed to be reshot. The rest of the band had been told to concentrate on laying down the tracks for the EP while Alik and Josh worked on some new video ideas. Alik had been bawled out by Parker about his behaviour at the festival and what that could mean for the band's reputation, not least putting future bookings in doubt. He was prepared to do whatever it took to make up for that mistake, even if it meant working twenty-four hours a day.

It was close to five o'clock when they emerged, both wired on coffee, and ravenous.

Mary was pottering around the kitchen, preparing for dinner when they came in.

"Hello, Mary," said Alik. "Is there anything left over from lunch?"

She tutted. "I'm sure I can rustle up some soup and bread, if that will do you for now?"

"That would be amazing." Alik gave her a big kiss on the cheek. "This is Josh, by the way. We're going to be doing a shoot later and need all the sustenance we can get."

"No-one told us about that." Billy wandered into the room. "I might have plans."

"You may not need to worry about changing them," said Josh, ripping into a piece of french bread that Mary had just put on the table. "The scenes we've been working on focus on Alik."

"No change there, then." Billy snorted.

Alik threw a bread roll at his head. "Josh thought of something that would work better than some of the original stuff we shot in the club and he's hoping that Edie will agree to be in it as well."

"Edie?" Billy frowned. "What's the story idea then?"

Josh sat down, pushing the storyboard towards Billy, with the rough sketches of what he envisaged. "You're more than welcome to come along and see how it works out."

Billy chewed thoughtfully on the bread roll Alik had thrown at him. "Might just do that. Has Edie agreed to do it yet?"

"Have I agreed to do what?" Edie wandered into the kitchen.

"We need a female lead for part of the video. Would you like to do it?" asked Josh. He pushed the storyboard towards her, briefly outlining that they were going to the beach for the shoot and she would be reacting to Alik.

Alik thought that it added gravitas to the request if it came from the director rather than her boyfriend, which was why Josh was asking her, not him.

"Really?" She squealed. "I'd get to be in a music video?" She twirled around the kitchen, hugging Alik, Billy, and Josh in turn.

"Can I take it that you're happy to do it?" Josh asked.

She nodded, smiling broadly. "What do I need to wear?"

"As little as possible," said Billy, with a wink.

Edie blushed "I mean; what sort of mood are you going for? I've got some options."

"Yeah, for once bringing practically your whole wardrobe on holiday with you might actually be of benefit," said Alik.

Josh stood up and ushered Edie out of the room. "Let's go and take a look, I don't want to miss out on the sunset."

CHAPTER THIRTY-ONE

"I need your help!"

Poppy's plea had come at somewhat of a bad time for Caro. The distraught bride-to-be had called Caro from Newcomen Farm practically in tears; there was no dress, she was too fat, Edie was driving her mental, and she needed her maid of honour. Now. Caro's initial refusal had brought about more tears and a slight tantrum, despite how many times she explained she couldn't just drop everything and head off down to Westbourne Deane.

"Poppy, I'm busy this morning with meetings, can we talk later?"

"Can you call me back as soon as you're free? I need you here!"

Caro rolled her eyes. Her friend had been great at not being Bridezilla, but it seemed there was some sort of imminent meltdown on the cards and she probably would have to go and pick up the pieces. She desperately wished that the morning would bring some success.

Caro and Nic were in the final throes of interviewing for their executive assistant, which had been a bit of a last-minute addition to The Indigo Lounge's staff list. They had realised that their original plans to try to do everything themselves - work rotas, paying staff, the HR elements of the business, finding bands to play, promotions, marketing, publicity, liaising with suppliers and so on - were likely to be beyond their capabilities. Caro's approach was more cash-in-hand and worry about the taxes later, based on her Mallorcan experiences, which wouldn't sit well with the UK tax office. They had decided to get in someone who could take on some of that more back office stuff, leaving them free to concentrate on the things they excelled in - like getting the punters in.

Whoever was selected had to be right. They would have a lot to deal with.

Caro was sitting in the VIP area on the balcony, listening to the builders banging about. Since the Blood Stone Riot video shoot, it seemed they had found "a few more things that need rectifying" as the foreman kept telling her, even though she thought things looked fine. She took a sip of the coffee that was in front of her and grimaced. It was cold, and she didn't have time to get another one before her next appointment. As she picked up the CV of the next candidate to come in, she heard footsteps on the stairs and got a waft of freshly-brewed coffee. Glancing up and expecting to see Nic, she was surprised to see that it looked like one of the candidates; a Starbucks cup in one hand and an expensive-looking handbag in the other. She was dressed smartly in a navy blue pencil skirt with matching heels and an eggshell blue satin blouse, making Caro feel distinctly underdressed in her black skinny jeans and cream blouse.

Caro's first though was that she was incredibly arrogant to bring her own refreshments to an interview.

The woman handed her the cup. "Nic thought you might need this," she said. "Americano, black, extra shot?"

Caro gave a reluctant smile. "Thanks, he knows me too well." She stood up and took the cup from her, realising she may have been a little hasty with her first impressions. "I'm Caro Flynn, and Nic Santino should be joining us shortly."

"He said he'd be up just as soon as he'd finished speaking with Danny. He was hoping to get a definite date from him."

Danny was the builders' foreman, and Caro had suggested that Nic have a word with him to see if he could get a different answer as to when they might actually have a finished club.

"I'm Amy Gold," the woman said. "Lovely to meet you."

They made polite conversation and Caro pointed out the bar and stage from the balcony and how their vision would work, until Nic appeared with a pile of paperwork. "Just a few things for us to go over afterwards, Caro. And this is one of the reasons why we need an assistant!"

"Okay, shall we start?" said Caro, taking a seat on the sofa and gesturing for Amy to sit opposite as Nic settled down beside her. "Why don't you start by telling me a bit about why working at The Indigo Lounge appeals to you?" She settled back, her pencil poised over Amy's CV. "And specifically working for Nic and I?"

There was a pause while Amy considered her answer. "I've been working as an executive assistant to the director of a successful PR company, so I know a little about working in a high-pressure environment. We work long hours and late nights and entertain a lot of clients. The Indigo Lounge would appear to offer a similar level of pressure, being in the entertainment sector. With it being a new venture, it would hopefully be both challenging and successful, something you can really see the results of." She paused to take a breath. "And as for working for you and Nic, well, I've done a little bit of research about you and know you worked together running a club abroad, meaning you already have an established partnership and in theory, there wouldn't be the same level of tantrums I've had to deal with."

"Don't be too sure," said Nic. "We can be quite difficult."

"I'm used to diva-like behaviour."

"Sounds as if you have already worked with Caro!"

They continued talking, questioning Amy about some of the difficult situations she had dealt with in the past and asking about her aspirations. She asked them intelligent, practical questions about the business and how they were doing in getting it up and running. Unlike a number of the other applicants they had seen, she didn't mention anything about the bands she might meet or the celebrities she might come into contact with. Caro was concerned that she didn't really understand the North Ridge scene and wanted to know more.

"Amy, everything you've gone through so far seems to be impressive, but we're a rock club, what do you know about that?"

Nic gave her a sideways glance, Caro's question was pretty direct, but it made sense to ask it. After all, if Amy preferred bubblegum pop, it may not work out.

"I like a lot of things, but I'm not the biggest rock fan. I know the importance of that market to The Indigo Lounge and I wouldn't be professional if I didn't realise that. I understand that Blood Stone Riot shot some of a video here and that can only be good publicity for you."

Caro scribbled a note on Amy's CV and passed it over to Nic. He read the message and nodded imperceptibly. "What's your notice period, Amy?"

"I'm pretty much available now. My current boss is on maternity leave and there isn't really anything else for me to do where I am, so I'm sure they'd be flexible."

"You don't want to stay until your manager comes back?"

"In all honesty, I don't think she will come back. She's been trying for a baby for such a long time and had to go for IVF in the end, it was all she ever wanted."

"Do you have any other offers or interviews in the pipeline?" asked Nic.

Amy shook her head. "Nothing concrete in any case. I've had a few interviews that I'm waiting for feedback on."

Caro and Nic nodded.

"Okay, thanks for coming in today, we'll get back to the agency in a couple of days as we have other applicants to see," said Caro. "It's been good to meet you."

"And good to meet you too." Amy stood up and Caro and Nic followed suit. They all shook hands and Nic escorted Amy back downstairs before rejoining Caro a few minutes later.

"What do you think?" He asked.

Caro looked up. "She's perfect, if a little too well-groomed. But we can soon knock that out of her!"

"Want me to make an offer?"

Caro nodded. "If she can start by the end of this week, that would be great. And I can go and deal with Poppy's insecurities for a couple of days."

CHAPTER THIRTY-TWO

Poppy met Caro at Westbourne station a few hours later, bringing back memories of Caro's visit to Gramercy Lodge. And dinner at Gallacher's. She hoped that this visit would be slightly less fraught than her previous stay.

"Oh, God, I'm so glad you're here!" Poppy threw her arms around Caro.

They took a taxi back to Newcomen Farm and Caro recognised some of the roads as they went through Westbourne Deane and out into the countryside. She hadn't seen or heard from Alik since the Wilde Park Festival and felt somewhat apprehensive about seeing him again, particularly after how the events had unfolded. Olivia had told her that she'd had to do some fire-fighting in the wake of the alleged assault incident, but everything had finally died down.

"Wow, are you sure they can fit me in here?" said Caro as they pulled into the driveway, observing the farmhouse and outbuildings.

Poppy laughed. "Wait until you see inside, you'll see there's plenty of space."

She wasn't wrong. Mary ushered Caro inside and took her upstairs to the top of the house where there was an impressive room kitted out with a slipper bath, a king-size bed, a cute window seat, and a tiny en suite. It was decorated in fresh greens and whites and had a calming feel to it, which was exactly what Caro needed. She quickly unpacked her overnight bag and made her way down to the kitchen, lured by cooking smells.

Caro entered the room and the first person she saw was Alik. He was deep in conversation with Josh and snacking on some delicious-looking homemade soup.

"Caro, can I get you something to eat?" Mary asked, as both Josh and Alik looked directly at her.

She nodded, taking the seat closest to Josh. "That would be great, thank you."

"What are you doing here?" Josh asked, giving her a hug.

"Ah, I heard you were shooting another one of your videos and wondered if you might need an assistant again." The shoot at The Indigo Lounge made an uninvited appearance in her head, Alik half naked, tied to a cross... Quickly, she dismissed those thoughts from her head as Edie walked into the room.

"Oh, hey, Caro," she said, eying her. "What are you doing here?"

"Poppy wanted some help with wedding stuff and suggested I come down. Well, demanded, more like. I think she's getting stressed about how close the date is now and..." Caro stopped herself and looked around the room. "Where is Poppy anyway?"

Mary set a bowl down in front of Caro. "She and Nate have gone out for the evening, something about a romantic meal together? I'm not sure whether to take that as a slight on my cooking."

"Nonsense, Mary, they probably just wanted some alone time. Your cooking is amazing." Billy entered the kitchen, throwing his arms around the housekeeper and giving her a big squeeze. Caro thought she saw him glance towards Edie as he did so, but dismissed it from her thoughts. "You guys ready to go yet?"

Josh checked the clock and looked out of the window. "We should probably go soon, I'm keen to make the most of the weather."

"Caro? Will you come along to watch?" Alik asked, his tone light as he looked towards her and Edie settled down next to him, dipping some bread into his soup.

Caro hesitated. She was here for Poppy's benefit, but having been abandoned as soon as she arrived, what choice did she have? Sure, she could go back to her room and hole up with a book or social media. Or she could go and spend some time with Alik.

"Sure, why not?"

CHAPTER THIRTY-THREE

There were still a few people left on the beach as Alik, Josh, Billy, Edie, and Caro made their way down to the shore less than three quarters of an hour later. Josh had insisted on shooting the scene himself on a small, handheld camera to get a more raw and moody feel to the footage. The sun was setting, creating a beautiful blood red and orange sky, the perfect backdrop for that part of the video, although the temperature was starting to drop.

"We're definitely going to get some good shots here," said Josh, checking his watch again and looking up at the sky.

Alik and Edie were getting ready, Alik gently stroking Edie's arm and whispering into her ear. He was conscious of Caro being there, watching them, and there was part of him that wanted to run over to her, throw her onto the sand, and screw her brains out. But he couldn't think about that now.

"Oi, lover boy, snap to it, we're starting to lose the light," said Josh, making his way back up from down by the water.

Alik extricated himself from Edie's grasp and stripped off his shirt, boots, and socks. Bare-chested and bare-footed, he offered up his wrists to Josh to be bound, in keeping with the theme of the previous part of the video. He knew that a certain amount of subversity would assist in promoting the band, plus by appearing half-naked throughout the video, it would certainly help to increase the female fan base.

"Not too tight, I hope." Josh secured the rope.

The singer shook his head. "You're okay, Josh, you're no dominatrix."

Edie, dressed in a peasant dress, shivered slightly. "It's cold out here, are we going to be long?"

"If you get it right first time we can be back at the house in less than an hour and out for dinner," said Josh. "There's no music playback or miming to do here, just you and Alik interacting."

He briefed the pair once again on what he wanted from the scene and pointed out the particular shots he needed. Alik and Edie went down to the edge of the water and Josh tried a couple of test shots before finding the background he wanted.

"Okay, go!"

On cue, Edie began walking along the shoreline, the breeze making her dress and long blonde hair ripple out behind her. Next, Alik dropped to his knees, crawling in her wake, his hands held up in supplication. The sea lapped around his legs, soaking his jeans, causing him to shudder involuntarily, raising goose bumps on his skin. His mind went back to scene they'd filmed in The Indigo Lounge when he'd been lashed to the cross, and the feel of Caro's touch; he remembered the feel of her fingertips caressing his skin and the smell of her perfume and a bolt of electricity shot down his spine.

At that moment, Edie turned.

The look that she and Alik shared was overwhelming, full of a mixture of lust and longing.

But he wasn't thinking about her. He was thinking about Caro.

Josh panned the camera from one to the other. "And cut!"

Alik fixed his eyes on the sand, willing himself not to look up at Caro. Edie helped him to his feet.

"Hey," she said, touching his cheek. "You okay?" She slipped an arm around his cold body.

He flexed his shoulders, shaking her off. "Sure, I'm fine."

Billy wrapped a blanket around Edie's shoulders. "Getting a bit chilly down here now, you want me to walk you back to the house? I think Josh wants to shoot one more scene."

Knowing the scene that they were about to shoot, Alik and Josh positively encouraged them to go - the less people around the better. Billy took Edie's hand and led her away, leaving Caro as the sole viewer.

Josh went up to the singer, starting him straight in the eye. "Do you want to do this now?"

"What? And miss out on this sky?" replied Alik. "I'm not looking forward to it, but the sooner it's done..."

* * *

They moved down to the edge of the water again and Caro turned to Josh.

"What's he going to do?"

"We wrote a scene where he's walking into the sea. It's the last scene where he realises he can't go on and he thinks it's the best way to go; 'you can bleed like cyanide, but I won't drown in your poison.'" Josh said, quoting the lyrics.

"But he's still tied up, he could drown!"

Josh shook his head. "He knows what he's doing, Caro."

Caro looked around the beach, looking for any lifeguards in case he got into difficulty. But apart from a few men kicking a ball around, there was no-one. She felt sick.

* * *

Alik was psyching himself up for the scene, staring out over the water, his mind whirling over a million thoughts at once. The temperature of the water had dipped suddenly towards arctic and his body was starting to shake. In the background, he heard Josh's cue and slowly began to walk into the sea. The icy water rose, covering his thighs, then his hips. A small current knocked him off balance, but he was determined to continue. The water reached up to his neck. He took a deep breath, closed his eyes, and immersed himself in the water. Everything went black around him. He counted to ten in his head and then broke the surface of the water, gasping for air. He struggled to the shore, collapsing on the sand.

Josh was by his side immediately, closely followed by Caro. Josh cut him loose from the rope. "What the fuck happened there? Are you okay?"

Alik looked beyond him, fixing Caro with the same look he had shown Edie earlier. The intensity consumed him. He needed to know how she felt, that she wanted the same as he did. In Greece, she had made it clear that it should just be a friendship; he wanted to know if things had changed.

Josh went to fetch a towel and Alik pulled Caro close to him, so the director couldn't overhear. "I need to see you. Have dinner with me tonight."

"I can't."

"Please, Caro," he said. "I need to explain."

Caro shook her head. "Alik, I'm so sorry, I just can't."

She pulled out of his grasp and walked back up the beach, away from him. He was vaguely aware of Josh wrapping the towel around him as he stared after her.

CHAPTER THIRTY-FOUR

As it turned out, they ended up going out for dinner after all. With Nate and Poppy already eating out, Mary had recommended the Dog & Duck on the outskirts of the village. Alik, Edie, Caro, Billy, Dev, and Josh found themselves in there amongst a group of locals who were clearly regulars, and who were almost hostile towards the strangers in their midst.

Particularly strangers who were dressed in denim and leather and had scary-looking tattoos.

Edie and Billy approached the bar together. Edie was trying to act casual around the bassist. Since the previous evening when they had been messing around in the pool, she found her mind wandering back to the festival and how he had made her feel: Hot, sexy and just a little bit dirty. She liked that feeling.

The barmaid began serving them, with a bright, nervous smile plastered across her face. "Hi Edie, what are you doing here?" She bit her lip, blushing furiously. "I mean, what can I get you to drink?"

Edie looked her up and down with some disdain. She wasn't used to being addressed like that, particularly by people who were serving her. She guessed that the girl recognised her from *Pretty Rich Things* and various magazine articles, although she looked highly unlikely to be able to afford anything that was stocked in The Magpie.

Billy laughed. "It's not often you get a personal welcome like that when you go into a bar you've never been to before, love. I don't even get that kind of welcome in my local. I'm Billy, by the way, and I think Edie's after your wine list, if you've got one."

The barmaid smiled. "Do you want to see the food menu as well? We've got some specials this evening." She turned around to pick some menus up from the bar behind her and Edie caught a glimpse of her bright pink g-string peeking out from the top of her cheap black polyester trousers.

"I'll just go and find the wine list," the barmaid said.

"Thanks, love, that would be great. We're starving and I bet you do a good pie in here," said Billy, flashing a cheeky smile. The same smile he had given Edie when he had been flirting with her. An unexpected sting of jealousy ran through her and she mentally shook herself to rid the feeling. Where had that come from? Why was she jealous of a slightly plump, plain barmaid?

Edie was still studying the wine menu when Poppy and Nate arrived, holding hands and giggling, both clearly a little worse for wear. She was surprised to see them; she'd expected them to head home after their romantic dinner.

They went straight to the bar and ordered. "Bottle of red please, something Spanish if you've got it, ideally a Tempranillo, thanks. We're with those guys over there." Poppy pointed to the table in the corner that housed the band.

"Hallelujah! That's the way to order wine!" said Alik.

Edie pouted. In defiance, she decided that she would have white wine and immediately ordered the most expensive bottle on the menu.

"I'll have to find it in the cellar," the barmaid told her, "so I might be a while."

In the time it took for her bottle to arrive, the rest of the band had downed two pints and Poppy was about to order a second Tempranillo. They agreed on what to order and it was pretty much pies all round - it seemed that the

Dog & Duck was renowned for its pie-making, and with fillings to suit all tastes, there was something for everyone. Except for Edie, who had decided to have the fresh sea bass with salad.

"How are things coming along with the wedding arrangements?" Edie asked Nate. Poppy was looking at her with daggers.

"All good my side," said Nate. "Got my best man sorted, got ideas for the stag, so I'm done." He gestured to Poppy with his glass. "This one, on the other hand, is in total chaos."

"Well, it's not my fault that Annie decided to leave me in the lurch. Thank God for Caro stepping in, otherwise I'd be getting married naked!"

"Yet another way to make the day memorable," said Nate.

Poppy punched him on the arm.

"We will find the most amazing dress, Poppy, I promise." Caro drained her glass. "More wine?"

Edie glanced between the pair. She suspected that the dress would probably be trashy or cheap, but refrained from saying anything. She put the last forkful of the overcooked fish into her mouth and swallowed it.

The plump barmaid who had seemingly allocated herself as their waitress as well - Bren, according to the badge pinned over her left breast - came to clear the table.

"Do you get many bands coming in?" Billy asked her as she carefully piled up the plates to take back to the kitchen.

She nodded. "We get a lot more... indie type groups though," she replied. "I think Bastille were here a couple of weeks ago."

"Must make your job more interesting, right? And I bet you get better tips as well."

Bren giggled. "Yes, sometimes."

They continued bantering for a few minutes, until Edie excused herself from the table and stalked off in the direction of the ladies. She couldn't believe the gall of Billy, to be flirting with such a non-threat in front of her. Again. She had also watched Alik and Caro carefully throughout the meal. They had barely spoken directly and when they did speak, Josh or someone else had also been involved. Not for the first time, she wondered what Caro was actually doing there. She checked her make-up and straightened the scarf she was wearing over her woollen dress, so it emphasised her cleavage. Applying another coat of lip gloss, she took a deep breath and headed back out into the bar. She wasn't watching where she was going, and barrelled straight into someone in the narrow corridor between the facilities and the main bar.

"Something tells me there's a bit of jealousy out there."

Billy had hold of her upper arms, steadying her. His firm touch sent a shiver down her spine.

She drew herself up and pulled out of his grasp. "And why would I be jealous of some nineteen-year-old barmaid? It's not as if you're going to sleep with her, is it?"

"I've got nothing else to do tonight..." he trailed off. "There's talk of going on somewhere after this. I'm going to head back to the farm, I think, maybe lay down a couple of things in the studio. How about you?" He ran a hand over her buttocks.

"I should spend some time with Alik."

Billy laughed. "Of course you should." He pushed her gently in the direction of the others. "I need a piss." And then he was gone.

Edie went back to the table, her mind whirling at what Billy had just suggested.

Nate was holding up his phone, struggling to get a decent 3G signal to look up the club that had been recommended. "Right, it's called The Pit, who's in?"

Poppy and Caro agreed immediately, while Josh and Dev declined. Edie glanced at Alik.

"I'm up for being out a bit longer, how about you?" he asked.

She pretended to think about it for a moment, as Billy returned to the table. He sat down and drained the last of his beer.

"Um, I'm a bit tired actually," she said. "I think I might head back too."

"Okay, no worries, we can go back."

Edie knew he was only saying that so as not to upset her. But Billy intrigued her, and she wanted to find out what was going on in his dirty little mind.

"I've got a bit of a headache," she said. "You go; I'll just get an early night." She gave him a lingering kiss goodnight, making sure that both Billy and Caro saw her.

CHAPTER THIRTY-FIVE

The courtyard was in darkness as Edie tiptoed her way across the gravel, trying to be careful. To her, each of her footsteps were like claps of thunder. As she turned the door knob, the scent of dope assaulted her nostrils, signalling that Billy was already there. Her heels clacked on the stone floor as she made her way into the studio.

Billy was lounging on one of the big black leather producer's chairs, a joint dangling from his lips, pupils already heavily dilated. "You took your time." He stubbed out the cigarette before grabbing her hand and pulling her onto his lap, his mouth on hers. He broke off for breath and looked her in the eye. "Take your dress off."

Edie stood up again, tossing her scarf at Billy and sliding out of her black wool dress. She was naked underneath, her nipples already standing to attention. She put her hands on her hips and smiled, twisting and turning for his benefit. Billy's eyes roamed over her naked body. He got up and manoeuvred her back towards the chair, pushing her into the seat. He tied one end of the soft cashmere scarf around her left wrist, before looping it around the back of the chair and then fastening the other end around her right wrist.

"Hey..." she protested. Her arms were pulled behind her, the length of the scarf making her position slightly uncomfortable but not painful. She twisted fruitlessly against the bonds. As she wriggled around in front of him, getting more and more aroused, she could see Billy's cock pressing hard against the zip of his jeans. Moving towards her, he gently traced a line around her breasts, taking one of the nipples between his thumb and forefinger and squeezing it tightly, causing her to squeal. He bent his head and took it in his mouth, alternately sucking, trailing his tongue and nipping with his teeth, his other hand moving towards her pussy. Edie felt herself teetering on the brink of orgasm and pushed herself towards him, wanting to feel him inside her; fingers, cock, tongue, she didn't care. He pulled back and took a step backwards.

"Jesus, don't stop," she said, struggling against the material holding her in position.

He gave a lazy smile. "Don't stop what, Edie?"

"You know what!"

"Do I?" He raised an eyebrow. "I want you to beg for it, Edie, I want you to tell me what you want."

"Please, Billy..."

"What?"

She arched her back, brazenly pushing her shaven pussy at him. "Make me come, Billy... please..." Her clit throbbed. "I want it... I want you... fuck me..."

She didn't recognise the person she was at that moment, restrained and controlled. Edie Spencer-Newman didn't beg for anything. If only Alik knew... As that thought came into her head, Billy lunged, his fingers delving into her wetness, probing, stroking, caressing, pinching. Her senses went into overdrive, pleasure and pain fusing together, shuddering as she finally reached a shattering orgasm. Billy unfastened one end of the scarf, setting her free. He stepped out of his jeans, struggling to free his cock and rested against the mixing desk.

"On your knees," he said.

She did as she was told, realising what he wanted, and crawled towards him, her arms aching from being in an unfamiliar position. The scarf trailed across the floor behind her. As she reached him, she placed her palms on his thighs.

"Tie your hair away from your face," Billy said. "I want to see what you're doing."

Edie obeyed and pulled her hair back into a ponytail, untying the scarf from her wrist and using the item to secure it. She took his cock in her mouth, feeling his hands on the back of her head, stroking her hair. It only took a few short seconds before he exploded in her mouth. Edie swallowed quickly, making a face. She sat back on her heels, and looked up at Billy. "Please, sir, I think I'd like you to make me come again, would you fuck me?"

A crooked grin crept across Billy's face as he pulled Edie to her feet, flipped her round and pushed her down over the mixing desk. The various controls pressed into her skin. He grabbed her ponytail, pulling her head back, and slammed into her from behind. She groaned as she felt the thick length of his cock inside her, grinding her mound against the edge of the desk. As he thrust into her once again, she was sure she saw stars.

CHAPTER THIRTY-SIX

The Pit certainly lived up to its name.

The slightly tatty exterior did nothing to draw customers in and the interior was no better: Dark, dingy, and distinctly dangerous. As Alik, Nate, Poppy, and Caro descended the stairs into the tiny, sweaty matchbox of a club that was pumping out System Of A Down, they certainly felt as if they belonged.

It was busy but they managed to cram themselves into a booth that was being vacated by a group of college kids, who nudged each other and pointed at Alik and Nate.

"Hey, didn't you play at the Wilde Park Festival? I saw your set online, it was awesome," one of the lads said. "Should have kicked seven shades out of that dick who was moving in on your bird."

Alik laughed. "She's not my bird, but thanks, I thought I did a good enough job of that. I got banned from the rest of the festival, remember?"

The boy nodded gravely. "Hope you play again though, might get to see you next time. Okay if I get a picture with you guys?" He gestured to his mates and they pulled Alik and Nate in for a shot that would no doubt end up all over their social media pages.

Once they'd done their rock star duties, Alik went to the bar, returning with four bottles of beer.

"It was beer or beer; they didn't seem to have much of a choice."

The music was cranked up, making conversation almost impossible. Another couple squashed into the booth with them and Alik was suddenly acutely aware that Caro was crushed up against him. His arm rested on the back of the seat and the angle meant that his hand kept brushing the back of her neck.

"I think I'm going to dance," Caro yelled, pushing her way out of the cramped space and out into the main body of the bar.

Poppy pushed him. "Go after her, you know you want to."

It wasn't much of a dance floor; more a space where people were milling around, sort of in time to the music. As Alik reached the periphery, he scanned the crowd for Caro. After a few moments, he found her, dancing in the centre of the floor, her hips swaying seductively to the music, her face hidden by her gorgeous mane of hair. He had never seen Edie lose herself in the moment like that. The music changed abruptly and so did Caro's movements; the harsh pulsating beat reverberating through his whole body as he watched her. The whole move seemed deliberately sexy, geared towards attracting the attention of any watching males.

And she was certainly doing that.

Alik pushed past the crowd and joined her. She flung her hair back and stared straight into his eyes, teasing him, drawing him in. She didn't resist as Alik slid an arm around her waist and pulled her body towards him as her eyes met his. They stopped moving. She lifted a hand to his face, tracing a line down his cheek and along his jaw, moving her thumb softly around his lips. His tongue flicked in and out, occasionally catching her skin.

"God, I really want to kiss you," he said, leaning close to her ear.

He felt her stiffen in his arms, desperate to touch her, taste her again, have her surrender to him.

"You usually tell me to stop now," said Alik, his voice low, his breath brushing the skin behind her ear.

"What if I don't want you to?"

Their lips hovered millimetres apart, teetering on the brink of something, maybe something they couldn't come back from.

"Caro."

He didn't get a chance to say anything else, as Caro's mouth was on his, taking command, her tongue insistent, probing. Alik's hand shifted to her buttocks, caressing the gentle swell of them, sliding his fingers in towards what he really wanted. He felt her gasp against him and he increased the pressure. His lips brushed down the side of her neck, a millimetre or so from her skin, causing her to shiver. A small circle had grown around them, leaving them alone - or at least as alone as they could be in a crowded club. No-one on the dance floor was really paying that much attention to them, they were all involved in their own mating rituals.

Abruptly, Alik drew back, grabbed Caro's wrist, and dragged her out of the bar into the corridor. He pushed her against the wall and kissed her again, hard, one of his hands cupping her breast, his fingertips toying with her. His dominance both scared and excited him and he could feel himself becoming aroused as he pressed against her.

Caro shoved him away. "Wait," she said, breathlessly. "We have to stop."

"What the fuck are you doing to me?" Alik said. "I thought it's what you wanted."

"We can't do this to Edie," she said.

"Come on, Caro, we're amazing together and you know it. Whenever we're around each other, you know how that feels, how much I want you."

"And don't think I don't want it too. Jesus, I'm not made of stone you know."

Poppy came over to them. "Um, Nate and I were thinking of heading back now."

Caro linked arms with her friend. "Good idea, let's go."

As the pair of them walked away, Alik sank back against the wall, shaking his head in frustration.

CHAPTER THIRTY-SEVEN

The following day in the studio, it was all Alik could do to stop thinking about Caro. When he'd got back, Edie was already asleep, snoring gently. He had lain beside her, tossing and turning for the best part of the night, his mind working overtime. Just thinking about what had almost happened in The Pit was giving him a hard on. He was glad that his role that morning simply involved him sitting behind a desk, listening to the others.

"Dude, what's with you this morning? That bass line is jumping up and down all over the place like Pharrell Williams or something. It sounds happy," said Alik, as Billy laid down the rhythm to 'The Imperial Kill.' It was meant to be a grinding, dirty backing track but it seemed that the bassist's mood was anything but. "Go again."

Alik rolled his eyes at Dion as he sat back in the black leather producer's chair.

"Billy, did you get laid or something last night?" asked Nate. "I thought I saw you flirting with that chubby barmaid." He sank down on a stool beside Billy, reaching down to get his guitar from its case on the floor.

Billy chuckled. "Ha, ha, you guessed it, mate. She was gagging for it."

Alik wasn't surprised. Billy's reputation in that department went before him, definitely the love 'em and leave 'em type; the band member with the biggest libido and the smallest heart.

"I might even hook up with her again tonight."

And if even Billy was getting together with someone, Alik realised he should probably try to make more of an effort with Edie. He had just left her to her own devices the last couple of days, although he had warned her that he was at the farm to work, not have fun. Well, not too much fun anyway.

* * *

Edie was lying in her bed trying to make sense of what had happened the previous evening. At the festival, she had felt vulnerable and out of place, watching Alik and Caro whispering together as if they were the couple, not her and Alik. The chance one-off with Billy there had been just that - or so she had thought. Her irrational jealousy the previous evening in the pub, of the plump, badly-dressed, barmaid had caught her off guard. And her behaviour in the studio had been totally out of character. She would never usually behave like that but with Billy it felt right. Her hand hovered over her phone. She toyed with the idea of calling Billy and getting a repeat performance. Replaying some of her actions in her head, she felt a flush come to her cheeks as she remembered kneeling in front of Billy and asking him to fuck her. With other men, Alik included, there had never been any need to ask, it had always just happened.

But even Alik didn't make her feel like Billy did.

Just imagining being tied up and having Billy manually manipulate her into coming was making her squirm. She felt herself getting slick between the legs, wondering what else he might get her to do if they ever got together again. Sneaking a hand inside her pajama shorts, she began stroking herself, gently bringing herself to a small, but satisfying, orgasm

There was a sharp knock on the door and it swung open. Poppy walked in.

Edie sat up, pulling her arms above the duvet and trying to ignore the throbbing in her clit. "Oh, hi, Poppy."

The other girl sat down on the bed.

"Caro and I are going into Westbourne Deane to get coffee, you want to come?" she asked. "There's not much going on today, looks like the boys are going to be locked in that studio for hours, probably until this evening."

Edie thought through her options for a minute, to stay in her room and think about Billy taking her in every which way possible or heading out with Poppy and Caro to talk about weddings.

"Give me half an hour and let's go," she said.

* * *

An hour and a half later, the three women were sitting in the courtyard outside The Deane Deli in the market place, drinking lattes and taking advantage of some late morning sunshine. Caro's eyes were hidden by a pair of sunglasses. She couldn't bear to look Edie in the eye after what she'd done at The Pit last night. A couple of giggling teenage girls came up to their table, having recognised Edie, and asked her for a picture. Caro and Poppy exchanged a glance as she posed politely and chatted to them for a few minutes. While they were still there, a young lad of about sixteen ambled up. He was dressed all in black, with Doc Martens and a couple of ear piercings.

"You're Caro Flynn, aren't you? I saw your picture in my sister's magazine. You're opening that club in North Ridge."

"That's right, The Indigo Lounge," replied Caro. "Is that that sort of music you're into?"

He nodded. "Yeah, I love Blood Stone Riot and Slipknot."

Caro stifled a giggle. She bet that Alik would love being put in the same sentence as Corey Taylor. "You must know that Edie is going out with Alik Thorne then?" she asked, gesturing towards Edie.

The boy gave Edie a cursory glance. "No offence, but I don't think you really go with him, you're a bit posh."

Poppy practically choked on her latte at the gall of the child, tears of laughter in her eyes. "Oh, Edie, the shame of having your love life dissed by a teenager!"

"Michael, stop bothering those ladies. We're going to be late for lunch, come on!" A woman, presumably his mother, called from the corner of the market.

"Could I get a picture?" Michael asked.

Caro smiled. "How could I refuse?"

* * *

As Michael walked away, Edie thought of his comment about her and Alik. Sure, the kid was only young, but even he could see that they were a mismatched couple. She wondered if he would think any differently about her and Billy. Turning her attention back to Caro and Poppy, she sighed, wondering how much longer it would be before she could have a glass of wine. She had no idea what the three of them were going to do until dinner.

"Hey, it looks like there's a bridal shop in Broadkeys." Poppy was flicking through a discarded local newspaper and waved the advert in Edie's face. "It could be fun trying on dresses, after all I am still looking for one. Hey, Edie, maybe you'll even get Alik to pop the question."

Edie didn't think there was much chance of that, considering that she was currently spending a lot more time thinking of Billy and he was probably thinking about Caro. "Sounds good. Do you think we'd need an appointment?"

As it turned out, Serendipity Dreams wasn't exactly very busy on a weekday afternoon in the early summer. When Poppy called to politely ask on the off-chance that they could be squeezed in for a fitting, they couldn't do enough to help her. The three of them had the place to themselves and the shop owner had arranged for a bottle of

Buck's Fizz for them to drink whilst trying on dresses. Edie and Caro made themselves comfortable on the plush, overstuffed, cream sofa, while the assistant helped Poppy with the dresses. There were creations in ivory, white, egg shell, snow, alabaster, pearl, chalk, anything they could think of. And there was silk, tulle, taffeta, satin, lace... Edie was getting a headache just watching all the choices, choosing instead to neck the free drink. Anything to get away from the fact that she was sitting there with Caro.

Poppy appeared every so often in a frock, twisting this way and that, showing the others the options. Edie hadn't seen anything that she liked, but then reminded herself that this wasn't about her, it was about finding Poppy the Perfect Dress. She nodded rather noncommittally at most of the dresses, until Poppy came out in a ruffled full-skirted off-white number with a boned, strapless bodice, edged with silvery lace.

"Oh, wow, Poppy." Edie sighed. "You look gorgeous! That dress is just perfect!"

"Yeah, um, you look lovely," said Caro, with slightly less enthusiasm.

"You look like a princess," said the assistant.

The bride-to-be frowned. "Are you sure? Isn't it a bit... frou frou?" The hint of Australian in her accent became a bit more pronounced as she expressed her concern.

"God, no! You want to be the centre of attention, don't you?" said Edie, jumping up and fluffing the skirt with her fingers.

"I feel like the centre of a toilet roll holder," said Poppy, under her breath. She turned to the assistant. "Um, how much would this be?"

A tiny smile crossed the assistant's face as she mentally did some sums. "That particular style is three thousand six hundred and eighty pounds."

Edie didn't bat an eyelid at the cost, although she noticed that Caro and Poppy did.

"It is a lovely dress," said Poppy, "but it's a little over the price range I had in mind."

"Let me buy it," said Edie. "It can be my wedding present to you."

Poppy looked at Caro, who shrugged in return, finishing off the remains of her drink. "I couldn't let you buy it, Edie, it's way too expensive."

"Nonsense, you want everyone to admire you on the big day. And think of all the little girls who would want to be you in that dress, marrying the talented, gorgeous rock star."

For a moment, Edie wondered who she was trying to convince, Poppy or herself - not that she thought for one moment that Alik would consider proposing to her.

"If you're sure...?" Poppy took one last look at herself in the mirror.

Edie nodded. "It will be my pleasure." She nodded towards the assistant, pulling out her purse and waving a platinum credit card in her direction. "Please make the necessary arrangements to have this shipped to North Ridge, I'll take care of everything."

CHAPTER THIRTY-EIGHT

In the days leading up to Poppy's hen weekend, Caro received a string of emails and texts from some of the hens crying off with various reasons why they couldn't come. There should have been ten of them altogether but when it came time to meet to go down to Brighton late on the Friday afternoon, there were only six: Edie, Olivia, Caro, Poppy, and two of Poppy's friends from London; Lara and Chrissy.

The plan was to check in to their hotel and then head to English's, the oldest seafood restaurant in Brighton, for dinner, saving themselves for a big session on Saturday. To get them into the swing of things, and compensate for the fact that it was actually quite an awkward group, Caro had bought a few of bottles of champagne for them to drink on the train.

"I can't believe some of the excuses that your friends gave me," said Caro as she poured herself another glass. "Who can't get a babysitter when they've known for weeks what the dates were?"

Poppy sighed. "I know, I'm disappointed too. But at least this pair stuck with me." She waved her plastic flute in the direction of Lara and Chrissy.

Lara grinned. "As if we'd let you down, babe. Not every day you get to hang out with a celeb." She gave a nod in Edie's direction. "I reckon we'll be getting VIP treatment the whole weekend."

Caro had taken to Lara immediately in the exchange of emails they'd had in the build up to this weekend. Lara had given her some entertaining snippets of gossip about Poppy's pre-Nate dating days. After the previous week's

Newcomen Farm adventures, she was glad there were some other people around.

* * *

Edie and Olivia were talking about The Magpie when their conversation was interrupted by Edie's phone. She briefly glanced at the screen before killing the call with a swipe of her recently-manicured nail. When it rang again, she repeated the move.

When it rang for the third time, Caro chipped in impatiently. "Just answer it, Edie, or put it on silent or something. I'm sure if Alik is that desperate to speak to you he'll leave a message."

"Sorry, I didn't realise that it offended you that much." Edie switched it to silent. She didn't want to divulge that Alik wasn't the caller, but Billy. And she couldn't really speak to him in public in front of the others. Staring at the phone, she watched as he called a few more times before giving up. Debating whether or not to go to the vestibule between carriages to call him back, Edie decided it would be easier - and less likely to arouse suspicion - if she just texted him back with a quick message. She fired off a *'Can't talk, I'm with the girls x'* missive and hoped that it would pacify him. She reached for the champagne bottle and wondered how long they had before they arrived in Brighton.

* * *

Caro had booked them into a quirky boutique hotel. Each room had a different theme and was beautifully-decorated to reflect the characteristics of that idea. Caro and Poppy's suite was boudoir-inspired, with totally frivolous decor, including framed frilly knickers adorning the walls and plenty of faux fur and vintage furniture. Olivia and Edie's room was 50's in style, dedicated to Bettie Page, with lots of leopard print and curved, elegant furniture, huge floor to ceiling windows and a balcony overlooking the square in front of the hotel. Lara and Chrissy's room celebrated all things Dolly Parton and Americana kitsch with plenty of gingham, plaid, and even a white picket fence painted on one of the walls.

They quickly unpacked and freshened up, before heading out to English's, nestled in the heart of the Lanes. They enjoyed a light-hearted, boozy meal, sampling some of the best food on the menu: Crab bisque, tiny parcels of lobster tortellini, massive tiger prawns, sea bream, and fish pie finished off with Calvados pannacotta and a bitter chocolate and mint terrine.

It had been Poppy's idea to go back to the hotel and play drinking games, rather than argue about which of the many bars and clubs that were in town to go to. Caro and Poppy wanted a rock club, Edie preferred pop or dance, and the others were trying to keep the peace.

"At least this way, we can all put our iPods on and all get a bit of what we want," said Poppy, as she opened another bottle of champagne.

* * *

Edie was chatting to Lara and Chrissy. She found them slightly crass, to say the least, particularly with some of the comments they had made about Poppy over dinner, but the bride-to-be didn't seem to have taken offence. And she suspected that she ought to at least make an effort as Poppy had been kind enough to invite her. She wondered if she would have been there if she hadn't just forked out for the wedding dress. Still, it wasn't worth worrying about now.

"Remind me what it is you do?" asked Edie.

"We work at Claire's Accessories," said Chrissy, taking a large sip of her wine. "That's how we met Poppy."

"Oh, right," said Edie. "Which store did you work in?"

Lara gave a loud laugh. "We're not shop assistants, Edie. I'm a designer and Chrissy's a buyer. She had the best-selling jewellery product last year that wasn't Disney-inspired."

Edie sat up a bit straighter. She hadn't realised that these two were quite so influential. Neither of them came across as she would have expected from people in the same industry as her. But she hadn't realised that Poppy had anything to do with fashion either. "I imagine that you've heard of The Magpie then?" she asked. "It was featured in *Aspire* recently."

Lara shook her head.

Chrissy nodded. "Yes, I've worked with a couple of suppliers recently that mentioned your shop. Seems like you've got some good success there."

Edie basked in the compliments as the three of them started discussing fashion trends until Poppy told them it was time to shut up and focus on her.

* * *

Caro set out six shot glasses and opened a bottle of tequila, pouring everyone a shot.

"Okay," she said. "It's time for that old favourite, Never Have I Ever." She paused as the others groaned. "I've prepared some questions, you pick one out and if you've done that thing, you need to sink your drink. Obviously you have to tell us what the question is."

"But do we have to divulge the situation?" asked Chrissy.

"Not unless you want to. Right then, lovely bride to be, you get to go first."

Caro shook the makeshift bowl - she'd actually emptied the ice down the sink and used the ice bucket, giving it a cursory wipe with a towel so the questions wouldn't get wet - and waved it in front of Poppy, who delved in.

Hooting with laughter, she took a shot. "Never have I ever flashed someone!"

Lara and Chrissy dissolved into giggles. Caro moved on to Olivia, who opened up her question and simply shook her head.

"Never have I ever ended up naked and can't remember why," she said. "I just don't do that sort of thing! I always know when I've had enough to drink."

"Are you sure about that?" Caro stared at her. "I seem to remember one night at The Roca Bar... Oh, no, wait, I know exactly what you were up to that night and you definitely knew what you were doing."

Next it was Lara and Chrissy's turn, both of them downed shots, sharing a little more than was necessary. The rest of them howled with laughter at the stories. Clearly working in fashion ensured that there were plenty of stories to tell. Caro came to Edie.

"Your turn."

Edie took her time in swirling the questions around before picking one. She read the question silently, before downing the tequila in her glass. "Never have I ever been told what to do during sex," she said quietly, avoiding everyone's gaze.

"Alik doesn't strike me as the dominant type," said Caro.

"What would you know about Alik?" said Edie. "Although you two are always off whispering together about something." She refilled her shot glass before Caro had chance to do so. "And isn't it your turn now anyway?" Edie grabbed the bucket and thrust it at her. "Go on."
Shaking her head, Caro took one of the cards and read it. Draining her glass, she looked Edie directly in the eye.

"Never have I ever slept with someone within an hour of meeting them. And God, he was good."

* * *

Edie decided that she wasn't going to stay up for much longer after Caro's question. She persuaded Olivia that it was late and the two of them should head off to their room as it would be a long day tomorrow. Olivia appeared grateful and the two of them disappeared.

Some time later, Edie lay in the dark, trying to get off to sleep. She had never shared a room with Olivia before and she was conscious of her movements, not wanting to disturb her roommate. As the sounds of the town settling down for the night filtered through the window, Edie's phone vibrated with a text message. Turning her back on Olivia, she held the device slightly under the covers so she could reply. The exchange of messages went on for a good five minutes before Olivia interjected.

"I didn't realise you and Alik were so needy," she said, sighing.

"It's not Alik," said Edie, without thinking.

Olivia propped herself up on one elbow. "Then who on Earth are you texting so eagerly at this time of night?"

Edie had been drinking since they had left North Ridge and was, perhaps, not thinking totally clearly. She admitted to Caro's best friend that she was in the middle of sexting her boyfriend's band mate.

"What?" Olivia sat bolt upright and flicked on the bedside lamp, flooding the room with light. "How did that happen?"

Edie covered her eyes to hide from the glare. Turning onto her back, she stared up at the ceiling and regaled Olivia with the events of the Wilde Park Festival and what had happened when they had gone to Newcomen Farm.

And how they had met up on a few occasions since, although it was getting difficult not to arouse suspicion.

"What are you going to do about it?" Olivia asked.

That was something Edie hadn't really thought about. She was enjoying the danger and the passion of her affair with Billy. Not to mention the totally hot, kinky, sex. She wasn't prepared to give it up. At least not yet. But at the same time, she also didn't want to break things off with Alik. There was a devilish streak in her that didn't want to do that and give Alik the opportunity to start a relationship with Caro.

"I don't know." Edie sat up suddenly and looked at Olivia. "You can't tell anyone about this. Especially not Caro."

* * *

After a leisurely start the following day, they all made their way to the Queens Cabaret Bar for their burlesque workshop. Edie was already on edge, wondering whether or not she could trust Olivia with what she'd told her about Billy. Olivia had been pretty quiet for most of the morning, and Edie had made sure that she was never on her own with either Caro or Poppy.

They were met at the bar by Pearl Delonge, who introduced herself as an international performer. She was dressed in an exquisite jewelled corset that wouldn't have looked out of place on Dita Von Teese, and ridiculously high sparkling heels. Her black hair was smoothed into perfect shape, and she had well-defined eyebrows and bright red lipstick. She looked like the whole package. Pearl instructed them to get changed and pointed to the stage, where she would meet them in a few minutes.

When they returned, Pearl was already playing some music that would complement the moves they were going to be learning.

"I'll start off with something relatively simple," said Pearl. "Now watch me."

The six of them, dressed more for yoga or pilates than burlesque, looked on as Pearl started to bump and grind along to the music. It was inherently sexy, without being too slutty. Despite their initial reluctance, it wasn't long before they were all giggling and moving like Pearl, waving large feathered fans around. Poppy and Caro were really getting into it, dancing back to back, playing up to each other, and pretending to kiss. Edie found it rather distasteful.

"You two are naturals!" Pearl said. "I should get you onstage with me tonight."

"Erm, I don't think so, but thanks. Neither of us is exactly the performing kind," said Poppy. "It's our other halves who like the limelight."

Edie immediately picked up on Poppy's comment. "What do you mean 'other halves?' Jonny isn't in a band."

"I know that but wherever there's a free ticket or a live gig, he's there. He's always first on the scene for new stuff," said Poppy.

"Not exactly the same as being the lead singer in an up and coming rock band though, is it? I mean, when did Jonny get the cover of *Roccia* magazine?" asked Edie, pretending to examine her nails.

"When did this become your-boyfriend's-got-a-bigger-dick-than-my-boyfriend?" challenged Caro, sipping from a bottle of water.

Edie knew they were getting close to dangerous ground and needed to do something to change the subject. "Pearl, how about you show us the shimmy move again?"

After the awkwardness of the lesson, they were grateful to escape to the showers and then head into the main bar and restaurant for the evening. They had a semi-circular booth in the centre of the room that faced the stage, decorated in deep blue velvet. An elaborate candelabra was the table centrepiece, strategically placed so they were all able to see the stage. Dinner was a fairly sombre affair, with not much conversation. They drank several bottles of champagne during the course of the meal until it came time for Pearl's show. They watched in awe as she went through her paces, recognising some of the moves she had taught them earlier.

"We could definitely do that," said Poppy, drunkenly waving her glass around. "We could form a new dance troupe."

Edie shuddered. She couldn't think of anything worse.

"Surely we should be playing some kind of truth or dare game, like we did last night," said Chrissy. "We are on a hen night after all."

"We could always play 'which member of Blood Stone Riot do you fancy the most.'" said Poppy. "I'll start: Nate, obviously! And Edie would obviously go for Alik."

Edie shifted nervously in her chair, avoiding Olivia's eyes.

Taking a sip of her drink, Edie nodded in agreement with Poppy. "Of course, Alik is definitely the one." Her eyes narrowed as she turned to Caro. "And what about you, Caro? Which member of Blood Stone Riot would you say was the most attractive?"

"Nate," replied Caro, without hesitation.

Poppy interjected. "Edie, let's just go back on your answer there. I thought you and Billy seemed quite close when we were in the studio...?"

Edie looked desperately at Olivia.

"If the marathon texting session last night was anything to go by, then I doubt anyone else but Alik would be lucky to get a look in," Olivia said, quickly. "Honestly, it took me ages to get to sleep because of all the beeping and vibrating."

"Are you sure that was just the texting?" said Lara, laughing. "Don't think we didn't notice you slipping off into that little erotic boutique place last night before we came back, Edie. Maybe you got Alik a little gift while you were there."

    Edie was silent. Billy had given her an instruction for their next meeting and she was merely obeying his request. Thank God they hadn't insisted on going with her. The sooner this weekend was over the better.

CHAPTER THIRTY-NINE

The text had been pretty direct. No niceties, no kisses, just a simple instruction.

Edie shivered in anticipation as the taxi delivered her to the outskirts of North Ridge, to a simple, no-frills hotel.

"That'll be a tenner, love," the taxi driver said.

She pushed a note at him and jumped out, her small bag bouncing against her hip as she tightened the belt of her stylish trench coat. She entered the hotel and smiled politely at the receptionist, pretending she knew exactly where she was going. Glancing to her right, she saw the tiny bar, which was empty. Except for one man sitting on a stool at the end, nursing a pint of beer. She walked confidently over to him, as best she could on dangerously-high black patent heels, and stood directly beside him.

"You're late," he said.

The smile disappeared from her face. "I'm sorry, there was traffic and it took ages."

Billy smirked.

"You obeyed the message so far then," he said. "Let's see if you did exactly what I told you."

He turned her to face him, pulling her into the space between his legs and hooking one around her calf, shielding her from anyone else who might be able to see. Slipping a hand beneath her coat, he ran his fingers from her knee, up to her thigh, tracing the lace tops of her stockings and between her legs, cupping her naked pussy in his hand. She quivered, her legs threatening to give way. She wasn't used to being touched in such a way where someone might see her. Abruptly, Billy removed his hand and moved to the lapels of her coat, tugging down the material until her bare nipple peeped from underneath. She went to cover herself, but he slapped her hand away, and did it himself.

"Good girl," he said. "Now follow me."

He stood up and put an arm around her waist, and led her towards the lift. As soon as they were in the lift, he told her to take off the coat. Edie glanced around nervously at the mirrored interior, checking to see how many floors there were. Would anyone would see her?

Taking a deep breath, she slipped the garment from her shoulders. Her semi-naked reflection stared back at her. She couldn't believe how it was making her feel; totally wanton and alive. Something she rarely felt with Alik. The lift pinged for their floor. Billy hurriedly pulled the mac back over her body, propelling her towards the room with indecent speed, his hand in the small of her back.

Billy placed the Do Not Disturb sign on the outer handle and locked the door behind them.

"What shall I do with you now?"

She stood there, looking around the sparsely-furnished room. There was a small double bed with what looked like a faux antique metal bedhead, a dressing table and chair, a kettle, two mugs, and the makings of tea and coffee. There wasn't a wardrobe, just hangers on hooks in the wall and behind the only other door in the room was the en suite. Basic.

"Do you want me to beg?" she asked.

"God, sometimes I wish I could gag you so you didn't ask stupid questions," he said, sliding in behind her. He placed a hand over her mouth, and pushed his fingers between her lips. Involuntarily, she started to suck, twisting her tongue around his finger. His other hand unbuttoned her coat again, ripping it from her body, leaving her standing there, naked but for the stockings and the heels. Her nipples were rock hard, standing to attention.

Billy drew away. "You are just so horny, you know that? Come here."

Edie moved towards him. He positioned her so she was standing at the foot of the bed. She braced herself against it with her shins. He spread her legs until they pulled uncomfortably apart and she was balancing precariously on her heels. He looped one end of the belt of her coat around the head of the bed and secured her wrists together with the other end so she was bent over, almost toppling forwards from the waist, her arms stretched out in front of her, pulled taut. She looked back at him over her shoulder, blonde hair tumbling across her back, catching sight of her own buttocks rising behind her. Her clit throbbed pleasurably as she twisted against her bonds. Billy chose to make her wait, deliberately taking his time in shedding his own clothes.

"You're taking too long!" she said, wriggling around.

"I could always gag you with my cock," he said

She made a face at him. He twisted her hair in one hand, pulling her head back, and gently slapped her arse a couple of times, before his fingers went to work on her. Within seconds, she was writhing underneath his touch, his fingers plunging in and out of her, her pussy so wet for him. When he stopped to position himself right behind her, she felt open and vulnerable. She needed something to fill the void. His cock slipped easily into her. He grasped her hips and thrust, banging right into her. Her body jolting against the bed. Edie was totally lost in the overwhelming feelings coursing through her body. She had never thought that rough sex or bondage would be her thing. She'd always thought she was far too good to debase herself like that. But it was making her come like she had never come before. And she loved it.

As Billy thrust into her once more, she cried out for him to go harder, deeper, again.

His hand cracked down on her bottom, causing her to squeal in excitement. The punishment made her contract around him, and she pushed back to encourage him further inside her. With a loud groan, he came. He sagged onto the bed and reached over to release Edie. She kicked off her heels, leaving on the stockings, and examined her wrists

"How am I going to explain those to Alik?" she said, as she settled onto the bed and spooned into Billy's naked body.

"You could always tell him that you spent the afternoon with his bandmate, tied to a bed, being fucked out of your mind," he said.

"Tempting, but perhaps not the best idea you've ever had."

"You don't want to know what ideas I've had, particularly the ones involving you," said Billy. "I bet they would make Alik freak out."

Edie's mind spun as she considered the sorts of things Billy could come up with. Even now, she was squirming as Billy held her in an almost loving afterglow, the fingers of his right hand gently stroking her breast.

"He would certainly freak out if he knew I was here with you... Ow!" Edie squealed as Billy pinched her nipple. It wasn't quite enough to distract her, though. "I told Olivia that we were seeing each other."

"You did what?" Billy increased the pressure on Edie's nipple and she gritted her teeth against the sharp pain. "Edie, it's just sex. I like shagging you, you're up for anything. It's easy."

Edie was stung by Billy's words as much as the physical ache in her chest. She struggled to extricate herself from his grasp, but his other hand grabbed her wrist. She knew that she was falling for him, despite her protestations. She knew that she wouldn't let just anyone do the things to her that he had done.

"How do you know she won't say anything to Caro? They are best friends after all."

"I guess I just have to trust her." Edie gasped as Billy let her go, the breath coming out of her in a rush. "And is it really so bad that I might be interested in you a bit more than just a quick fuck?"

Billy laughed. "Get real, Edie, that's all we've done; sucking and fucking. We're hardly stepping out together." His quaint turn of phrase appealed to her.

"What if we were? Would it be that awful?" It was then that Edie knew she wanted more than just the physical stuff with Billy. He was very different to Alik, more attentive to her at least, and he excited her.

Billy pushed her onto her back, looming over her, his dark eyes boring into hers. "I don't think it would be awful at all, it just depends how badly you want it."

She grabbed one of his hands and pulled it between her legs, letting him feel how wet she was again. "Oh, I want it, Billy, I want you." All thoughts of Alik were banished from her mind as Billy started working his magic again. As wrong as she knew it was, she gave herself up to the sensations running through her body.

CHAPTER FORTY

After the not-so-unexpected drama of Poppy's hen weekend, Caro was glad to have something else to focus on apart from the opening of The Indigo Lounge, and moving into her new house was a welcome distraction.

She'd spent a lot of time over the previous weeks choosing furniture and bedding and other household essentials, and her credit card was groaning under the weight of it all. The last couple of days had been a whirlwind of activity as she coordinated various delivery drivers and arranged everything where she wanted it, before changing her mind an hour or so later and moving things around herself. A last-minute decision to have a house-warming party had created even more chaos, and she was now arranging shop-bought party food into bowls and making sure there was enough beer in the new fridge.

"How many people are you expecting?" Jonny asked, swiping a handful of crisps from one of the bowls on the kitchen table. "You've got enough here for a small army." He'd been there all afternoon, ostensibly to "help", but had spent most of the time sprawled out on the sofa watching music videos.

Caro ran a hand through her hair, wondering if there was time for her to jump in the shower before everyone arrived. "Everyone" included Alik. She had avoided him since their last near-miss at The Pit, and had simply texted him and Edie an invite for this evening. She had butterflies in her stomach thinking of him here, in the house that he had helped her choose.

"Just making sure we don't run out of anything," she said. She decided there was time to freshen up, and went to the bathroom. As she stripped off and dived under the large rainfall shower head, she remembered Alik commenting that it was big enough for two, and an image of his naked body crept into her head. Shaking it from her mind, she quickly lathered shampoo over her head, hearing Jonny call up the stairs that Olivia and Nic had arrived already. She hurriedly finished her shower, roughly towel-drying her hair, and picked out a pair of black skinny jeans and a simple blue and white patterned top. Shoving her feet into a pair of espadrilles, she quickly applied a layer of tinted moisturiser, mascara, and a slick of pink lip gloss. There wasn't time to dry her hair properly, so she grabbed a band from the drawer and pulled it up in a messy bun, tendrils escaping round her face.

"You look hot," said Jonny as she came into the kitchen. He slipped his arms around her waist and nuzzled her neck.

"Thank you," replied Caro. It wasn't often that Jonny complimented her.

Olivia passed her a bottle of champagne. "For the stock."

Caro gratefully accepted it and added it to the stash that was already chilling in the fridge. She got a cold bottle and passed it to Jonny to do the honours. He duly obliged and passed out glasses to the four of them.

"Cheers!" said Olivia. "To your new home and the future success of The Indigo Lounge!"

* * *

Alik and Edie arrived hand in hand, some time after everyone else. Alik remembered the last time he'd been at the house, when Caro had first seen it. Now fully-furnished in Caro's style, it looked even better than it had back then.

There was a mix of modern and vintage furniture, depending on which room you were in, and it suited her perfectly. Tightening his grip on Edie's hand, he went into the kitchen, where Nic and Olivia were chatting.

"Evening, guys," he said. "Great place, isn't it?"

"You should know that more than the rest of us, mate," said Nic. "After all, you helped her choose it."

Edie gave Alik a sideways look. "What does he mean, you helped her choose it?"

"Alik didn't tell you about his house-hunting expedition with Caro?" asked Nic.

"No, he didn't." Edie's tone was cool. "When was this?"

Alik rolled his eyes at Nic. Although he hadn't deliberately chosen to keep this from Edie, it hadn't been something he was prepared to shout about. "Ages ago. Olivia couldn't go with her, I think there was some crisis at The Magpie you needed her for, and Nic had meetings at the club. We didn't think it was safe for her to go alone."

"It was a house viewing, Alik, not a war zone," said Edie, pouting.

"You're seriously that bothered about it? It's not like I hooked up with her in a hotel or anything."

"Who's hooked up in a hotel?" said Billy, joining the group. He had his arm around a young girl with bleached-blonde hair and a micro skirt. "Alright, Edie?" He leaned across Alik and kissed Edie on both cheeks, which wasn't a Billy thing to do at all. "Guys," he said, acknowledging the others.

Alik felt Edie stiffen beside him. "You'll definitely be at The Indigo Lounge tomorrow for rehearsal?"

Billy looked at the girl he was with. "As long as I don't get distracted by this one." He ran a hand across her arse, then playfully slapped it while she giggled in response. "We should go and mingle." And the pair were gone.

"He's a piece of work, isn't he?" said Alik, shaking his head.

Nic nodded in agreement. "He certainly gets through them. I don't know what a woman would see in a man-slut like that."

Alik looked between Edie and Olivia. "Ladies, any thoughts on that?"

Edie shuddered. "Urgh, I don't know how any woman would let herself be sweet-talked by him. I mean, he doesn't exactly look... clean."

Alik laughed. "I just hope he gets himself tested regularly. I bet Parker wouldn't want to be hit with a bill for an STI."

* * *

Edie cornered Olivia in the garden. She'd been trying to keep her distance from Billy, but it was proving difficult. When he'd kissed her in front of Alik, she had felt her nipples hardening and her crotch spasming. It had been a couple of days since their hotel meeting and she needed to see him again. But first, she needed to speak to Olivia.

"Have you said anything about me and Billy?" she said, checking there was no-one in earshot to hear her.

"To who? Edie, I'm not going to tell Alik if that's what you're worried about. I thought you did a good job of covering yourself earlier."

Edie sighed in relief. She had hoped that her attraction to Billy wasn't obvious, but she couldn't be sure if anyone else would notice her treacherous body reacting. "Thank you for not saying anything."

"I don't like it, Edie. I don't like keeping your secrets."

"I know, and I'm sorry. I'm not about to dump Billy."

"Why not, Edie? Alik's your boyfriend, not Billy." Olivia was, as ever, the voice of reason. "You need to think about what you're doing. And not leave me in the middle of things. Look, I'm going to find Nic. Why don't you come with me and spend some time with Alik?"

"I will, just give me a minute."

Edie went inside and headed upstairs towards the bathroom. She needed some time to think. She found herself standing by the window in Caro's bedroom, staring out over the canal.

"What are you doing up here?" Billy asked, making her jump.

She turned slowly, uncurling her body, the danger of the situation turning her on. "Just thought I'd check out the view. You can see right across the city from here." She glanced around behind Billy. "Where's your little tramp anyway? Shouldn't you be with her?"

Billy laughed, a low, throaty sound. "Oh, she's here alright."

Edie's mouth fell open.

Billy smirked. "I've got a use for that." He abruptly grabbed her and pulled her into the walk-in wardrobe, closing the door behind them and pushing Edie against it, so she was trapped. Her breath was already coming in short gasps as one of his hands encircled her wrists and drew them up and over her head. The other pushed up the short skirt of her dress, exposing her lacy knickers. His fingers traced the crease at the top of her thigh and she shifted her legs apart slightly, pushing herself towards him.

"Patience," he whispered in her ear.

"Billy...please..." The heat between her legs increased as his fingers gently stroked her.

"Oh, babe, what I wouldn't do for a quickie here, but we need to be quiet. We couldn't have Caro or Alik finding us, could we?" He silenced her with a kiss, his tongue probing the inside of her mouth before pulling her dress back down and releasing her, her arms falling limply to her sides.

Billy looked her squarely in the eye. "This is getting dangerous. Every time I'm near you, I want you, I need to be inside you. Then I remember you're with him." He spat out the last word. "I think you're right, we should be together. One day."

Billy barged past her, leaving Edie staring after him.

* * *

It was close to two in the morning when Olivia and Nic, the last people remaining, left. Caro closed the door behind them, went into the living room, and dropped down onto the sofa.

"Jesus," she said. "I guess that's a bit of a dry run for The Indigo Lounge then."

Jonny appeared with two more glasses of champagne. "Get this down you," he said. "You really have been the hostess with the most-est this evening." He had clearly been indulging in something that night, his pupils were huge and he was slurring his words a little.

Caro reached eagerly for the glass. It had been a fantastic evening, reacquainting herself with some old North Ridge faces and enjoying chatting with her guests. Just like the early days at The Roca Bar. She briefly thought of Mariella and wondered what her friend was doing now. She was so caught up in her own thoughts that she somehow managed to miss her mouth and spill most of the champagne down her front, causing her top to cling to her. "Shit!"

Jonny placed his own glass on the table and sat down beside her. "Here, let me help you with that."

He reached over and hooked the garment over her head, revealing her voluptuous breasts. His hand trailed across their dampness, his thumb brushing across her nipple as he reached around to unhook her bra. Caro let out a sigh as he continued to torment her relentlessly, their bodies intertwining as they got into a more comfortable position. He replaced his thumb with his mouth, alternately flicking his tongue and sucking, driving her towards the edge. She wriggled out of her jeans and knickers, feeling the cool leather of the sofa directly on her skin as Jonny shed his own clothes, his lithe body on top of hers. Wanting a release, Caro reached down and took Jonny's cock in her hand, guiding him towards her.

"Wait," he said, scrabbling for his jeans and taking a condom out of his wallet. He rolled it on and resumed his position, sliding gently into Caro.

She grabbed his neck and pulled him towards her, wanting him to be more forceful, wanting him to take control, much like Alik had. She tried to banish the thought from her mind. She was with Jonny and he was here now. She had to forget about Alik.

CHAPTER FORTY-ONE

Alik had gone to The Vegas to see Dagger Drawn play the night before The Indigo Lounge opening. He was close friends with Ben, the lead singer, and the two bands had often supported each other on out of town gigs. Edie had told him she was doing something with Minty and that she wouldn't be back until much later. The regulars at The Vegas barely batted an eyelid as he sat at the bar, watching the band, waiting for Ben to finish so they could catch up for a beer.

Out of the corner of his eye, he saw Jonny Tyler at the other end of the bar. He was with a girl, likely a student given her approximate age and dress. Jonny had his arm around her and was whispering something in her ear that was clearly the funniest thing in the world based on her reaction. He tried to ignore it, but their actions got more amorous and he watched as Jonny went in for the kiss, while groping her arse. Within seconds, there were tongues.

Alik slid off his stool and walked over to them. He grabbed Jonny's jacket and pulled him off the girl.

"Hey, what do you think you're doing?" the girl said.

"Go and buy yourself a drink, sweetheart, I need a chat with Jonny." He pushed a ten pound note at her, still keeping a hold of Jonny's coat.

The girl huffed, but did as she was told. Alik relinquished his grip and turned to Jonny.

"What the hell was that all about?" The promoter asked, dusting himself off. "You got designs on her yourself?"

"Where's Caro?"

"Probably working, that's all she does these days."

"And you should be supporting her. Tomorrow's a big night for her."

"Yeah, I know, but I'm in Barcelona. I'm promoting a new club there."

Alik resisted the urge to punch him. How could he consider being somewhere else?

"Are you and Caro serious?" Alik asked.

Jonny shrugged. Very non committal. And the answer that Alik wanted.

"If you want to make it work with her, I wouldn't expect to see you here tonight with your tongue down some other girl's throat."

Again, Jonny shrugged. His total indifference toward Caro made Alik furious. And made him think. The occasions when he and Caro had been together, her insistence on purely being friends and nothing more, was because he was with Edie. She was, technically, a free agent.

But he was with Edie.

The words reverberated in his head. Everything that had happened recently made him want Caro even more.

He knew what he had to do.

When The Indigo Lounge opening was over, he'd tell Edie the same thing.

CHAPTER FORTY-TWO

The Indigo Lounge was eerily quiet and empty. The aroma of new leather and freshly-laid carpet hung in the air.

It was hard to believe that in a few hours it would be packed with punters and musicians, enjoying the opening night bands, taking advantage of the special offers and, hopefully, spreading the word to others in order to continue the success.

Caro and Nic were carrying out last-minute checks on the bars and the VIP areas, making sure that all the drinks were stocked, glasses were clean, and surfaces were shining. Amy was running around with a clipboard, barking orders at anyone that would listen. The security team, bar crew, glass collectors and cleaners had all been briefed. Everyone was ready.

The only one who wasn't ready was Caro. She was still dressed in her jeans - her caramel hair pulled up into a topknot - having made a few last minute amendments to the layout, which meant she had ended up crawling about on her hands and knees as she rearranged some of the soft drinks behind the bar.

"Caro, what are you doing?" Olivia's voice cut through the air.

Caro picked herself up off the floor, brushing some dust off her jeans. "Just finishing off a few things," she said, meekly.

"You have rafts of staff to help you do that. And you're not even dressed!" Olivia took her by the elbow and marched her upstairs to the office.

"I could hardly wear my opening night outfit to change barrels though, could I?" Caro protested.

Caro's dress was hanging up, a beautiful plunge v-neck mirrored dress, that had a heavily hand-embellished front and sleeves, with a plain Georgette black back. She planned to team it with a pair of Christian Louboutin metallic silver pumps. She had a pair of silver Converse stashed in the office for when her feet inevitably started to hurt too much later.

She stripped off her jeans and t-shirt, and was standing in front of Olivia in just her underwear - something black and lacy from La Perla - when Nic walked in.

"Jesus, Caro, I know we want to attract the punters, but we're not running that kind of club," he said.

"I know, but Olivia reminded me I really should be ready by now."

"You should." Nic gave her a quick kiss on the cheek. "Olivia, the guys from *Roccia* magazine are downstairs and they're waiting for their exclusive. Alik's waiting backstage for you." His phone buzzed. "And Amy's just found an issue with a spelling mistake on a poster...I'll see you later." He was gone just as quickly as he'd appeared.

Caro swiftly sprayed on some deodorant and perfume and slipped on her dress. Twisting her hair back up into a tousled, sexy, ponytail, she applied some make-up, before presenting herself to Olivia.

"Will I do?" she asked, twirling around in front of her friend.

Olivia laughed. "Gorgeous. Jonny will be eating out of your hand."

"Oh, he's not coming. He's promoting some club in Barcelona tonight. We sort of fell out over it and I'm not sure I'll be seeing a great deal of him any more." Caro was very matter of fact in her explanation. Their relationship had always been one of friends with benefits, but since Caro had returned to the UK, there had been a possibility that it could have turned into something more. Jonny was, Caro reflected, one less complication she didn't need right now.

Olivia slipped her arm through Caro's. "Let's go."

* * *

Edie twirled around in front of the mirror, admiring her reflection; the way her freshly blown out blonde hair gleamed under the bedroom lights, the beautiful sheen from her gold sheath of a dress, cut high on her thigh and the sparkling new shoes - a gift from Alik - although he hadn't done much of the choosing.

She knew she looked good.

Her phone buzzed with a message. Expecting it to be from Minty, she opened it, realising too late that it was from Billy. And detailed exactly what he wanted to do to her that night. She shivered in anticipation.

"Who was that?" asked Alik, coming into the room. He looked gig-ready in tight dark grey jeans and a fitted t-shirt. As usual, he had a change of clothes for after the set stashed in a bag.

"Oh, just Olivia, saying she's already at The Indigo Lounge. Just wondering where we were."

Alik nodded, checking his watch. Edie knew he wouldn't want to be late for sound checking - being that Blood Stone Riot were playing last, they would usually sound check first. "Sure, we should go."

Edie pouted. "Oh, okay." She said softly.

"You look amazing," he said without really looking up.

The pout instantly changed to a beam. "Thank you, honey."

CHAPTER FORTY-THREE

Several hours later, The Indigo Lounge was flooded with people. There was a mix of university students, local townies, and a variety of ages from teenagers on one of their first nights out to punters in their fifties who had been clubbing for decades. That was the beauty of the rock scene; it attracted both ends of the spectrum and everything in between, all coexisting in total harmony. Both Nic and Caro were secretly pleased, and surprised, that so many people had turned up, despite Olivia's insistence that it was never in doubt.

Firstly, she'd pointed out, punters always loved a new bar, and secondly, when you had a shit hot band line-up that was topped by Blood Stone Riot, you were always likely to get the crowds. The band's set had been phenomenal; short, tight, and appropriately dark. They'd thrown in a few old favourites - cover songs they used to do in the early days of the band - to really whip the crowd into a frenzy. Alik had been outstanding, and also managed to get through a set without taking out someone in the mosh pit, something that Poppy had reminded him of the minute he'd come off stage. It had been Olivia's idea to run teasers of the 'Bleed Like Cyanide' video throughout the set and the screens that were showing music channels were also being interspersed with a few shots as well. Already people were beginning to talk about the video, way before it had even been released.

* * *

With the live music over, Caro and Nic were working the floor, making sure that everyone was having a good time. Everything was running smoothly. There were queues at the bar and queues for the toilets, but manageable ones in both cases, and no-one seemed to be complaining. Their head of security had reported a bit of a ruckus when he had turned a small group of men away because the club was actually full, but they had finally seen sense and moved on somewhere else.

"You should be proud."

Standing on the balcony of the VIP area surveying the throngs of people below and lost in her own thoughts, Caro jumped. Turning towards the owner of the voice that had just whispered in her ear, she saw Alik, holding two glasses of champagne. He'd changed after the band's set, now dressed in black jeans and fitted dark blue shirt that clung to his torso, unbuttoned enough to reveal his tattoos.

"I mean it," he continued. "You and Nic should be really proud of what you've made happen here." His eyes swept over her. "And you look incredible." He passed her one of the glasses and gently touched her forearm.

A bolt of electricity shot up towards her neck, making her shiver, despite the heat of the club. She had almost forgotten how much of an effect he could have. "Thank you," she said, softly. "You were pretty amazing too."

They stood there for a moment and the rest of the people in the club melted away. Caro remembered all the times she and Alik had almost been together, recent memories of The Pit coming to the forefront of her mind.

"Is that for me?" Edie swooped in and grabbed the glass that Alik was holding. "I'm so thirsty! I didn't realise you could work up so much of a sweat in a rock club. Things seems to have gone okay tonight, haven't they, Caro?"

Caro mentally compared their outfits.

Edie in gold, Caro in silver; the winner had been decided.

*　*　*

Some time later, Alik broke away from the group of women in the VIP lounge to take a breather. Edie had been there to start with, entertaining them with tales from *Pretty Rich Things* and persuading them to check out The Magpie. But she had disappeared what felt like eons ago and Alik was starting to struggle for conversation.

He sought out Caro, gesturing to her that he wanted a drink after he'd been to the VIP facilities and she nodded.

He pushed to door of the gents open, seeing it was empty except for one of the cubicles. As he glanced towards the door, he noticed a pair of gold, glittery heels just poking out from beneath it. A pair of heels he was very familiar with. Particularly as he had bought them.

"Edie?" he called.

Wondering what the hell she was doing in the gents, he gently pushed the door open and was met with the sight of Edie in front of Billy, sucking him off. He met the eyes of his bassist, a mixture of anger, disbelief and disgust clouding them.

"What the fuck?"

Edie collapsed on the floor, coughing. "It's not what it looks like." She scrambled to her feet and rearranged her dress.

"What's up, mate? She never do that to you?" said Billy, zipping up his jeans. "I reckon there's a lot of things she didn't do with you, she's fucking filth."

Alik looked between the pair, unsure as to who he was more appalled with. Edie, for apparently cheating on him with one of his best friends - a band mate, for Christ's sake - or Billy, for moving in on his girlfriend.

"Alik, it hasn't been going on long..." Edie went to grab his arm, but he pulled away.

"It shouldn't have been going on at all," he replied.

Billy smirked. "I'm going to get some drinks, anyone joining me?" When neither Alik or Edie moved, he shrugged and headed out of the room.

"Alik, I'm sorry." Edie said.

As he looked at Edie standing in front of him, Alik knew that the decision he had made the previous evening had been vindicated. Even though the circumstances in which it had come about hadn't been what he had anticipated.

Edie batted her eyelashes at him, eyes that glistened with unshed tears. Crocodile tears as far as Alik was concerned.

"We're done, Edie," he said, flatly.

She clutched at his arm. "It was a mistake, it only happened a couple of times..."

"A couple of times too many! Edie, you were supposed to be my girlfriend."

"Ha! For all the time you've been pining over Caro bloody Flynn and you say I'm meant to be your girlfriend?" Edie said. "You took *her* to Greece, protected *her* at the festival, and don't think I missed the way you were looking at her all the time we were at Newcomen Farm. It's difficult to compete with that."

In his mind, Alik knew there was no competition. He should always have been with Caro, and regretted not making it happen sooner.

"Billy made me feel special, he wanted to be with me, Hell, he *wanted* me." Edie's tirade against him continued. "I don't have to play second-best to another woman or even a guitar with him, he's totally into me."

"Of course he is," Alik said.

"I suppose you'll go running to her now," she said, crossing her arms.

Alik sighed. "Even if I was, it would have nothing to do with you. It's over."

He made his way back to the bar where Caro was quietly chatting with Poppy, trying to comprehend what he'd just seen. He downed the drink that Caro had waiting for him and gestured to the barman for another, before sinking that in one as well. As he asked for a third, Poppy grabbed his wrist.

"Hey, slow down, I know we're all celebrating tonight, but we want to remember it in the morning."

"You might want to remember it, Poppy, but right now I'm trying to erase the memory of seeing my ex-girlfriend with my bandmate's dick in her mouth."

Poppy almost spat out her drink. "What?"

"You heard. I just found Edie and Billy in the VIP gents and she was sucking his cock."

"It might not have been the first time..." said Poppy.

"Oh no, I've found out it wasn't. Edie told me so herself. Happened a couple of times apparently."

"We, um, maybe thought something happened at Newcomen Farm when you guys were recording. She was acting really oddly." Poppy glanced at Caro.

Alik finally got his third drink, savouring the taste of the whisky more on this occasion. He looked Caro directly in the eye, wanting her more than anything, but knowing that now wasn't the right time. He wasn't in the right place, in the right frame of mind to be anything but angry. And she didn't deserve that. He didn't want it to represent just a revenge shag, which is what it would amount to if he did anything with her tonight. He slammed the empty glass down on the bar and stared blindly into the main body of the club.

"I need to get laid."

CHAPTER FORTY-FOUR

In the days that followed his discovery of Edie and Billy together, Alik had pretty much turned into a hermit. After getting horrendously drunk and hooking up with some random groupie the night of The Indigo Lounge opening, he had retreated to his flat and spent the next week ordering in take-away, drinking anything he could get his hands on, and writing songs.

All the anger he harboured was being channelled into new work, some for Blood Stone Riot and some to add to 'Girl From The Blue.' There were pieces of paper scattered all over the living room; covering the table, sofa, and floor, as lyrics just came flowing out of him. The best thing he'd written was called 'Poisoned Rationality', which tried to detail his balanced emotions about his relationship, or former relationship, with Edie. He had moments of crashing rationality, when he was able to compartmentalise the fact that they were from two different worlds and had been drifting apart for a while, to poisonous thoughts about how long it had been going on for, how many times they had been together and how much he wanted to hurt them.

And then interspersed with that were thoughts of Caro and what he should do with his feelings for her, now there could be an opportunity for them. But would she see it as being second best? Taking a sip from a beer can on the table, and coughing when he realised that he'd managed to put a cigarette out in it, he heard someone hammering on the door.

He dragged himself up from the sofa and headed to the front door.

"Oh, and you look like shit." Nate barged past Alik into the flat, surveying the detritus of discarded pizza boxes, noodle cartons and plastic boxes that once contained curry - and probably accounted for some of the t-shirt stains. "Where the hell have you been, mate, we've been worried about you. You're not answering your phone."

Alik shrugged, rubbing his bloodshot eyes. "Where do you think?"

Nate cleared a place on the sofa and sat down, picking up one of the leaves of paper. He scanned over the lyrics, some words angrily crossed through, lines arrowing where words and phrases should go. "Poppy told me what happened," he said. "Have you spoken to Billy?"

Alik gave a harsh laugh. "He's last on my list right now." The bassist had tried to call on several occasions, but Alik had rejected him each time. It had been the same with Edie.

"You guys need to sort it out though. We're due to start the promotion around the EP soon."

"What do you want me to say? 'Thanks for shagging my girlfriend, Billy, I hope you and Edie are really happy together?'" Alik started shaking beer cans, trying to find one that had some left and also wasn't contaminated. "Not going to happen."

"What went wrong with you and Edie anyway? She was starting to become more involved in band stuff."

"Yeah, and I wonder why that was."

"What are you going to do about Caro?"

Alik met his friend's eye. "What do you think I should do about Caro?"

"I know that the two of you have been circling each other for ages. And that you're happier talking about her than you've ever been talking about Edie. And that you seem very comfortable in each other's company. I suggest you stop wasting time and get on with it." Nate cast his eye over

Alik's appearance. "Although I also suggest you take a shower first and clean up. You stink, mate."

* * *

Alik was ridiculously nervous. More than when he had performed on a stage in front of the crowd of hundreds at the Wilde Park Festival. More nervous than when he and Nate played their first ever gig at some tiny pub in the back end of nowhere to about nine people.

He had been pacing up and down his living room for the last ten minutes, picking his phone up, putting it down again. And repeat.

Now that the dust had settled and things had become calmer for everyone, it was time to make a move.

He needed to go for what he had always wanted over the last few months.

It was just one call. One invitation. But it was an invitation that could be thrown back in his face and rejected out of hand without a second thought.

He wasn't sure he could handle the rejection.

But if he didn't make the call, he would never know the answer.

Would that be the better alternative?

"Oh, for Christ's sake, man, just do it," he told himself, loudly.

Picking up his phone again, he located Caro's number in the contacts list and called it. It rang and rang without going to answer phone and just as he was about to give up, she answered.

"God, sorry, Alik, I couldn't find the phone. Lost it in the bottom on my handbag." She sounded slightly out of breath.

"Um, hey, no worries." He paused. "Look, it's been a while since I've seen you," he said, "and I was wondering whether..." There was another chasm of silence. "Well, if you maybe wanted to go out sometime. Just us."

She didn't answer immediately. What if he'd read the signals wrong?

"If you don't want to, it's fine. But after everything..." He hoped he didn't sound desperate.

"No," she said. "I would love to. It's about time, after all. When?"

Alik thought that asking her out that evening would be too keen, too teenage. And she would probably be working anyway. "Would Nic let you out tomorrow night?" Then he mentally kicked himself for making it sound as if she needed someone else's permission to go out.

Caro laughed; that low, throaty laugh that ultimately turned him on. "I'm sure I can arrange to be free. What did you have in mind?"

Alik racked his brain. Most of their working lives revolved around clubs and music. It needed to be different. "How about The Reading Room?" he suggested.

"Sure, sounds good. I'll meet you there at eight?"

"Great, looking forward to it."

As he ended the call, he found himself punching the air in excitement. Oh God, now it was really getting teenage.

CHAPTER FORTY-FIVE

Alik was the first to arrive the next evening.

The Reading Room was one of North Ridge's most prestigious restaurants. As the name suggested, it was situated in a building that had previously been used as a library. A beautiful, high-ceilinged room that had ornately-decorated, carved wooden bookshelves and pillars. It was tucked around the corner from North Ridge's train station and because of it's proximity, the bar area was usually frequented by commuters grabbing a quick drink before their journey or workers from the nearby office buildings taking time out before heading home. It was usually pretty busy and that night was no exception.

Alik found an empty table at one side of the bar and ordered a bottle of Argentinian Malbec and two glasses and proceeded to wait.

And wait.

He was about three quarters of the way through the bottle when Caro appeared. Standing up, he kissed her politely on both cheeks as she struggled out of her coat.

"Sorry I'm late," she said. "Problems at work."

She didn't elaborate and Alik didn't want to push it. After all, tonight was meant to be about them and not the band or the club.

"You look lovely," he said, casting an eye over her outfit of tight black leather trousers, a simple black top, and a gold two-tone sequin bomber jacket layered over the top.

"Thank you, so do you."

The waiter appeared and poured Caro a generous glass of the wine, finishing the bottle. "You want another?" he asked in heavily-accented English. "And some menus?"

Alik looked at Caro. "What do you think?"

She shrugged in return. "I don't mind, how about you? Are you okay with red?"

"I will bring you another bottle and the menus," the waiter said. "If you drink and eat and enjoy yourselves, that's good, and if you don't, you still pay."

It broke the tension and Alik and Caro both laughed. After everything that had happened between them, it still felt a bit odd being alone, just the two of them. On a real date.

The waiter brought their menus and showed them to their table. A few heads turned as they walked into the main restaurant. Alik knew the type of diner that usually frequented The Reading Room was someone who was in a certain salary bracket, wore a certain type of clothing and spoke a certain way. He and Caro certainly didn't fit that mould. He wasn't surprised when a couple of people nudged each other as they recognised the couple.

They sat down, staring at the menus and taking in the muzak that was playing in the background. Alik felt himself being stared at, and he started to feel a little uneasy about his choice of venue. After a few moments he set down his menu. "I was trying to do something different here, stepping out of our comfort zone, but..."

"I think I know what you're saying," Caro replied. "I'm not sure I want to find out what snail porridge tastes like." She pulled a face.

"What do you think? Shall we do a runner?"

They looked around to see if the waiter was anywhere in sight and agreed to leave. Caro went first, pretending she was going to the ladies. After a couple of beats, Alik followed her. Once outside, they burst out laughing.

"God, I'm so sorry," Alik said. "It wasn't meant to be like that. I wanted us to have a good time, but it's not really our scene is it?"

Caro shook her head in agreement. "I know where we can go."

* * *

Across the other side of town, the less salubrious side, was Pink Ginger. Unlike its hipper cousins, The Indigo Lounge and The Vegas, Pink Ginger catered for campness and cheese, with an underlying measure of gay. When Alik and Caro walked in there was again a definite sense of excitement in their arrival. Standing on the bar was a flamboyantly dressed guy, with spiked bleached-blond hair dressed in skin-tight black and white trousers, teamed with clumpy biker boots and a bright purple Kiss t-shirt. He was pouring tequila down the throat of an equally-blond guy, dressed in a muscle t-shirt and cycling shorts and being cheered on by the surrounding crowd. Out of the corner of his eye, he spotted the pair and grabbed a microphone.

"Gentlemen and gentlemen, it seems we have a couple of interlopers from the other side," he said, causing everyone in the bar to turn and look at them. "Blood Stone Riot's Alik Thorne and The Indigo Lounge's Caro Flynn. Let's hope Miss Flynn isn't on the lookout for new staff, otherwise you might lose me!"

There was a chorus of boos as they made their way to be served. Downing a couple of shots of tequila each, they found a table and watched the throbbing dance floor, men gyrating with men, women pirouetting with women and the occasional couple like themselves, standing on the sidelines. As the night wore on, and the place became more packed, the essence of lust began to permeate the air as things got dirtier. Bodies were crushed together and the temperature was rising. The music changed - Suede's 'Animal Nitrate' - and suddenly the whole bar was singing along.

"What does it take to turn you on?" Alik whispered in Caro's ear, his hand caressing her buttocks. His body was thrust up against hers and she could feel that he was already starting to get turned on.

They had waited so long for this.

The lingering looks, the snatched kisses, the moments where they'd been together but knew they couldn't take it any further, even though they both wanted to.

Now that time had arrived.

For several minutes, they just stared at each other, looking deep into each other's eyes. Alik leaned forward and met Caro's lips, his tongue gently probing into her mouth, as he reached round to the back of her neck and pulled him close to her. She kissed him back, hard. The kiss lasted for eons, both of them slightly out of breath as they broke off.

"Why are we wasting our time here?" said Caro. She grabbed Alik's hand and dragged him out of the club.

They practically ran across town to Caro's house, barely making it through the front door before they were tearing each other's clothes off, slamming against the wall, such was their urgency. They fell onto the sofa and Alik took a moment to appreciate Caro's body once again. She looked up at him, her eyes full of desire; there was nothing more she wanted. And she wanted him now. She traced her fingernail around his nipple ring and he tensed in pleasure. He made her wait, holding his cock just outside of her, gently probing, but not fully entering her. Her nails raked down his back and she drew him into her, rocking against him as she climbed towards the peak.

Like their night in Mallorca, it didn't last long, but the intensity was almost paralysing.

It felt so right. The distractions of other people, of work, simply faded into the background as they enjoyed each other.

Caro pulled a throw over their naked bodies as they lay there afterwards, basking in the almost ethereal atmosphere of what had just happened.

"How was that, *Nate*?" she said with a giggle.

"Definitely better than it was with *Olivia*," he replied, rewarding her with the tenderest kiss she had ever received.

They laughed, cosying up together under the throw, enjoying the silence of the house and revelling in the calm of their own little world.

A calmness that wouldn't last for long.

CHAPTER FORTY-SIX

"I've changed my mind about the dress," said Poppy.

Caro and Poppy were at Montgomery Hall with Lucia, Poppy's wedding planner from the venue. Montgomery Hall was a nineteenth-century country mansion, with thirty-two acres of garden, elegant bedrooms, and conservatory dining. In the 1400s, it had been the home of the Seymour family, passed down through generations, witnessing lavish parties attended by various members of royalty, before the original house sadly burned down around 1840. Beautifully rebuilt and restored, it was set to be the setting of a new period drama, with both the BBC and ITV fighting it out to be the one that would turn it into the next Downton.

They had been there to go over the final plans for the day, checking on seating arrangements and flower displays with some of the other suppliers who were also there for the day. Lucia and Caro stared at each other in horror. After all the other mini dramas that Poppy had come up with over the past few days, this was just another one to add to the list.

"What do you mean you've changed your mind?" Caro asked.

"As if I'd want to accept a gift from that cheating whore!"

Lucia looked between the two of them. "And that would be?"

"Edie," said Caro, sighing.

The after-effects of Edie and Billy being discovered in a compromising position were still creating ripples within the rest of Blood Stone Riot and their entourage. Poppy had flatly refused to be in the same room as Edie, which was causing some issues particularly with the premiere of the 'Bleed Like Cyanide' video coming up. Her loyalty to Alik and Caro was strong, but this was perhaps taking it a step too far. Her decision to change the dress at this late stage meant she would have to find something off-the-peg, as there wouldn't be enough time to get something made-to-measure.

Lucia simply nodded. "I'm not sure I can help with the dress at this point, but how about we look at the seating instead?"

Poppy grabbed the plans from Lucia's hand, reaching for the red marker pen that was on the table. She scribbled out the whole of the top table and started again, putting just herself and Nate, Caro, and Alik on it and drawing another one as far away as possible that only had Billy and Edie on it. "There! They can sit in the other room as far as I'm concerned."

"Poppy, you can't just add another table like that," Lucia said. "For a start, we can't fit more than ten tables in the room."

"Then perhaps they shouldn't come," Poppy said, pouting.

Caro screwed up her eyes. In some ways, she agreed with Poppy, but she knew she wasn't totally blameless herself, although at least she and Alik hadn't got together properly until after he had split up from Edie.

"You can't just un-invite them, Poppy. Not least because the band are playing at the reception."

"Maybe we should get married on a beach somewhere instead with just you and Alik as guests."

"What would that solve?" said Caro. "Just another reason for Edie to get away with what she's done without having to face up to the consequences? I'm sure we can come up with something that can keep the peace, right?" Taking the table plan, she quickly sketched out a new one on the back, that placed Billy and Edie a safe distance from the top table but still made them feel part of things. "Look, this might work."

Poppy scanned the new scenario. "That might be okay."

"Then let's see what else we can sort out. Lucia, do you have the final menus?"

* * *

A couple of hours later, Poppy and Caro were in Caro's office at The Indigo Lounge, sharing a bottle of wine.

"What do you want to do about the dress then?" Caro asked. "We can go to a few shops this afternoon if you want? Amy can hold the fort here. We're not open until later tonight anyway."

Poppy took a sip of her wine. "I don't want to trek round places explaining why I need a dress so quickly. Do you think we can find something on the internet and then just go to one place?"

"I don't see why not. I bet Amy would be able to help out as well, let me give her a shout."

Caro called Amy into the room and quickly explained the problem. They both fired up their laptops and started searching. Poppy moved between the pair, checking out pictures on sites, looking at prices, and making the odd phone call when she saw something she particularly liked. The White Room in Henlake seemed to have the best choices and was prepared to open especially for Poppy that afternoon; she would be the only bride in the shop. She hadn't explained fully why she needed a dress just a couple of weeks before her big day, but they had been fairly understanding.

"What will you do with the other dress?" asked Caro.

"Burn it?" replied Poppy. "I thought I could send it to Edie and ask her whether she would wear it when she married Billy, but that's probably a bit childish, right? I don't want to return it and have them refund her. She doesn't get away with it that easily. I don't know really. Do you want it?" Poppy was rambling, waving her half empty wineglass around, the remains of her drink threatening to splash out over Caro's laptop.

"Oh, God, no, it was hideous!" said Caro, far too quickly. "I mean, I know we all said it looked great and that, but in all honesty you looked like one of those toilet roll holders from the seventies. Plus I have no intention of getting married."

"Yet," said Poppy.

"Alik and I have only been on one date."

"Mmmm." Poppy nodded. "One date, but how many near misses before that?"

Caro rolled her eyes. "Too many to even count."

CHAPTER FORTY-SEVEN

After a couple of months in production, Josh O'Brien was finally happy with the results of the video for 'Bleed Like Cyanide' and deemed it ready for public consumption. To celebrate the premiere, he had hired out the cinema at Cerise - a boutique hotel in the centre of North Ridge bordering one of its parks - and invited the band, Parker Roberts, Griffen, and Olivia. It would be the first time that Alik and Edie would come face to face after he had discovered her with Billy, as well as the first time that he and Caro would be going out as a proper couple in the company of the rest of the group.

It had disaster written all over it.

* * *

Edie and Billy were curled up in bed.

"Do we really have to go tonight?" Edie reached under the covers for Billy's cock. "We could she stay here."

Billy flipped her onto her back, leaning over her, his dark eyes teasing. "We could, but I've been summoned. Parker Roberts has spoken." He bent down, his lips finding hers. "I need to shower."

He slid out from underneath the duvet and Edie admired his muscled, tattooed, back as he walked naked to the bathroom. Since everything had come out, they had become a proper couple. Billy was happy to accompany Edie to her socialite events, something that Alik had never been comfortable with. The sex was as mind-blowing as ever, with Billy putting her into positions she had never dreamed of and bringing her darker fantasies to reality. He spent a lot of time at her flat, which was a lot nicer than his, but sometimes disappeared for hours on end, turning up eventually after seeking out Leo Kendrick.

Billy's phone vibrated with a text and Edie didn't hesitate in checking it. The message was from Leo, stating that he would be there in ten minutes with the goods Billy had asked for. It wasn't that she minded his drug-taking, after all it wasn't as if she were an angel in that department. Her concern was that it was getting more frequent.

"You didn't tell me Leo was coming over," she said, waving the mobile at Billy as he came back into the room. He had a towel wrapped around his wet body. Drops of water glistened on his chest.

He swiped the phone from her hand. "Who said you were my secretary?"

"I thought it might about tonight," she said. "You said you were going to cut back."

"And I will. Once this evening is over."

She hoped he was telling the truth.

* * *

Alik and Caro arrived first, with Nate and Poppy. Dev wasn't far behind them. Alik sometimes felt sorry for him as everyone else seemed to be paired up, but he always insisted he was fine and didn't need anyone. He assured them he was happy in his online relationship with a Latvian singer, but no-one had ever met her.

Poppy, so close to the wedding now, was super excited about everything and in an effervescent mood. She got chatting to everyone and anyone who would listen, most recently to the waiter who was milling around with trays containing glasses of champagne and nibbles.

Nate and Alik were chatting quietly about some of the new material Alik had been writing and how they could get into the studio to start recording it. Whether it was new Blood Stone Riot material or not remained unspoken. Caro was chatting with Josh, getting some inside information on how the video clip had turned out and enjoying the intellectual director's company.

Alik saw Parker arrive and waved him over, with Olivia not far behind him.

"Alright, mate?" Alik held out a hand. "Long time no see."

"Now you're behaving yourself, I don't need to be around as much," replied Parker.

"I need to talk to you about some of these press junkets," Parker said, waving Olivia over. "I want you and Nate doing *Roccia*, biggest title alongside *Kerrang,* and still on the shelves with a big online presence. I think the best idea is to keep you and Billy apart for the time being."

"What? You think the scandal hasn't already been in the gossip rags too much already?"

Parker laughed. "I don't have time to be reading that nonsense, the less I see of it the better."

"Alik's been working on some new material," said Nate. "For when we're super successful with the first EP and need some more stuff."

"Sounds good, we'll need more music for the album. When do I get to hear it?" asked Parker.

Alik hesitated. He wished that Nate hadn't mentioned the new songs. Some of them were still quite raw, particularly the one about Edie's betrayal. He wasn't sure if he was ready to air them to anyone else yet, even though Nate had been treated to a sneak preview. "Soon, I promise. They're still a bit rough at the moment."

They heard the door crash open and turned to see who had arrived.

Billy swept over to Alik, gathering up the singer in a big bear hug. Alik could smell the alcohol on his breath and extricated himself from the embrace.

"Alik! How's it going? You missing this little beauty yet?" He gestured towards Edie and swiped a glass of champagne from the passing waiter.

Alik's eyes narrowed as he looked at Edie. "Hardly, Billy, hardly."

* * *

Edie felt Alik's gaze on her and flushed with embarrassment. She slunk over to Olivia and grabbed a drink.

"I knew we shouldn't have come," she said quietly, so no-one except Olivia could hear. "I told him not to drink before we came out, but he wouldn't listen."

She plastered on a smile as Caro and Poppy approached them.

"Edie, how lovely to see you," said Poppy. "How are things with you and Billy?"

Edie could tell from Poppy's tone that she wasn't being sincere. "We're good. So good. It's so refreshing to be in a relationship where there isn't another person involved," she said, with a pointed glance at Caro.

"Glad to hear it," replied Poppy. "Of course, you know Caro and Alik are finally together."

Her smiled wavered slightly. Edie knew that it had been coming, but to hear it said out loud was still a kick in the teeth, even though she had been the one to betray Alik. "About time, really, I always knew there was something between them. They make a good couple."

"How kind of you to give your blessing." Caro's smile didn't reach her eyes. "Now I really must go and speak to Josh." She swept past Edie heading towards the director, leaving Poppy and Edie together.

"You're some piece of work, Edie," said Poppy, once they were alone. "All this time we thought you and Alik were a great couple and you were shagging around behind his back with one of his best friends! I suppose I should be grateful it wasn't Nate."

Edie lowered her head. "I didn't mean for it to happen, Billy was just...being friendly and flirting a bit when I was feeling low. I guess he kind of took advantage of me initially."

"You didn't think to tell him to stop because you were seeing Alik? Whatever happened between you shouldn't have been done when you were still with someone else. You can't deny that you cheated."

Edie couldn't help but think that Alik had done exactly the same thing with Caro. But now wasn't the time to have that debate with Poppy. She knew that Poppy's loyalties were with Caro. It was plainly obvious to Edie that she and Poppy would never be friends, even before all of this had happened.

"I'm with Billy now, Poppy, you had all best get used to it," she said, as strongly as she could muster. "Now, if you'll excuse me."

* * *

Josh clapped his hands and brought everyone together. "First of all, I want to thank you for coming along this evening. And secondly, for everything you did in order to get this film clip to be as fantastic as it is. You'll probably be embarrassed to see yourselves up on the big screen, but stick with it. If you'd like to find some seats, we can get started."

The assembled crowd obediently filed into the rows of seats; Alik and Caro front and centre. Billy pulled Edie towards the back row, making some comment about what he'd be getting up to if the clip was dull.

The opening chords of 'Bleed Like Cyanide' filled the room, along with the first shots of the clip taken from the set at The Indigo Lounge, the camera panning round, taking in the various implements of torture and the women who were tormenting Alik. He felt ridiculous seeing himself up on the screen like that. Caro squeezed his arm, leaning in close to his body. The action comforted him. He couldn't believe how long they'd waited to be together - it felt so right. He tried to ignore the whispers and sniggers coming from Billy's direction, tolerating them for the sake of the four-minute video.

When the final shots of Alik on the beach faded away, there was a moment of rapturous applause, followed by some deliberate, slow-hand clapping from Billy.

"And there he is," Billy said. "Alik Thorne in all his glory, the centrepiece of this band."

Alik swivelled to face Billy. Edie shrank back into the seat beside him.

"Your point being?" said Alik. He already knew the answer, but he wanted Billy to say it.

Billy stood up and walked down the steps and loomed over Alik. "The celebrated, feted, awarded frontman, whilst the rest of us are hidden in the shadows and never allowed to see the light of day."

"If you're behaving like that, is it any wonder?" said Alik. "Your behaviour hasn't exactly been exemplary recently."

"And don't think that these things don't go unnoticed by the guys at Numb," said Parker. "There's already been enough drama around this band and that's even before you've had anything released."

At the mention of the record company, a silence descended over the room. Alik knew Parker had the power to really make or break their ambitions. Anything they did was going to be scrutinised heavily. Something Billy seemed to have forgotten.

"Alik, Parker... is there anyone who doesn't own me? I'm done." Billy threw open the door and stalked out of the room.

The tension between those remaining was palpable, and after a beat Edie followed Billy.

"What is his problem?" Caro asked, taking one of the left over glasses of champagne from the table.

"Where should I start?" Alik sighed and took her hand. "Let's go."

They walked out of the cinema and into the hotel foyer

"I could do with getting away from here," Alik said.

"Me too. And I know just where we can go."

CHAPTER FORTY-EIGHT

When Caro and Alik arrived at the airport the following day, Mariella was waiting for them.

"You look amazing!" The Norwegian blonde threw her arms around Caro. "And happy. Is this Alik?"

Caro nodded and Mariella drew back, looking Alik up and down. "He's perfect for you."

"I'm glad you approve," said Caro, laughing.

They put their bags into Mariella's car and set off. As Mariella drove them through the streets, Caro pointed out various landmarks and venues of her time on the island; bars she had frequented and restaurants she had been to. They came into the village, past the marina and the beach Caro and Alik had walked along when they had first met.

"I assume we'll be spending some time at Juju's?" asked Alik as they drove past the bar where they had first laid eyes on each other.

"It would be wrong not to," replied Caro. She kissed him on the lips.

"Hey, I don't want to spend this whole time being a blackberry," said Mariella.

Caro and Alik frowned at each other for a moment, until Caro laughed. "Oh, you mean gooseberry! I'm sure you won't, there must be someone you're seeing?"

Mariella blushed as she screeched to a halt in front of the apartment building. "There might be someone. If you're good, I'll let you meet him."

Since Caro had left, Mariella had moved out of their shared flat and into a more spacious one-bedroom place. It was light and airy, and if you stood on tiptoe on the balcony, you could just about see the beach. There was a large open-plan living room with space for a dining area, a tiny galley kitchen, which suited Mariella and her complete ineptitude in the catering department, one huge bedroom with a massive bed, built-in storage, an en suite wet room, and a tiny bathroom. There was still some evidence of the time that Caro and Mariella lived together in the decor and accessories: Rugs and scarves that covered the furniture, the wooden wind chimes that hung outside on the balcony, and a porcelain iguana.

"How long have you been living here?" asked Caro, dumping her holdall on the floor by the sofa.

Mariella counted on her fingers. "About six weeks. I got a great deal on this place and I missed you too much in our old flat."

"Awww..." Caro pulled her friend in for another hug. "I missed you too. Life seems so much simpler out here." She glanced meaningfully at Alik.

"What brings you here anyway?"

"Needed to get away from the bright lights of North Ridge for a bit and this seemed like the best place to be," said Caro. "Let's just say things got a bit heated and we needed to be somewhere else."

Mariella was staring intently at Alik. "Wait a minute, you said something about Juju's. Are you the mysterious man Caro spent her last night in Mallorca with?"

Caro and Alik exchanged a telling glance and smiled at each other.

"I knew it! She's never usually that secretive about her conquests."

"Well, he was called Nate when I first met him," Caro said.

Mariella screwed her face up. "You had another name?"

"Let's just say we played each other quite well that night," said Caro. "Although who knows, if we'd been more honest with each other at the start, things might have been very different."

* * *

For the next couple of days, Caro and Alik did little else apart from sleep, swim, eat, drink, and make love. The pace of life on the island was much more relaxed than it was in North Ridge, and without the stresses of being around Billy and Edie they were able to enjoy themselves and chill out.

One afternoon, they found themselves on one of the beaches, away from the centre of town. Having had a leisurely lunch at one of the hotel restaurants - a delicious paella - they were sitting at the back of the beach, sheltered slightly from the intense heat of the sun.

"You were really reticent about getting involved with me," said Alik, as Caro played with the sand, letting it run through her fingers and tracing shapes where it fell.

She nodded. "It wasn't right. You were with Edie and I swore to myself I wouldn't do that again."

Alik frowned. "What do you mean, again?"

Caro took a breath.

"I was seeing someone once. He was married."

She told him everything, how the relationship with Josep had started, how he had been less than honest with her and naively she had carried on with him. How it had all ended with Josep's death and the subsequent wrangling with his wife.

A single tear fell down Caro's cheek. Alik lifted a finger and wiped it away. He gently tilted her face towards him and kissed her. It was the gentlest, most loving kiss they had ever shared.

She pulled away. "We were on this beach, and we argued. Then he left me and I never saw him again."

Alik's face changed. "The 'J' doesn't stand for Jonny, does it?"

"What are you talking about?"

Alik reached around and traced the tattoo on the back of her neck. "It's for Josep, isn't it?"

The tears started to fall again as Caro nodded, remembering her first true love. As she sobbed in Alik's arms, she thought how lucky she was to have found her next.

CHAPTER FORTY-NINE

Caro sat at her desk, making some amendments to a flyer for an upcoming promotion. It had been tough coming back from Mallorca. She and Alik had had such a relaxed time, and she enjoyed showing him around the island. Mariella had been so welcoming as well. Caro had a sudden pang of sentimentality. She did miss the place.

She had half an eye on her inbox, when she noticed a sudden influx of new emails; mostly social media notifications. She scanned the messages and started to feel sick at some of the content. There were the ones that called her a money grabbing whore, those that said what they'd do to her if she needed more money, ones that out and out said she slept her way to the top.

One of them contained a link.

She clicked on it and was directed to *The Goss'* website. Her jaw fell as she read the article, written by their features editor.

We know that Edie Spencer-Newman likes a rocker! Since splitting up with Blood Stone Riot's lead singer, Alik Thorne, Edie has become involved with the band's bassist, Billy Walker. The Goss *got the latest on the* Pretty Rich Things *star's complicated love life.*

Edie told us that her relationship with Alik was difficult and she felt that she was often sidelined by his career and supposed friendship with club owner Caro Flynn. "It felt like I was being pushed aside for his career and he was spending more and more time at The Indigo Lounge with her," the socialite said.

Caro shook her head. She knew that Edie was playing the victim and was pushing the blame onto her and Alik. But she also knew the truth. She carried on reading.

"When I found out how Billy felt about me, I was flattered. I thought it was too soon to get involved with someone again, but he managed to persuade me otherwise..."

Caro had enough. She scanned the rest of the piece, not really taking in the words - she knew that they were false, anyway. Then she came to the second part of the article. The sub story showed a grainy picture of Caro and Mariella outside The Roca Bar, celebrating with a few of the locals. The headline screamed at her: *Caro Flynn - shady past exposed!*

Alik Thorne's new girlfriend may not be the no-nonsense businesswoman she appears. The Goss *has uncovered news reports that the bar Caro Flynn owned in Mallorca was gifted to her by a former, married, lover. Josep Leon owned The Roca Bar just outside Alcudia and Caro started working there as a mere barmaid. Her affair with the renowned local businessman was kept under wraps. But when Leon died suddenly after suffering a fatal heart attack, his recently-changed will meant that his wife lost out on the bar and his younger lover gained it. Despite being challenged by Consuela, his wife, Caro retained the bar and it became one of the most popular bars in town. We wonder how much of that was down to its attractive owner?*

She felt sick as she read on, recognising some of the words from the articles that had appeared in *Mallorca Daily Bulletin* and *Talk Of The North*. Without reading the remainder, she grabbed her phone and dialled Olivia's number. Olivia answered on the third ring.

"What do you know about this?" Caro asked.

"What are you talking about?"

"Edie's article in *The Goss*. You must have seen it."

"No, I've been working on a Blood Stone Riot press schedule. I haven't had the opportunity to look online. Plus, *The Goss* isn't my preferred website for news."

"Let me ping it to you."

Caro copied the link and pasted it into an email to Olivia. She pressed send and sat back in her chair, waiting for Olivia to receive it. There was silence on the other end of the line.

"Jesus, Caro, I had no idea," said Olivia.

"You should see some of the comments I've had from people who have read it and made their own assumptions. I think the nicest one said something like 'scheming bitch sleeping your way to the top.'"

"Has Alik seen it?"

"I don't know. He does know about Josep and me though." Caro gulped down some water, eternally grateful that she had taken the opportunity to tell Alik the truth about her relationship with Josep. Had he found out like this, their relationship would have been on the rocks before it had even begun. "I thought you might know why Edie had done it. She and I have never been friends, but I don't know what she thought she would achieve with this. I guess she's trying to damage my professional reputation now."

"I'm sorry," said Olivia.

"You have nothing to be sorry about! You didn't write it." Caro sighed. "I need to speak to Alik. Do you think you could mention it to Parker? I'm sure there will be a few trolls out in force."

"Sure. I'll come in to the club after work. We can get a drink."

After Caro hung up, she reread the two articles, wondering how Edie was so bitter about how things had ended up. She had got what she wanted, after all. She scrolled through her contacts list and found Alik's number. It went straight to voicemail. Deciding it would be best if she didn't leave a message, she tapped out a text message that assured him everything was okay, but that he needed to read the story. She added the link to the message and pressed send.

* * *

Edie swept into The Indigo Lounge that evening, closely followed by Minty. She scanned the VIP area, which seemed quieter than normal, as did the rest of the club. Caro wasn't anywhere to be seen. Probably hiding away, thought Edie. She was pleased with the results of the article. There had been lots of messages of support for her and she'd seen some of the choice words that had been directed at Caro. She headed over to the bar.

"Bottle of champagne, please," she said.

The barman stared past her, choosing instead to serve the woman standing to her left. When he'd poured the two pints of cider she'd requested and taken her money, Edie tried again.

"Bottle of champagne, please."

Again, he ignored her, busying himself with wiping down the bar.

"Excuse me, I'm waiting to be served." Her voice grew indignant.

Edie turned around, looking for someone in authority to complain to, and came face to face with Caro. "Your bar staff need to learn some manners," she said. "I've been waiting to be served and he's completely ignoring me."

"Good work, Simon," said Caro. "I'll make sure you get a decent tip for that."

She took Edie's elbow and steered her towards one of the tables in the corner, out of earshot of the majority of people in the bar, leaving Minty on her own. Edie extracted her arm from Caro's grip and sat down, Caro taking a seat opposite her.

"He's not serving you because you're not welcome here," said Caro. "In fact, you're barred."

Edie was taken aback. She had never been barred from anywhere, especially not a seedy little club like this. "What?"

"You heard me, I don't want you in here," said Caro. "And neither does Alik."

"Oh, darling, I'm sure he's very upset having found out about your sordid affair in Mallorca, but he should know I'm here for him."

Caro smirked. "I know you found out about Josep with the intention of splitting Alik and I up. But I beat you to it, Edie. He already knew. I told him last week."

Edie's jaw dropped. That had been the true motive behind her interview. She had found the news reports online and simply pointed the reporter from *The Goss* in the right direction. She had hoped that Alik would find out that his beloved new girlfriend had also cheated with someone and wouldn't want anything more to do with Caro. Just like he had with her.

"It's not very busy in here tonight, is it?" she asked. "I imagine people will have read about you..."

"Edie, it's Tuesday. It's never busy on a Tuesday," said Caro. "And if you think that a silly article about something I did years ago is going to influence the type of people that come in here, you're wrong. I doubt many of them have ever even come across *The Goss*."

Edie sat back, knowing she'd been defeated.

"I think it's time you found somewhere else to drink, don't you?" Caro turned on her heel and walked away.

Edie stared after her, shooting daggers at Caro's retreating back. "It may not have worked this time, but I will find a way to ruin you."

CHAPTER FIFTY

"Now are you sure you can't see my pants?"

Poppy twirled round in front of the mirror, twisting this way and that as she examined her reflection in minute detail. The delicate, off-white vintage wedding dress had an intricate lace overlay that covered her shoulders and chest, with a fitted embroidered bodice. In contrast to the top half, the ruffled peplum waist draped into a waterfall hemline that fell beautifully to the floor. Peeping out from beneath the hem were Christian Louboutin heels. Her hair was half up, half down, with soft curls pinned into the back with the rest of it trailing loosely over her shoulders. The last-minute changes she had made to her outfit, despite everyone else thinking she had gone loopy, were justified. She looked gorgeous and completely natural.

Caro laughed. "No, babe, you definitely can't see your pants. As if we'd let you have VPL on your wedding day!" She wasn't anywhere close to being dressed, prancing about the bridal suite in her own underwear, occasionally swigging from a champagne bottle. The hair and make-up woman, who was one of the official suppliers to Montgomery Hall, sighed heavily as she tried to get Caro to sit still for five minutes so she could finish her work.

Lucia, who was managing the day to the absolute second, popped her head around the door. "You have around thirty minutes, ladies. People are already starting to arrive. You look amazing, Poppy, very you. And Caro, unless you're planning a new career as a glamour girl, then I suggest you hurry up and get dressed."

Caro plonked herself on the chair in front of the mirror and the hair and make-up lady finally pounced on her. "Not like I haven't had those offers since Edie's article in *The Goss*," she said. "And some of the fees were quite tempting."

"You won't make a scene today thought, will you?" Poppy's face radiated concern.

Caro shook her head. "Of course not. I simply intend to ignore her."

Caro knew that despite Poppy's bravado, she was nervous about the whole day. The majority of guests attending were Nate's friends and family, and when Poppy's mother had refused to come - they couldn't afford flights for the whole family, and it was either everyone or no-one - Poppy had been in pieces.

There didn't need to be any more drama or upsets.

* * *

"Mate, have a drink," said Alik, as he watched Nate pace around his room. "You know she's going to turn up. In fact, you know she's already here."

Both men were dressed in traditional morning suits, with a contemporary slimmer fit, a French navy fabric in a lightweight wool and mohair mix, although they were now regretting the stiff collar and cravat ensemble. Being a slightly bolder blue, it was an alternative to classic navy, which had looked very dark, verging on black, and hadn't complemented the shade of green that Poppy had chosen for Caro's maid of honour dress. It was all very different to their usual attire, though. Trying to loosen his cravat, Alik wished they had chosen a beach wedding.

"What if she's changed her mind?" Nate said.

"Why would she do that?"

"Because brides have last-minute nerves."

"Sounds like it's you with the last-minute nerves," said Alik.

Nate and Poppy's relationship had always been straightforward. Poppy had appeared in Nate's life some two years ago, initially as a groupie, but as she followed them around on tour, it became apparent she was more serious about Nate than it seemed on the surface. She had an easy-going nature, able to befriend pretty much anyone, and everyone liked her. She had always made friends with the conquests of the other band members, no matter how long they lasted in the group.

Alik knew there would be no second thoughts for her at all. Nor for him and Caro.

He checked his watch. "Come on, mate, it's time to go."

* * *

Alik couldn't take his eyes off Caro while Poppy and Nate said their vows. She looked absolutely ravishing in the jade dress and cream fur stole.

The ceremony itself was fairly short, and was full of laughter, emotion, and a few tears as they read out the vows they had written themselves. Before long, they were husband and wife. They walked arm in arm down the aisle, to a round of rapturous applause, Alik and Caro behind them.

"You know," said Alik, gently kissing Caro's nose. "We make such a good maid of honour and best man that people will soon be asking when we're getting married."

She laughed. "One step at a time."

"I could very easily already be in love with you," he admitted.

She kissed him back, a smile practically breaking her face. "And I you."

Alik cast a glance around them, watching as Poppy and Nate were congratulated by an ever moving queue of guests. "I guess we have a bit of time before we have to be the dutiful best man and maid of honour again, don't we?" he said, a cheeky smile crossing his face. "Because I'm desperate to know what you're wearing under that dress."

Caro pretended to look shocked, but failed miserably. Alik grabbed her hand and pulled her up the stairs towards their room, hurriedly pushing her inside and slamming the door shut behind them. She sank onto the edge of the bed, kicking her shoes off.

"No time for resting," said Alik. He fell to his knees in front of her, gently tracing her ankle, running his fingertips up her calf, under her dress and along her inner thigh. As he got close to the top, he felt Caro tense and sensed her disappointment when he withdrew.

"Now, this is a very beautiful outfit and you look absolutely stunning in it, but I think it's time you took it off." He was already shedding his own suit jacket and shirt, the inks on his chest at odds with the sharp cut of his trousers, with a pair of Calvin Klein boxers peeping over the top.

Obediently, Caro unzipped her dress and stood to let it fall to the floor, the material pooling around her feet. She delicately stepped over it, placing the garment carefully on the chair so as not to crease it. Alik watched her every move intently, his eyes dilating at the sight of her semi-naked body.

"Well?" She pirouetted a couple of times, giving Alik the full effect of the emerald green bra and panties, her hair tumbling wildly around her shoulders.

His answer was to pick her up and throw her onto her back on the bed. He sat down beside her, tracing the line of her breasts above the cups of her bra before gently easing them from their casing. She looked up at him as he lightly began stroking her nipples, alternating between using his fingertips and his tongue, occasionally sucking or biting them. Caro's hands moved between her legs.

"Wait," he whispered, circling her wrists with one hand and pulling them away. "I want to be the one to make you come."

Alik shifted position, kneeling between Caro's legs and unknotting the bows that held her knickers together, revealing what he really wanted. He bent over, kissing her stomach, the insides of her thighs, every so often his hands reaching up to her nipples again to maintain the perpetual stimulus. He carried on teasing her, conscious of when she was on the brink and lessened off just enough to stop her plunging over.

"Jesus, don't stop," she said, shaking. "I'm so close."

"I know you are, sweetheart, but doesn't this feel good?" He lapped at her clit again, varying the pressure as she started to spasm beneath him.

"Oh God, I can't help it!" The strength of her orgasm forced her to collapse back against the covers, panting heavily.

Alik pulled off the remainder of his clothes, feeling his cock get even harder as Caro unclasped her bra, her voluptuous breasts springing totally free. He started to reach for her, but she turned the tables.

"I think it's my turn to be in control, don't you?"

Pushing him onto his back, Caro straddled him, lowering herself onto his bulging erection, just the tip of his cock inside her, tantalising him. He tried to move further inside her, but she stopped him.

"Remember the video shoot? How hot I got you then? Imagine you're still tied to that cross and I'm there, in front of you, naked and on my knees, waiting to take you into my mouth and suck you off with all those people watching us."

Alik stiffened beneath her as his imagination started to work overtime as a real life, fully naked Caro towered over him.

"Fuck me, Caro," he groaned. "I need to be inside you."

Caro eased herself down, impaling herself fully on his shaft. Alik reached up to cup her breasts in his hands, his thumbs alternately rubbing, tweaking and pinching her nipples, causing her to contract around him. They rocked in unison, Alik thrusting up into Caro as she ground down on him, fingers entwined as they soared towards the peak, Caro clutching at Alik as a second shattering orgasm ripped through her body.

They lay, breathing heavily, a tangle of limbs and bedclothes until they heard a gentle knock at the door.

"Caro? Alik? Are you okay?" Lucia's voice came through loud and clear. "We're ready for the wedding breakfast now and need you for speeches."

"Sure," replied Caro in an overly perky voice. "We'll be down shortly, Alik was just helping me with my dress."

"Not longer than five minutes." Lucia was firm.

Caro laughed. "If she'd have been five minutes sooner..."

"We could have asked her to join us?"

"You're incorrigible."

"You bring out the worst in me. And the best." He pulled her towards him, claiming her mouth in a passionate, lust-filled kiss.

CHAPTER FIFTY-ONE

Edie approach Caro after the wedding breakfast. Caro was deep in conversation with one of Nate's teenage cousins. They had been discussing the merits of each member of a famous boy-band and deciding which one they would go for, if the chance ever arose of course.

"Caro?" said Edie, touching her arm. "Can we talk?"

Nate's cousin muttered something about going to ask Poppy the same boy-band question and disappeared as Caro turned her attention to her lover's former girlfriend. Having downed what felt like several bottles of champagne, and still on a high from her earlier entanglement with Alik, Caro's head was starting to feel fizzy.

She eyed Edie with suspicion. This wasn't Edie-like behaviour at all. Since Caro had barred her from the Indigo Lounge, Edie and Billy had barely hung around with the band - except for official, Parker-approved, events or rehearsals. Caro wondered how much that had to do with Poppy binning off the original wedding dress, or whether it had more to do with Alik. Either way, it had been quite nice not to have to put up with her.

"I don't think so, Edie. What could we possibly have to talk about? Maybe you've found another skeleton in my closet that you want to share with the world," said Caro. "Or maybe you're trying to split me and Alik up again. You're a poisonous witch, Edie, and I have no idea what Alik ever saw in you. Or what Billy sees in you now."

Despite her earlier promise to Poppy, Caro was enjoying telling Edie what she really thought. She was about to continue when she saw Olivia heading their way. "I told

Poppy I wouldn't make a scene if I saw you today and I'm true to my word. Unlike some people." And she walked away.

* * *

Drawing back her shoulders and composing herself, Edie headed off towards the ladies, determined not to let anyone see she was shaken. Pushing open the door, she was relieved to see that only a single stall was occupied. She pulled out her compact, dusted a little more blusher across her cheeks, and reapplied her lip gloss. As she was about to leave, she saw Poppy coming out of the stall.

"Nice dress," she said. "Although I doubt it cost the three and a half grand I parted with in Broadkeys."

"You're right, Edie, it didn't. But when I found out what you'd done to Alik, I couldn't wear it. It didn't seem right that I should accept a gift from someone who doesn't rank loyalty amongst one of her top five things in a relationship."

Edie laughed. She expected this from Poppy. "You could say the same about your maid of honour as well."

"Caro has nothing to do with this," said Poppy. "It was my decision to change the dress. I didn't want something that had been paid for by someone who was looking to buy my friendship."

"Poppy, we've never been friends."

"You're right about that. I just tolerated you for Alik's sake, like all the other groupies he'd been with. I don't know why I even agreed to let you come today."

Edie's tone was saccharine sweet, but laced with underlying venom. "Does Caro fall into that category too? Another little groupie for you to tolerate?"

Poppy shook her head. "Caro was more of a friend to me in the first few minutes we met than you ever have been. Everything has to be about you, doesn't it? Even now, you're here feeling sorry for yourself because I'm wearing a different dress to the one you thought I should be wearing." She headed for the door. "Get over yourself, Edie."

As a gaggle of drunken women entered the room. Edie leaned against the wall, Poppy's words washing over her. She knew that there just might be an element of truth about what the bride had said.

After a couple of minutes, she went to look for Billy. He was sitting outside on the grass, a bottle of beer in one hand and a cigarette in the other.

"Don't you think you've had enough to drink?" Edie asked. Blood Stone Riot were due to play a short set as part of the evening's entertainment, and it wouldn't be good if the bassist were drunk. Again.

"When did you become the nagging girlfriend?" Billy spat.

"I just thought..."

"Well don't."

Edie sighed. "Can I get you another drink instead?"

He nodded and she went to the bar, where Alik was also waiting to be served. She saw him take a sparkling mineral water and down that in one before asking for another.

"Hello," she said.

He barely acknowledged her, merely nodding in her direction.

"How are you and Caro doing?" she asked.

"What do you care, Edie?" he said. "I know what you tried to do. And that was low, even for you."

"It must have been awful for you, finding out about her affair."

Alik narrowed his eyes. "I could compare it to finding my so-called girlfriend on her knees with one of my best friends. But I won't. What Caro did was in her past and she had the decency to be honest about it."

"Honest? Ha! Maybe if you'd been more honest with me, then I wouldn't have had to fight for the affections of someone more interested in a guitar or another woman."

"If that's the way you want to look at it, Edie, you do that. I hope you are Billy are very happy together."

And he stalked off without a backwards glance.

* * *

Alik decided to try the gents one last time in the hope of finding Billy before they were due to play. He didn't want to let Nate and Poppy down over some stupid argument with his ex. He flung open the door and glanced in, unwanted memories of finding Edie and Billy at The Indigo Lounge filling his head.

"Billy, where the fuck are you?" he said, yelling over the top of the one cubicle door that was closed. He hoped he wasn't in for a repeat performance.

There was silence in response. He stalked over to the door and hammered on it with his fist. The door swung open to reveal Billy bent over the cistern, shopping big fat lines of coke.

Billy turned to look at him, his eyes bloodshot and red. He smiled lazily, clearly off his face. "It's good stuff, man, you should have some." He lifted a bottle of beer to his lips and took a hefty slug, before resuming his position and lifting the rolled up twenty pound note to his nose again.

Alik shook his head. "Come on, Billy, it's their wedding day, do you really think Nate and Poppy need this shit?"

"I didn't think anything could spoil their party," said Billy. He nodded to the lines on the cistern. "It came from a reliable source."

"I'm sure it did."

"You've become so fucking straight since you hooked up with *her*," said Billy. "You don't know how to have fun any more."

"Mate, I know how to have fun."

Billy stared him straight in the eye. "Then prove it." He offered him the rolled up note.

Alik hesitated for a moment before accepting. It had been a long time since he'd last indulged. Once wouldn't hurt. He bent down over the cistern and swiftly inhaled one of the lines that Billy had cut, feeling the hit almost immediately. Then, with a sly wink, he leaned over again.

* * *

Alik and Billy walked out of the Gents together, laughing, the animosity between them seemingly forgotten, masked by the effects of the cocaine. Nate signalled to them and they made their way to the small platform that was doubling as a stage. Their gear was crammed into the tiny space and Dev was squeezed into one corner behind his drum kit.

"You two seem as thick as thieves," said Nate, as he tuned up his guitar. "Made friends or something?"

"Definitely something." Billy threw his bass strap over his head and joined Nate in the tune up.

After a few minutes, they were ready. Poppy had taken it upon herself to be the MC and encouraged as many of the guests as possible into the room.

"Ladies and gentlemen," she said. "My wonderful husband and his equally wonderful bandmates would like to play a few songs in honour of our nuptials. They have promised to keep it clean. Or at least as clean as they can. Please give it up for Blood Stone Riot!"

Alik had decided that they would stick to covers, mostly to keep the peace. Running through a swift, pacy ten song set they played some Aerosmith, Extreme, Skid Row, old nineties favourites that many of the audience recognised.

When they got to 'I Remember You,' Billy tried to ad lib his piece and ended up bumping into Nate, sending the guitarist tumbling to the ground. There was an almighty screech of feedback, which caused several members of the audience to shriek.

"What the fuck are you playing at?" Alik said, as they got to their feet and tried to pick up from where they left off.

"This idiot trying to get centre stage as per usual." Nate pushed Billy in the chest.

"I thought that was more your style," said Billy, ducking out of the way.

Poppy jumped in and took the microphone from Alik. "Thanks guys, great set!" She turned to the crowd of guests. "If you want to shake your thing on the dance floor, the DJ will be back in five."

The guests melted away and Poppy turned to Billy. "Thank you so much for making a scene, that's exactly how I want people to remember my wedding day." She shoved the microphone back to Alik. "If you need me, I'll be dancing with the other children."

Alik went to confront Billy.

"What?" Billy shrugged. "These things happen."

"Not if you weren't trying to over play your part."

"Oh, because I'm just the rhythm section and don't figure in the important plans for this band." He stripped off his instrument and thrust it at Alik. "Maybe you can learn to play this as well if I'm not wanted."

Alik and Nate exchanged a glance and watched Billy head off towards the gardens, swiping another beer from the bar as he went.

CHAPTER FIFTY-TWO

Much later, Alik and Caro were sitting outside, taking advantage of the still-warm evening and taking a breather from the general chaos inside Montgomery Hall after Blood Stone Riot's short set. There had been a mixed reaction, unsurprisingly, from the assembled guests.

Not least because of the onstage row.

"I could kill him," Alik said. "Of all the times to fuck up like that and he has to do it on his bandmate's wedding day."

"Yeah, but I think I know why," Caro said. "You scored, didn't you? I can tell by your eyes. And I'll bet Billy had something to do with it."

Alik couldn't look at her.

"Caro, I..."

He didn't have chance to say anything else. Nate came running across the lawn towards them, urgently calling Alik's name.

"Nate, what's the matter?"

"It's Billy. There's been an accident."

Alik searched his face to see if he was joking. "What kind of accident? Is it serious?"

"We don't know. We need to get to the hospital."

The three of them made their way to the porch, where Poppy and Lucia were waiting. Lucia had arranged for someone to pick them up, but had persuaded Poppy and Caro that they should stay at the reception. Reluctantly they agreed, on the proviso that someone kept them informed of what was happening.

Upon arrival at the hospital, Alik and Nate were directed to one of the relatives' rooms just off the main A&E waiting room and told that they would get news when there was anything to tell. The two of them sat there for what seemed like eons. There was the occasional sound of a doctor calling out for assistance or a telephone ringing, but otherwise it was horribly quiet. Neither of them spoke.

Alik flicked through one of the old magazines on the table, barely registering what was on the pages until he came to a photograph of Billy and Edie at an event. A sickening thought came into his head.

"Hey, do we know if Edie was with him?"

Abruptly, the door opened and a doctor came in, holding a clipboard. The two of them stood.

"You're the friends of Billy Walker and Edie Spencer-Newman, yes?" the doctor asked, her eyes darting between them.

They nodded mutely.

"Ms Spencer-Newman will be okay; she has a few bumps and bruises. She was, at least, wearing a seatbelt and the airbag was deployed. But mostly we are concerned about the baby, so we'll be keeping her in for a few days to monitor her condition."

Alik and Nate stared at each other. A baby. Alik shook his head.

"Seatbelt?" he said, quietly. "You mean he drove? But he wasn't, I mean we had been...we were..." He trailed off.

"What about Billy?" Nate asked.

"I am so sorry," said the doctor. "We did all we could for him."

"What?" Alik's voice cracked. "What do you mean you did all you could?"

Nate moved towards him, placing a steadying hand on his arm. "Alik, Billy didn't make it through," he said softly. "He's..."

Alik looked between Nate and the doctor. And then back again.

"I'm sorry, I can't do this." He turned and ran from the room.

* * *

By the time Alik and Nate got back to Montgomery Hall, there were barely any guests left. Lucia was still there, manning the bar. She looked quizically at the pair as they walked in. Alik shook his head.

"Poppy and Caro are in the drawing room," she said, pointing to the room across the hallway. "I'm sorry about your friend. Do let me know if you need anything."

"Are you going to tell the girls or shall I?" asked Nate.

"I'll do it." Alik's stomach churned at the thought. "We need to tell Dev as well."

"I'll call him after we've spoken to Poppy and Caro."

They found the bride and her maid of honour curled up on the sofa, talking quietly. There was an almost empty bottle of champagne on the coffee table in front of them.

"What happened?" asked Caro.

Alik sat down on the arm of the sofa next to her. All he wanted to do was gather her in his arms and tell her that everything was fine, it would all be okay. He put a hand on her shoulder, as much to steady himself. Nate gathered Poppy in an embrace, pulling her close to him.

"Billy..." His voice cracked. He took a deep breath as he closed his eyes and tried again. "He didn't make it," he choked.

He felt Caro reach for his hand, squeezing it tightly. When he looked at her, there were silent tears falling down her face.

"What about Edie? Was she with him?"
"Yes."

"Is she...?"

Nate took over. "A few cuts and bruises. She was wearing a seat belt and the airbag deployed, which helped her." He glanced over at Alik. "Although we did find out something else."

"Edie's pregnant."

CHAPTER FIFTY-THREE

Edie opened her eyes, slowly, wondering where on Earth she was. Her entire body ached. It hurt to even breathe. The sterile scent of disinfectant assaulted her nostrils, and it was all she could do not to throw up. As things began to come into focus, she realised that she was in hospital.

Then her memory returned with a vengeance. They had been at Nate and Poppy's wedding, arguing, then driving, then... The crunch of metal, the stench of petrol, everything twisted in the wrong way, Billy screaming, making sounds that Edie didn't think could be human.

She sat up suddenly, yelping as the pain coursed through her. Where was he? She had to get to him. She tried to stand up, but her legs wouldn't hold her and gave way, leaving her in a crumpled heap on the floor.

The sound of her landing was enough to send two nurses scurrying over.

"What are you doing out of bed?" one of them said. "You should call for one of us if you want something."

"I need to see Billy," Edie said.

The two nurses exchanged a glance, before one of them answered. "Let's get you more comfortable, shall we?" she said, helping Edie her up and getting her back into bed before tucking the blankets back around her legs. "We'll get the doctor to come and talk to you."

"I need to see him now!"

Edie strained to listen to what the nurses were discussing as they walked away from her, but they were talking so quietly that it was impossible to hear. One of them disappeared out into the corridor. The other one stayed with

Edie. As she waited, she looked around the small ward, pristine and white. All four beds were occupied; the other three by elderly women who stared vacantly into the distance, either drugged up on medication or sleeping.

A handsome dark-haired man in his early fifties, clad in a smart suit, waltzed into the ward, the nurse who had gone to fetch him trailing in his wake. He stood at the end of Edie's bed and removed the notes from the holder, scanning them briefly. He nodded at the nurse, who pulled the curtains around the bed, cordoning them off from the others.

"I'm Dr Glover," he said, with the soft burr of a Scottish accent. "I understand that you've just woken up."

"Yes," said Edie. "I want to see Billy."

"Do you know what happened to you?" he asked.

"I, I think so. We had an accident?" Little bits were coming back to her, what was on the radio as they drove, the silly things they had said to each other.

He nodded. "That's right. You were very lucky, wearing a seatbelt probably saved your life. And the baby too."

"Baby? What baby?"

"You did know you were pregnant, didn't you? Even though it's only a few weeks?"

She shook her head. She touched her stomach, running her hands over the gentle swell of it. She had dismissed her recent slight weight gain and recent bloating as water retention. She had no cravings, her periods had always been irregular anyway, although she hadn't been so careful about taking her pill lately. "Does Billy know about the baby?"

Dr Glover sighed gently.

"Edie, I'm so sorry to have to tell you this, but Billy didn't survive the crash. His injuries were just too severe and he'd lost a lot of blood. We tried to revive him, but I'm afraid we couldn't."

Edie was silent, until tears fell down her cheeks and she began to sob.

* * *

"Visitor for you, a lovely young gentleman." One of the more cheerful nurses, a round, middle-aged lady with apple pink cheeks, breezed in with yet another jug of fresh water and set it down on the pedestal beside Edie's bed. She cleared away the untouched afternoon tea tray and bustled away without passing comment on this occasion - she was always going on at Edie to eat. Especially for the baby's sake.

Three days in hospital and Edie was slowly going out of her mind. Initially devastated at losing Billy, her grief had turned to anger, and she pushed away anyone that came to see her. Not that many people had. She found that being stuck in a four-bed ward with three elderly women alternately coughing and snoring was driving her mad. She kept begging to be moved to a private room, but she had been told there wasn't one available. She had already read all of the magazines in the hospital shop. She broke down every time she saw a picture of her and Billy, and she didn't have a phone or an iPad to entertain her because Olivia hadn't yet come in with some of her own things to make her stay more bearable. The nurses were encouraging her to get out of bed and move around or take walks around the unit, but it either hurt too much or, realistically, she couldn't actually be bothered. She spent a lot of time curled up in the foetal position, turned away from everyone, staring at the wall, clutching her stomach, protecting her baby and wondering how everything had all got so messed up.

With an effort, she turned around and opened her eyes, and was stunned to see Alik.

"I guess you were the last person I expected to see," she said. "What are you doing here?"

"I...we wanted to see how you were." Alik hovered between the doorway and the bed, his eyes darting to the other women in the room.

"It's okay, they usually take a nap around this time, they're not dead," Edie said, as she propped herself up against the pillows. "Otherwise they'd be rather excited to see a nice young man."

Alik looked Edie directly in the eye as he sat down on the chair beside her bed. "We need to talk about something," he said. "The baby."

Edie felt sick. "How do you know?"

"The doctor told us the night you were brought in. Did Billy know? Is that why you were arguing?"

Edie didn't reply straight away, remembering what the doctor had told her about how far along she might be. "Alik, the baby's yours," she said.

The words hung in the air.

"What are we going to do?"

"I don't know."

They sat in silence for a few moments, each lost in their own thoughts.

* * *

Caro waited for the break in conversation and forced a smile as she waltzed into the room in. She dropped a perfunctory kiss on Edie's cheek and placed the bag she was carrying on the bed.

"We thought you could do with some of your home comforts," she said. It was a strange enough situation being nice to Edie in any case, let alone after hearing that she was carrying Alik's child. "I asked Olivia to go over to your flat and pick out some decent clothes, as well as get your iPad and a couple of good, trashy novels, as you've probably run out of things to read. She said she'd come in later, but was going over to The Magpie first to check that everything was okay."

"I take back what I said earlier," said Edie. "Caro is definitely the last person I expected to come and visit me. Thanks for bringing my stuff in, but I think I'd prefer it if you left now." She turned her back on the couple.

Alik shrugged. "If that's what you want."

"You said Olivia was coming in later, that's fine, but I'd like to be left alone now."

Alik reached for Caro's hand as they left the ward, but she pulled away.

"What are you going to do about the baby?" she asked, without looking at him.

"You heard us? I'm sorry, Caro."

"Being a new parent will be tough if you're trying to juggle gigs and tours," she said.

"There won't be much of that anyway as the best bassist I've ever known has just been killed in a fucking car crash," he said. "There might not even be a band anymore. I have no fucking idea what's going to happen now."

Caro stopped and turned to look at him. He'd had a haunted look about him since the accident. Her heart contracted as she realised what he meant to her, and how much she loved him.

"I have to go," she said. "I need some space."

"You can't, we have to talk about this."

"What is there to talk about? Until you know what you're going to do, there's no point."

"Caro, please..."

She was already walking away from him, hurrying down the hospital corridor, her eyes glittering with unshed tears. "I can't do this, Alik, not now." She ran. "I'm sorry."

The nausea that had been held at bay by her anger took hold as she burst through the exit and out into the fresh air. She leaned against the wall and tried to breathe steadily. She inhaled deeply and bent over as she retched.

CHAPTER FIFTY-FOUR

Alik fell into a routine over the next few days. He would spend the morning playing guitar or writing lyrics and would then go and see Edie in the afternoon. The creativity helped him to stop dwelling on the loss of Billy, and the thought of the baby gave him some sense of purpose. Caro was spending more and more time at the club, citing staff issues, but he was convinced that she was avoiding him. Or at least avoiding the situation. He still didn't really know how she felt about the baby and the tie that he now had to Edie. They hadn't discussed it at any length. And he wasn't brave enough just yet to address it.

He scribbled down some words that seemed appropriate for the song he was working on about Billy and their friendship. It was tentatively titled 'The Lost Boy'. He stopped for a moment, remembering the last time he'd seen Billy. He gave a deep sigh as he looked at the words again, knowing he also had to write something for the funeral. Billy's parents had asked if he would do a eulogy. He started to scrawl a suitable tribute on a clean sheet of paper.

Needing a distraction, he texted Edie to see if she wanted anything and she immediately responded with a list of magazines. He smiled to himself. While still being her usual high-maintenance, demanding self, she was actually being quite nice. Glancing up, he saw it was time to head over to the hospital.

He grabbed his jacket, phone, wallet, and keys and headed out the door. It was a nice enough afternoon and he chose to walk over to North Ridge Hospital. Some air and some exercise would do him good. It would also give him chance to think about everything. Forty minutes later, he arrived, his mind more frazzled then when he had left home. Maybe he was the one that needed some help.

The same cheery assistant who had seen him buy the contents of the magazine shelf the previous day greeted him as he went up to the counter with another pile. *Tatler*, *Vogue*, *Vanity Fair*, *Harper's Bazaar*. The bigger and glossier the better. Just as Edie liked them.

"Good thing we got new issues in today. Your girlfriend a bit of a reader, is she?" the woman asked as she rang the purchases into the till.

Alik nodded. "Something like that, yes." He handed over his card. "Thanks." He headed off to the wing where Edie had recently been moved to, having secured a private room for her recovery.

When Alik walked into her room, Edie was sitting up in bed. She smiled brightly at him, looking happier than she had done in days. He deposited the stack of magazines on the bedside cupboard.

"You had better take your time with those," he said. "I don't think there's anything left for you to read in the hospital shop."

"I won't need them for too much longer, the doctor has said I can go home tomorrow."

"Hey, that's great news!" He watched her smile fade.

"I don't want to go back to an empty flat alone," she said.

He sat down in the chair beside her bed and took her hand. "I know it will be hard..."

"You know me, Alik, I'm not very good at looking after myself."

Alik couldn't disagree with that. "We'll be there for you."

Edie screwed up her face. "Who will? Caro? Poppy? I can't see either of them wanting to cook chicken soup for me. Not unless it was laced with arsenic."

She had a point. Edie hadn't exactly endeared herself to them with her actions. But he didn't like the idea of Edie being on her own either. "Perhaps I could come and stay with you for a bit, just until you're back up on your feet properly. And I would be around for baby stuff too. What do you think?" The words were out of his mouth before he'd thought them through.

Edie's eyebrows knitted together. "You? You would really do that?" she asked.

Doubts were already starting to creep into Alik's mind. He hadn't meant to be so impetuous, even though it was an idea that made sense. But an idea that would send Caro into orbit. He should have discussed it with her first. There was a look of relief on Edie's face and he realised that it was too late to backtrack.

"Yeah, sure, why not?"

Edie squealed and threw her arms around his neck. He imagined that Caro would have a similar reaction.

Although her hands would likely be around his throat.

* * *

Alik went straight to The Indigo Lounge from the hospital. There was no point in delaying telling Caro about his offer to help Edie out. He pressed the buzzer and waited. After a couple of minutes, Caro came to the door.

"Oh, it's you. I thought you were a delivery driver," she said, turning her back on him and walking into the bar. "Or Nic. He's gone to pick something up from the printers."

It was strange being in the club when it was closed. Right now Alik would have preferred it if there were some other people around. Caro walked up the stairs to the office and Alik followed her.

"How's Edie?" asked Caro.

"She's coming out of hospital tomorrow."

"Thank God for that, at least you won't be trekking there every day to see her."

"About that..." Alik paused. "I need to tell you something."

Caro sat down on the sofa and Alik settled next to her.

"I've offered to go and stay with her for a bit, until she's feeling better anyway."

Caro didn't reply. She simply stared at him, her face impassive. The silence went on for longer than was bearable. Alik was desperate for her to say something, to let him know how she felt about it. If she agreed, if she hated the idea. Anything.

"Caro?"

"What?" She stood up, pacing the floor. "What can you possibly expect me to say to that?"

Alik watched as she tried to wipe a tear from her eye. He got up and went to her. He grabbed her by the shoulders and made her look at him. "Caro, she's just lost her boyfriend, she's having my baby. I can hardly abandon her, can I?"

Caro wrestled herself out of his grasp. Tears fell down her cheeks. "Don't you think I know that? But after everything she's done to you, how she tried to split us up..."

"She didn't though, did she? We're still together."

Caro's words stung. "Only just, Alik, only just."

* * *

"Do you think I'm being unreasonable?" asked Caro.

She had invited Olivia and Poppy over to talk through Alik's decision, because she knew she wasn't dealing with it very well. They had already got through one bottle of wine and were halfway through a second, although Caro was drinking the lion's share.

Olivia was playing devil's advocate as usual. "Think about it, Caro. If it were you, wouldn't you want someone around to help you."

"Maybe. But couldn't that have been Minty or one of the other Stepford friends? Why did it have to be Alik?"

"Um, maybe because he's the father?"

Deep down, Caro knew Poppy was right. But to have Alik seemingly push her aside just as they had worked everything out and become a couple hit her hard. She was aware she had distanced herself from him once she'd found out about the baby. And thrown herself into her work as usual. Maybe this was her fault after all. She drained her glass and poured another.

"Hey, take it easy," said Poppy. "I know this isn't easy, but this won't help in the long run. It's the funeral in a couple of days, perhaps you can talk to Alik after that? Let him know what you're really feeling."

"You think I should offer to help out too?"

"I didn't say that. But by the sounds of it, you and Alik haven't exactly discussed this properly. You need to find out from him why he wanted to help Edie," said Poppy. "For all you know, she might have forced him into it."

"Edie can be very persuasive when she wants to be. I should know!" added Olivia.

Caro sighed. "You're right. I'm getting myself worked up when I don't know the full reasons behind it. I reacted badly when he told me and didn't give him chance to explain." *Just like I did with Josep,* she thought to herself. *And look what happened then.*

CHAPTER FIFTY-FIVE

The day of Billy's funeral dawned sunny and bright. After a week's worth of rain, the weather had finally picked up and the sun had come out. Although that did little to lift the mood of those present.

There had been vicious rumours flying around about Billy: His apparent womanising, his involvement with drugs, that he was about to be thrown out of Blood Stone Riot, that he had been arguing with Alik Thorne. The speculation was endless. And then, of course, there was his relationship with Edie. The same Edie that was pregnant by Alik Thorne - another little gem that had been revealed by *The Goss* in the last few days.

"What if there are press at the service?" said Edie, as she pulled on a vintage Chanel jacket.

Alik sighed. "If there are, I'll handle it. We need to be going soon, are you ready?" he asked gently.

Edie swept her hair up into a high ponytail, looking at her reflection in the mirror. She looked perfect - if a little gaunt - in a striking black skirt suit and spiked heels, her appearance not giving any indication that she was pregnant. "Do I look okay?"

"You look incredible."

Tears filled Edie's eyes. "Thank you for being with me. I don't think I could have got through this without you."

Alik put his arms around her, gathering her in for a hug, before releasing her and gently stroking her belly. "I'll be here for you," he said, and for a moment, Edie wondered whether he was talking to her or the baby. "Come on, we need to go."

They drove in silence to the crematorium, passing a few fans gathered around the entrance wearing home-made Blood Stone Riot t-shirts with Billy's picture on it. Edie stared at them as they went past, wondering who they were and how long they had been there; why they had chosen to come.

* * *

Alik parked up and the two of them made their way to the front of the building. Gathered in the ornately-fashioned doorway were Billy's family, mingling with the remaining members of the band. Caro was chatting quietly to Parker Roberts, who nodded at Alik as he and Edie joined the others.

Alik's eyes kept straying towards Caro. She had shut him out recently. He was grateful that Parker appeared to be the one looking after her and that she hadn't sought solace with Jonny Tyler.

There was a signal for them to move inside.

It was their turn to be processed - get the grief and tears over with so another group could go through the same thing. There was nothing personal about it. They trooped inside, wondering where to sit, whether they should all be together. Eventually, after an awkward moment and some shuffling of seats, they found places and braced themselves for what was to come.

The vicar stood up next to the wooden casket, adorned with a simple bouquet of lilies. Edie started snuffling, clutching hold of Alik's arm as the two of them sat closest to Billy's family. Alik's blood ran cold and he stared straight ahead as the vicar began to speak softly about Billy's life - if he made eye contact with anyone, he knew he would lose it.

There was barely any noise as the vicar went through his short service.

Alik stood up at the end, and walked slowly to the front. He placed a hand on the casket and waited in silence for a moment. Taking a deep breath, he turned to face the mourners.

"We all knew Billy in different ways," he said. "He was a true friend. A loving, if somewhat wayward, son." He acknowledged the Walkers. Billy's mum had a handkerchief covering her face. "A caring, if somewhat undependable, boyfriend." His gaze fell on Edie, who was trying not to cry again. "But still a friend. A true, true friend." His voice wobbled and he steadied himself before continuing. "But most of all, there was the music. The most important thing in his life was the band, and he achieved more than he could have ever believed possible in such a short space of time." He paused, taking another deep breath. "The void caused by this tragic accident will be hard to fill and no-one will ever be able to replace him."

* * *

Caro listened to Alik, her heart breaking. She desperately wanted to comfort him, to hold him, to tell him that it was all going to be okay. When she looked up at last, the casket was making its slow journey behind the curtains, never to be seen again.

One of the ushers gave another signal and it was time to move on.

As they filed out of the chapel into the garden, the sun blazed down, and the assembled group milled around looking at the flowers people had sent. Caro distanced herself from the main crowd, choosing instead to stand by the walled garden and read messages of sympathy for another family. Turning her back on the sight of Edie clinging to Olivia, sobbing, she tried to compose herself.

She felt someone beside her and breathed in the familiar scent of Alik's aftershave.

"How are you?" she asked.

"Been better." Up close, she could see that his eyes were tired and bloodshot, and he wasn't as clean-shaven as she would have expected. She wanted to support him, make it better, but something held her back. "You?"

"Coping, it's been a lot to take in," she said.

He nodded. "Caro, I..."

Edie appeared in front of them. "Sorry to interrupt, but Alik we need to go now."

Caro forced a smile. "Of course, I'll see you later."

And they were gone.

* * *

After the funeral service, Caro and Nic had invited everyone back to The Indigo Lounge. The sign on the door read 'Closed for a private function', but there were still a few people who came to see what was going on, trying to peer through the windows.

Billy's parents and assorted family gathered on one side of the room, with the band, and Poppy and Olivia sat in the other. Edie was dividing her time between the two sets of people, the strain of the day beginning to show.

Alik had already made heavy inroads into the alcohol, helping himself to a bottle of single malt whisky from behind the bar.

"Mate," said Nic. "If you're going to drink us dry, at least do it with the cheap stuff."

"Whatever," Alik said, taking a glass and stalking off in the direction of the VIP bar for some privacy. He was slightly put out to see that Edie had got there before him.

"Sorry," she said. "I just felt I needed to be on my own for a while. Everyone's being so nice."

"I know how you feel." He sat down on the sofa and poured a hefty measure of whisky into the glass. "Want some?"

She shook her head, covering her belly with her hands. "I don't think this little one would appreciate it somehow. Although Daddy is a bad influence."

Alik forced a weak smile, mentally punching himself for trying to encourage a pregnant woman to drink. He swigged a mouthful directly from the bottle. "How are you doing really?"

"It's hard," Edie said. "Everyone else has been asking me exactly the same question all day, almost as if they have to, and I feel like a robot when I answer. I know you've been amazing and been there for me, but I can't help feeling as if everything that happened that night was my fault and they should be blaming me."

"What makes you say that?"

"We were arguing. About you. Billy kept going on about how being with me somehow meant that he'd got one over on you, that suddenly you weren't perfect and didn't have everything you ever wanted. And that he could have Caro any time he wanted."

Alik bristled. There had always been a rivalry between the pair, which went back years, to the early days of the band and the nights they had spent sleeping in the back of vans. Or, if they'd got lucky, on the floor of someone's house whilst the other one got the luxury of the girl's bed.

Edie continued. "We were in the car and he was yelling at me. I told him to slow down, that I wanted him to stop, but he wouldn't listen. And then something ran into the road and he swerved…" Her voice trailed off.

Alik took her hand in his. "It's not your fault, no-one blames you, how can you even think that? Billy shouldn't have been anywhere near a car that night, he'd been drinking and was totally off his face. I should know, I was doing it with him. You know what he was like, you couldn't tell him not to do anything because he'd go ahead and do it anyway."

Edie laughed softly. Her eyes filled with tears, threatening to spill down her cheeks again.

Alik was suddenly aware that he was caressing the back of her left hand, gently soothing her. He pulled back, not wanting to give Edie the wrong signals.

"Oh, God, I miss him so much!" Edie said. "I know we hadn't been together all that long, but we just clicked, we just kind of got each other I suppose. It was different than it was with you." The tears were now flowing freely, running unheeded down her face. Her shoulders started to heave as she sobbed uncontrollably.

Alik took her in his arms, holding her close to him, gently stroking her long hair, breathing in her scent. He was acutely conscious of her closeness and the way her body felt against his. After a few moments, she drew back, breathing deeply and snuffling, staring deep in Alik's eyes.

"God, I must look awful," she said, blinking.

"You're gorgeous, you know that." Alik wiped the tears from her eyes with his thumb, streaking mascara across her cheek.

Their eyes locked. Edie's hand closed over Alik's, guiding him down to her lips. He traced the outline of her mouth before she drew his index finger in, sucking gently on it. Alik felt his groin stirring, strangely turned on by the situation, grief mixing with need. He felt her reach down to the belt on his trousers, then reach for his cock and he tensed, growing hard under her touch.

"What the fuck..." he said.

"Ssshhh. Just let me make it better. I need you, Alik."

"Jesus, what are you doing?" He pushed her away, confused, the emotions of the day coupled with alcohol on an empty stomach overwhelming him.

"It's called grieving, Alik," said Edie. "And being pregnant makes me horny."

"I said I'd look after you, but I can't be with you like that again. You should go, I need to be on my own."

After Edie left, Alik lay there for a long time, staring at the ceiling. He was in need of a cigarette but couldn't be bothered to move. Edie's behaviour was erratic, no doubt her hormones were all over the place because of the baby, not to mention whatever she was feeling over Billy's death. He knew he was doing the right thing in standing by her, but missed Caro deeply. He didn't know what to do.

He grabbed the neck of the whisky bottle, raised it to his lips, and began to drink.

CHAPTER FIFTY-SIX

Despite everything that had happened at the wake, Alik insisted on accompanying Edie to her booking appointment. Things had been strained between them and he had found himself going out every night to make sure he wasn't giving Edie the wrong message. He was helping her out as a friend, as the father of her baby. He was being responsible. He wasn't about to be her boyfriend again. He had an escape route planned in any case, as he needed to be in London for a meeting with Parker and Griffen later that afternoon. Edie had initially resisted, saying she would be okay on her own and being vague about what the appointment would entail. He almost regretted his decision the moment they walked into the waiting room at North Ridge's independent private hospital. Heads swivelled around to check out the new arrivals. His eyes fell on the back issue of *The Goss* with Edie's interview lying on the table. But he couldn't think about Caro at this moment. This was about his and Edie's future. He was apprehensive and excited at the same time. He knew his life would be different, but there were plenty of other rock stars that managed to juggle a tour schedule and fatherhood. If there was to be a tour now. That was something else he couldn't think about.

Edie made the receptionist aware of her arrival and came to sit down next to him.

"I hope you're ready to answer lots of questions," she said.

"Probably not the same type of ones I get asked in press interviews, right? I'm not going to questioned about my preferred guitar brand am I?"

Edie shook her head. "She's more likely to ask about family history of genetic conditions."

"Right." He racked his brains, trying to think if there was anything he could remember that might affect the baby.

A short, dark-haired woman with a broad smile walked down the corridor from the consulting rooms and addressed the waiting room. "Edie Spencer-Newman?"

Edie jumped up. "Yes, that's me."

"I thought I recognised you from the picture in that magazine. Do come with me," she said. "And is that your partner?" She looked at Alik.

"I'm the father," said Alik. "But we're not together. I'm Alik Thorne, nice to meet you." He didn't want Edie to think otherwise either. He stood up, following them down the hallway. They went into a light, airy room, decorated in calming hues, with a desk, several comfy looking chairs, and a sofa.

"Edie, I'm Patsy Crane, your community midwife. You'll see me at all your appointments throughout your pregnancy starting with today's welcome visit." Patsy took a seat behind the desk and gestured for Edie and Alik to sit opposite her. She offered them some water and poured a glass for each of them. "Right, let's get started."

Patsy opened up the file in front of her. She admitted she preferred to handwrite her first set of notes as people tended to remember things later in the appointment and her computer system wouldn't allow her to go back.

Alik couldn't keep up as Patsy fired questions at Edie. When was her last period? Have you been pregnant before? Are there any genetic conditions in your family? What do you do for work? They just kept coming.

"And what about your lifestyle? Do you smoke? What about alcohol?" Patsy put her pen down and looked between the pair. "I am aware of your accident and that your pregnancy was discovered when you were admitted. There was a high level of alcohol in your bloodstream then, but I hope you've changed your ways."

Alik knew Edie had been religious about doing things right. Since she'd left hospital it was all clean-eating and juicing; nothing stronger than green tea had passed her lips in the past couple of weeks. He, on the other hand, had been out most nights and woke up with a hangover most mornings. He should probably turn over a new leaf too.

Edie nodded. "Yes, Patsy, I have. This baby is important to me and I want to make things work with Alik. We could do with a fresh start." She reached for his hand and squeezed it. She gave him a small smile.

Patsy nodded. "Good, good. Now, just a few more questions."

Alik tuned out as Patsy concluded her interrogation. There couldn't have been anything that she now didn't know about Edie. The midwife took some blood, explaining that they would be used to check Edie's iron levels, blood group, and to screen for the risk of Down's Syndrome. He hoped everything would be normal.

"Last few things and then we'll go and do a scan," said Patsy.

"Really? That happens today?" Edie looked surprised.

"Of course, by the date you gave me for your last period, you'd be at least twelve weeks by now." Patsy looked at Alik. "And I'm sure you'd like to see the little one, wouldn't you?"

Alik nodded, a mixture of excitement and fear bubbling away in his stomach. That would certainly make things real.

"Right, tell me when you're ready and we'll go down to the scanning suite. I need you to drink all that water and let me know when you're ready to pee," said Patsy.

Alik screwed up his face. "Too much information!"

Edie gulped down the rest of her water and refilled her glass. She repeated the move and then declared she was ready.

Patsy stood up and showed them the way to the scanning suite. Edie settled down on the bed. Alik stood beside her, not quite knowing what to do with himself or where to stand. Patsy sensed his awkwardness and pointed to a chair. He sat down and took Edie's hand as Patsy pulled up Edie's top and rubbed some gel onto her stomach. The midwife ran a small handheld device over Edie's tummy, her eyes fixed on the screen. She moved the device several times, each time reviewing what she saw on the monitor, without saying anything.

"Edie, are you sure about the date of your last period?" asked Patsy, eventually.

"Um, they are pretty irregular..."

"Why? What's wrong?" asked Alik.

"Looking at the size of the embryo and the heart rate, it would appear you are only seven weeks pregnant, not twelve."

Alik mentally calculated the dates in his head. And as he made eye contact with Edie, he knew she had been doing the same.

He dropped her hand as if he'd been burned. "You bitch," he hissed, getting to his feet.

Patsy looked between the two of them. "I'm guessing this is news to you?"

"Damn right. Could you leave us alone?" asked Alik.

The midwife left the room, closing the door behind her. Edie grabbed some tissue and cleaned the gel from her stomach. "Alik, I can explain..."

Alik faced her. "You don't need to explain; I know exactly what's happened. The baby isn't mine. It's Billy's."

He looked up at the ceiling, trying to control his rising anger. "You lied to me, Edie. Again."

"But I only did it because..." Tears started to fall down her cheeks.

"I don't care why you did it! You know what I gave up for you, what I lost. That was one of the hardest decisions I've ever made because I thought I was going to be a father. And now I find out it was all a sham."

"We can still be a family... I'm sure Billy would have wanted that."

"Billy wanted to fuck my girlfriend while she was still with me. Or did you forget that?"

Alik paced around the room, wrestling with a myriad of emotions. The elation he had felt when he thought he was about to see his child was replaced by burning resentment. Edie watched him.

"I need to get out of here," he said, reaching for the door handle.

Edie sprang up from the bed and stood in front of the door, blocking his exit. "Please stay, let's talk about this."

"I don't think there's anything to discuss." Alik's face was contorted with rage. "Get out of my way."

He pushed her to one side and walked out.

CHAPTER FIFTY-SEVEN

Alik had tried several times to get through to Caro on his journey up to London. But each time he called, it went straight to voicemail. He was desperate to talk to her, to tell her what he had just discovered. It needed to come from him. He had also tried to cancel the upcoming meeting, but Griffen insisted it was a crisis meeting and not showing up could jeopardise what might happen next for Blood Stone Riot. As Alik walked to their offices, along Carnaby Street towards Broadwick Street, his head was swimming. Distracted, he wondered what the area had been like in its heyday. He remembered reading that the likes of *Kerrang* and the long defunct *Raw* had had their offices at the end of the street, above some dubious-looking shops. He could imagine the journalists and bands enjoying the close proximity to Soho for debauched nights out and long boozy lunches. At the head of Broadwick Street stood the Numb Records premises, in a building that also used to house a number of women's magazines - some had long gone, but others were thriving in the digital age and had transformed their business operations as a result.

Having pretty much come straight from the booking appointment, he hadn't had chance to freshen up and, as a result, he looked dreadful. With at least a week's worth of beard covering his face, hair that had grown lank and straggly, and dressed in ripped jeans and an old, beaten-up, donkey jacket, it wouldn't have surprised him if someone had pressed a pound into his palm and told him to go and get a cup of tea. It was no wonder the security guard had confronted him as he entered the foyer and demanded to know what he was doing there. After a brief explanation, he was pointed in the direction of the lift. Out of the corner of his eye, he spotted the receptionists sneaking a glance at him and whispering to each other.

Griffen was already waiting in the same meeting room they had been in before when they first met Parker. He cast an eye over Alik's appearance and tutted. "You could have made an effort; this meeting could go either way."

A young intern poked her head around the door. "Can I get either of you a drink at all?" she asked.

"Two coffees, please," said Griffen, ordering on Alik's behalf. "And make his strong."

She disappeared, leaving them alone again.

"What did you mean by 'this meeting could go either way'?" asked Alik.

Griffen sat down. "Parker called me to discuss some options. I'm not sure you're going to like them."

Alik didn't get the chance to respond as the door swung open, admitting Parker Roberts followed by the intern with the drinks. She placed a tiny cup of espresso in front of Parker and two larger mugs of coffee on the table for Griffen and Alik, gesturing to the one that was meant to be stronger.

Parker drained his coffee in one gulp, placing the small cup carefully back in the saucer, before steepling his fingers together and turning to Alik. "I am so sorry about what happened to Billy, such a tragic accident. I didn't get chance to speak to you at the funeral."

Alik nodded, sipping the too-hot coffee.

"This does leave us with a bit of a dilemma," Parker said. "The EP is due out soon and at the moment, Blood Stone Riot is a three-piece, which means we can't tour it properly or invest in a lot of heavy promotion. We have options of course. Replacement, which worked for the likes of Metallica, AC/DC and Slipknot, or we can sit on it. My preference is to find a replacement. The EP is ready to go and if you needed to do any live gigs, you can always get a backing track or hire a session musician. I can think of a few that would work."

Alik interjected. "We've worked way too hard on this to just let it rot in a studio somewhere, and Billy wouldn't have wanted that. But we can't just replace him like that."

Griffen nodded. "Alik's right, Parker, it should be such a waste to let the EP go to ground. And the contract..."

Parker waved his hand. "We would work something out in terms of the contract."

Alik felt a knot of nausea gather in his stomach, like a heavy iron fist. The thought of replacing Billy, even though he knew it was the right thing to do, left a sour taste in his mouth.

"There is another interim solution." Parker reached into his suit pocket for his phone, placing it on the table. "This has come into my possession." He fiddled about with the device, preparing it to play something. When the music filled the room, Alik was horrified. It was an extremely rough demo of 'The Girl From The Blue'. Upon hearing it for the first time, as a listener rather than performer, he realised how the song had developed since he'd first come up with the idea. As the chords faded out, he was met with the familiar opening riff of 'Poisoned Rationality', his "break-up" song, and then after a couple of minutes 'The Lost Boy'. He hung his head and wiped away a tear as the emotion of the song hit him.

Griffen's face was unreadable.

As the last strains of 'The Lost Boy' died away, Parker looked between the pair. "This stuff is good. It's different though, it's not Blood Stone Riot material."

Alik knew that. He had never intended it to be for the band, most of it was simply for him.

"We could release this whilst you look for a replacement for Billy."

The word 'replacement' hit Alik again like a punch as he realised that the artist development manager was for real. That message was getting through loud and clear.

Parker continued. "Look at Corey Taylor or Frank Turner, they both had successful careers in one band or genre and were able to flip it to appeal to an alternative audience. I know you already have some exposure with a different type of press from your relationship with Edie, which means you could build on that. I'm sure we can get an exclusive with Rick Hills at *Aspire*."

Griffen nodded. "That would seem to be a sensible option. Alik?"

"I need some time," he said. "How long have I got?"

"The EP was due out at the end of next month. If we're going to replace it with the solo material, we need time to record those three songs and get a marketing and PR campaign around it."

"Olivia could help with that," Alik said, although he wasn't anywhere near to making a decision. "I'll think about it," he said, finally. "Do you need me anymore?"

Parker shook his head. "I've got a couple of things to discuss with Griffen, but you know what you need to think about and I suggest you go and do that. Call me when you've made that decision."

Alik left the building, his heart heavy. He needed to speak to Nate and Dev about the decision, but he had a sneaking suspicion that Nate might have been the one who had made Parker aware of the new material. After that meeting and the events of the morning, if there was ever a time he needed a drink, it was definitely now.

CHAPTER FIFTY-EIGHT

Caro was sitting cross-legged on her bed, leaning against a wall of pillows, a bottle of Jack Daniels propped against her thigh and the remains of a roll-up beside her in the ashtray. Her iPod was blaring a demo of Blood Stone Riot's EP and Alik's voice was singing only to her. Strewn across the duvet were the latest copies of *The Goss*, as well as bank statements and shift rotas from the club.

She looked at the pictures in the magazine of Edie out at various events, showing off her barely-there baby bump, seemingly loving every moment of it. The accompanying verbage was full of sympathy about the tragedy of Billy's death and providing advice for the yummy mummy to be, particularly as she had just been announced as the brand ambassador of the new *Bump!* Maternity clothing range. And it was full of praise for Alik, supporting her after the terrible times she'd been through. There was some speculation that this was why he had seemingly split with Caro.

Truth was they hadn't spoken about it.

Caro hadn't seen Alik since the funeral. Caro had said she was too busy. But she couldn't get the image of Edie and Alik out of her head. How she had discovered them kissing in the VIP bar. And how she'd run away as soon as she saw what was happening.

Caro fired up a new browser window on the laptop in front of her. After a swig straight from the bottle, she tapped in a search string and reached for her credit card.

CHAPTER FIFTY-NINE

Alik lifted his head from the pillow and wondered what had crawled into his mouth and died. As he came around, he realised he wasn't alone, and there were two other bodies in the bed with him. And they were all naked. Glancing around he saw some nondescript, generic student room, empty bottles and cans, and an overflowing ashtray.

He carefully manoeuvred his way out of the bed, trying hard not to wake the two sleeping beauties - Christ, were they twins? - and stumbled across the room, thankful to find there was at least an en suite. Locking the door behind him, he took a piss and stared at his reflection in the mirror above the sink. He looked dreadful; red-rimmed, bloodshot, eyes, puffy face, definite signs of hangover and other recreational abuse. Seeing there was at least one clean towel in the room, he stepped into the shower. As the water pounded over his head, he tried to piece together the events of the previous evening. After the meeting with Parker and Griffen, he had headed into Soho and started drinking, alone. There he had got talking to a couple of American tourists who recognised him from the YouTube leak of the 'Bleed Like Cyanide' video. The next thing he remembered was a bar in Camden, lots of beer, a number of hot girls trying to give him their phone number - although not the ones currently in the bed he had slept in - following someone into a random house party, playing guitar, being offered poppers and God knows what else, then the rest of it was a bit hazy. And that was an understatement. How he had got from Soho to Camden was a mystery, but clearly he had interested these girls enough for something to happen, but again he had no recollection of what. Reaching for a bottle of shower gel, he lathered his body, trying not to move his head too much.

All he knew was that he needed to get out of the house. And quickly.

Despite his attempts at stealth, both of his companions were awake when he re-entered the bedroom, and looking like they wanted a repeat performance of whatever had gone on.

"Hey baby," one of them said, lifting the duvet and giving him a full view of her naked body. "Why don't you come back to bed?"

"It's cosy in here," said the other. "Last night was so much fun."

Alik glanced around the room, trying to identify which jeans were his in the tangle of clothes that lay on the floor. He was relieved to see that his wallet and phone were still sitting on top of a chest of drawers. "Thanks, but I need to get off."

"But we can get you off." The pair started cosying up and fondling each other.

It was all Alik could do not to throw up as he hastily pulled on his jeans and grabbed what looked like his t-shirt from the pile by the bed. Snatching his belongings, he bolted from the room, checking the unfamiliar surroundings as he found his way down the stairs and out of the front door.

Gasping in cool air in an attempt to calm his stomach, he made his way towards what appeared to be a main road. Checking his phone, he saw a dozen missed calls from Olivia.

She answered on pretty much the first ring. "Where the hell are you?"

Alik checked around him, looking for some kind of sign post or identifying landmark. "Um, somewhere in London," he said. "I think."

"When did you last speak to Caro?"

He had a vague recollection of leaving her another rambling voicemail at some point during the previous evening. Although he couldn't be one hundred percent sure of the content. "Last night, maybe early this morning. I needed to tell her something."

"What time?"

"Sorry, Olivia, I don't remember."

He could almost feel her breath in his ear as she huffed down the line at him. "What's happened?"

"She's gone, Alik."

"Gone where?"

Again, the exasperated sigh pierced his eardrum. "If I knew that I wouldn't be asking you! Just let me know if you hear from her."

After Olivia ended the call, Alik found Caro's number in his recently-dialled contacts and pressed 'call.' It went straight to voicemail. He tried again. And again. The same result. Trying her work landline, he was frustrated to get an identical answer. It took all of his patience not to hurl the phone into the road.

The thought that he might have lost her for good, combined with the previous night's excesses building up in his system, made him turn around and vomit into the nearest garden.

CHAPTER SIXTY

Caro knew it was early, but she couldn't help pounding on the door of the apartment. No doubt the neighbours would start complaining at any minute, but she really didn't care. Just as she was about to begin hammering on it again, the door cracked open a couple of inches and Mariella's blonde head peered out.

"What the hell are you doing back here? Are you okay?" she said, flinging the door open wide and ushering her friend inside. She apologised in Spanish to the elderly gentleman who lived in the apartment next door and had come out to see what all the noise was about.

Caro shook her head, a fresh wave of tears engulfing her. She allowed Mariella to lead her into the living room and collapsed on the sofa, pulling her knees up to her chest.

"What's going on? Everything alright?" A muscled Adonis with an Australian accent wandered in from the bedroom, naked, and Mariella scurried over to him.

"Might be best if you head back to bed, babe," she said, tactfully covering him with a t-shirt that had been draped over the back of the sofa. "I've got this."

He kissed the top of her head, yawning, and did as he was told. Mariella went to the kitchen to put the kettle on, coming back shortly with two very strong cups of coffee, one of which smelled distinctly alcoholic. Caro blew on the steaming mug of coffee, inhaling the brandy fumes. A weak smile crossed her face at Mariella's thoughtfulness. Her friend curled up on the opposite end of the sofa and waited until Caro was ready to talk. They sat in silence, sipping their drinks, listening to the sounds outside as the island started coming to life.

"Okay," Mariella said. "The last time you were here, you were with Alik and now you're here on your own, so I'm guessing that it must be something to do with him. Am I close?"

Caro nodded.

Taking a sip of the disgustingly strong alcoholic coffee, she began to talk, the whole story tumbling out about how she had wound up where she was now.

"I didn't know where else to go," she said.

Mariella reached out and hugged her. "You are always welcome here, we can go back to how things were."

She was true to her word. Within a few days, Caro was back working at The Roca Bar, the easy familiarity and the constant cheerfulness of the tourists a welcome distraction from everything that had happened.

It almost felt like home again.

CHAPTER SIXTY-ONE

Alik arranged to meet Olivia at The Green Tree, one of North Ridge's most popular cafes, a couple of days after his London bender. After repeated fruitless attempts to get hold of Caro, he desperately hoped that Olivia knew where she was. He ordered a coffee and waited, trying to evade the looks of the customers who were staring at him, knowing that he looked dreadful. Whatever he'd done on that night out was still having an after-effect on him. He browsed on his phone, scrolling through pictures of him and Caro, reminding himself of the good times they had, the happiness he felt when they were together. Something that had certainly been missing of late. Edie had been trying to reach him and had left him several messages begging him to talk to her. He had ignored all of them, scared by the depth of disgust he felt towards her. And scared that if they talked in person, he would do something that he would deeply regret.

The door finally swung open and Olivia entered. She looked full of purpose and determination as she strode across the floor. Alik was filled with confidence that she would know something. But as she dropped down into the chair opposite him, that confidence evaporated.

"Before you ask, I still have no definite idea of where she is," said Olivia. She waved at the waitress and ordered a latte. "It's possible she's gone back to Mallorca, but I can't get hold of Mariella."

Alik sighed heavily. He had suspected the same thing and wanted to go out there himself to look for her. Caro needed to know the truth. And although she deserved to hear it first, he also needed to confide in someone else before he burst.

"I found something out a couple of days ago," he said, "that changes things. Again."

The waitress placed Olivia's latte on the table and she immediately reached for it. "Go on."

Alik decided not to bother with the detail and went straight in. "Edie lied. The baby is Billy's. She's only about seven weeks pregnant, so it can't possibly be mine."

Olivia's jaw dropped and Alik watched her take several sips of her drink, trying to digest the news. "I knew she was capable of some deceitful behaviour when she told me she was seeing Billy, but this?" Olivia hung her head. "Alik, I'm sorry, I should have told you about the affair when I found out."

"Yeah, you probably should have," agreed Alik. "We wouldn't be sitting here now having this conversation, but I can't blame you for what she did. Although I guess you probably kept Caro's involvement with me a secret from Edie too."

Olivia nodded. "I got stuck in the middle of the two of them, a bit like you did." She took another sip of her latte. "I'll try Mariella again. And maybe you should just head on out there."

"You're right. I don't know why I'm sitting here just talking about it." Alik drained his coffee. "Would you talk to Edie? Maybe she needs to speak to Caro, too. Explain herself and why she did what she did. I don't trust myself around her at the moment."

"Of course. I'll head over there now. Call me when you know anything."

Alik watched Olivia leave, a sense of urgency suddenly kicking in. He grabbed his phone and fired off a few texts before turning his attention to flights.

* * *

Edie settled down on the sofa, a mug of ginger tea on the table in front of her. Apparently morning sickness wasn't confined just to mornings for her. She'd been shopping for baby stuff in Henlake for most of the day before meeting Minty for a catch up. Her friend had wittered on endlessly about what diet she was trying, which Edie was far too polite to mention didn't seem to be working. Minty asked her loads of questions about the baby, her plans for decorating the nursery, what she was going to call it and how she was getting on with Alik. It had been exhausting. That was before the awful traffic coming home. She ran her hands over her stomach.

"You're tiring me out already," she said. "And you've not even been born yet." Her eyes wandered to the baby magazines scattered next to her on the sofa, wondering which one of them had the best tips on sleeping. Idly, she flicked through the TV channels, trying to settle on something mindless enough to keep her attention for a little while before it was an acceptable hour to go to bed. An old *Sex & The City* re-run was just starting, so she settled for that, snuggling back into the cushions and half closing her eyes.

When she heard knocking, she thought it was on the programme, but when the knocking became more insistent, she realised that it was her own front door. She wondered who would be coming to see her at this time and hauled herself up off the sofa. Checking the door spy-hole before opening it, she saw Olivia standing on her doorstep.

She opened the door. "Hi, what are you doing here?" she asked.

Olivia didn't reply and barged straight past her into the living room, sitting down in the armchair. Closing the door behind her, Edie resumed her place on the sofa.

"I was with Alik this afternoon," said Olivia.

Edie felt the colour drain from her face. She thought she might throw up.

"He told me everything. How could you do that to him? And to Caro? I know you were jealous of what they had, but you were screwing around with Billy. You didn't need to take it any further, it was done."

A single tear crept down Edie's cheek and she swiped it away. She didn't want Olivia to see how upset she was, she needed to stay strong. "Caro had everything, didn't she?" she said. "The successful career, the man that wanted her. Her, not me. If I couldn't have him, then I didn't want her to either."

Olivia shook her head. "And to think I covered for you over your affair. I didn't realise just how vindictive you could be, although I should have guessed after you did that article on Caro."

Edie laughed through her tears. "Jealousy works in mysterious ways."

"You've destroyed my best friend's happiness. Not to mention my trust. Just like that." Olivia clicked her fingers.

Neither of them spoke any further. Somewhere in the distance, Carrie Bradshaw was championing the merits of strong female friendships and how lucky she was to have Miranda, Samantha, and Charlotte. Listening to the words, Edie knew she had a choice. She had to do the right thing. For once.

"You need to make this better," said Olivia. "You need to tell Caro the truth."

CHAPTER SIXTY-TWO

Caro stretched, adjusting the tie string on the bottom of the minuscule turquoise bikini that she'd just bought. Fleeing North Ridge late at night had meant that she hadn't packed properly and simply thrown a few clothes into a bag. Clothes that were not necessarily appropriate for the late summer weather of Mallorca. Having been persuaded by Mariella that she needed to give herself a break and not just be holed up in the apartment when she wasn't working, she had packed a bag and headed to one of the nearby hotels to pretend to be a tourist for the day. Behind her sunglasses, she surveyed the pool, watching the families with pre-school age children splashing about in the water, carefree and laughing, and couples canoodling on the sun loungers. She flicked her iPod onto shuffle and regretted it seconds later when Alik's voice whispered in her ear as he sang 'The Girl From The Blue'. Ripping the headphones out, she picked up her book instead and tried to concentrate on that. Despite Jackie Collins weaving a plot line that was only slightly less complicated than her current life, she soon found her mind wandering: Alik and Edie, the baby...

The book soon went the way of the discarded iPod and she sipped her freshly-made margarita instead and returned to watching the children playing, something so easy and so innocent.

A shadow fell over her from behind, blocking the sun, and she glanced up, expecting to see Mariella.

But it wasn't Mariella.

"Hello, Caro."

Edie was dressed in a simple broderie anglaise maxi dress, her head covered with a large straw hat. She looked slightly ethereal and angelic, her golden blonde hair pooling around her shoulders.

For a moment, Caro wondered if she were hallucinating and the apparition in front of her could simply be put down to too much sun and margaritas. When Edie placed her bag on the floor and gently sat down on the end of Caro's sun lounger, she knew it was real.

"What the hell are you doing here?" said Caro, pulling herself into an upright position.

Edie took a deep breath. "Poppy and Olivia tracked you down and Mariella said you were here," she said. "There are some things that I need to tell you." Her voice cracked as she spoke.

"Like what, Edie? What could you possibly have to say to me?"

"I don't really know where to begin."

"Then it looks like you've had a wasted trip, Edie." Caro reached into her bag and pulled a navy blue lace shirt dress over her bikini, suddenly feeling a chill.

"Wait." Edie placed a hand on Caro's arm. "It's about the baby."

"I'm sure you and Alik will be the best parents ever."

Edie swallowed. "Alik isn't going to be involved."

"You're doing this on your own?"

"It isn't fair to Alik. He isn't the baby's father. Billy is." A single tear trickled down Edie's cheek.

"Sorry, what? Did I just hear you say *Billy* is the father? After everything you said at the hospital and at the funeral? How could you lie to Alik like that? It wrecked our relationship, what we had, everything!" Caro's voice rose as her anger increased. "Why would you do that?"

Caro was pleased to see that it took a moment for Edie to gather herself before she replied.

"I was jealous, Caro," said Edie. "I have been since the day I met you. You had everything - a successful business, a brilliant best friend, and you had Alik's attention. From the first time we met at The Vegas, I knew that something had happened between the two of you, although he never told me where or when. When Billy started flirting with me at the festival and showed some interest, it was nice to know that someone else could be attracted to me."

"Why didn't you finish with Alik then?"

Edie shrugged. "I liked the attention."

Caro took off her sunglasses and fixed Edie with her violet eyes. "What happens now? We just hug it out and become best friends?" Caro chewed thoughtfully on the arm of her sunglasses. "What do you want to happen now?"

"I don't know."

"You spent a lot of time creating this mess, but have no clue as to how to sort it out. That's brilliant, Edie, just brilliant." Caro couldn't work out how to feel. She was desperate to find out how Alik was, how he wanted to move forward. Then she remembered that she had been the one to push him away, once she'd found out about the baby.

"I know we can never go back to the way things were."

"It's not as if we were friends in the first place." Caro's tone was deliberately harsh. She didn't want Edie to have an easy time of it. She wanted to make her suffer as much as she had. She wanted to know where Alik was. "You ruined my relationship. I can't just forgive you like that."

"I'm not expecting that. At least not yet."

Caro's laugh was hollow. "Not yet? Can you hear yourself, Edie? I'm not sure I can ever forgive you."

They fell silent, the only sound being that of children splashing around in the pool and screaming with pleasure as they played in the sun. Edie struggled to her feet. Without saying goodbye, she walked away.

Caro watched her retreating figure and slumped back into the sun lounger, exhausted after everything she had just heard. She drained her glass and signalled to the waiter that she needed a refill. She scrolled through photos of her and Alik on her phone. Pictures of them at gigs, in Mallorca with Mariella, at The Indigo Lounge, at Poppy and Nate's wedding. Before things had gone wrong. She called his number, but it went straight to voicemail. She hoped it wasn't too late to make things right between them.

CHAPTER SIXTY-THREE

Caro had finally been persuaded by Mariella to go out and they had gone to Juju's for a few drinks, in the vain hope that the familiarity of the bar would relax her. Caro had told her everything about Edie's visit to the pool, but she was in a dark place and didn't know what she should be feeling. There was obviously some relief at finally knowing the truth, but she didn't know what she should be doing with that information.

Caro took a long sip of the glass of rosé in front of her, the delightfully-chilled Rosé Mortitx wine that she had missed while being back in North Ridge. She'd certainly been drinking enough of it since her return to Mallorca.

"What are we doing here anyway?" she asked Mariella, as the host started preparing the evening's entertainment.

"Hey, I know how much you like this place, we just thought it would be good to get you out of the apartment." Mariella wrapped her arm around Trent, her Australian Adonis. The couple had been so good to Caro since she landed on their doorstep, and she was eternally grateful for their love and understanding. It can't have been easy for them, in the first flushes of romance, to have a blubbering wreck turn up and basically live on their couch. She really did need to start thinking about what the future held.

It was open mic night again, with person after person getting up and covering a recent chart hit. A lump formed in her throat as she thought back to the last time she had been there.

Mariella tapped her on the shoulder and rolled her eyes at Caro as a bunch of teenage boys took to the stage and attempted to sound something like One Direction. They certainly had the looks, however it wasn't a sound that was likely to have Simon Cowell losing any sleep over signing them any time soon. Caro smiled weakly in return. She knew they meant well in trying to get her out, but all she could think about was curling up on the sofa with another bottle of wine and trashy TV that didn't require her to think.

The sound of an acoustic guitar caught her attention, but she had her back to the stage. She recognised the chords instantly.

Spinning around, she saw Alik on the stage, leaning towards the mic. He was dressed in a pair of black jeans and a tight-fitting indigo shirt, unbuttoned to show off his tattoos.

"I remember being here some time ago," he said. "And I tried this song out on an unsuspecting crowd. There have been some changes since then, both to the song and to my life, but I'd like to try it out again."

'The Girl From The Blue' kicked in and it was all Caro could do to stop the tears falling unheeded down her face.

After everything that had happened, everything that Edie had confessed to that afternoon, he was here.

Singing that song.

She glanced over at Mariella, who had a knowing smile on her face and gently pushed her towards the stage. As she made her way through the audience, Alik didn't take his eyes off her and continued singing.

Singing the song that had brought them together in the first place, and was inexorably drawing them together again.

There was a tumultuous round of applause as the song ended and the crowd there realised something was going on. Alik held out a hand and pulled her onto the stage.

"Ladies and gentlemen, meet Caro Flynn, the inspiration behind that song. I met her here all that time ago, fell in love with her and pretty much changed all the lyrics so they were about her."

The crowd clapped even harder and Caro felt herself dissolving into tears. She ducked her head in embarrassment and jumped down off the raised platform, making her way outside. Alik passed his guitar to someone behind the bar and followed her outside, down to the beach.

They stood at the edge of the shore, the water lapping around their feet.

"Edie came to see me," Caro said. "She told me everything."

"I know," said Alik.

Caro nodded. A tear fell down her cheek as she thought about a future that didn't have Alik in it.

Alik turned her towards him and reached forward to brush it away, his thumb gently caressing her lips. "It's always been you, Caro," he said, softly. "Ever since that first night at Juju's, it's always been about you."

CHAPTER SIXTY-FOUR

Six weeks later

The Indigo Lounge was closed for a private function, but this time in happier circumstances; Caro's homecoming party.

Caro and Alik were back from Mallorca, although Caro was toying with the idea of splitting her time between The Indigo Lounge and The Roca Bar. Having spent a little time working at the bar again, she realised she missed it more than she had initially thought. She had briefly spoken to the new owners about the possibility of buying it back. But first she needed to have a long discussion with Nic about what the future held.

Alik had been in negotiations with Nate and Dev, as well as Parker. They had come to the conclusion that Blood Stone Riot should continue and they were going to start looking for a new bassist. Alik had also agreed to record some of his solo material as the band took a short hiatus, to keep momentum and interest.

Edie had lots of bridges to build, some of them easier than others. The Magpie had really taken off thanks, in part, to the introduction of a very successful maternity range and an expansion into childcare products. She had dropped out of public life for a while, choosing instead to decamp to Gramercy Lodge for a quieter pace of life. She occasionally kept in touch with Alik. She was having a baby boy and had already decided to call him Billy Junior.

Poppy and Nate were talking to Nic and Olivia about their plans for an extended honeymoon. They were looking forward to travelling around the world, with an extended stop in Australia to see Poppy's family.

Even Dev was there, with his Latvian girlfriend, Yulia. Everyone had been surprised when they realised she actually existed. It seemed the two of them were very much into each other. Dev was planning to take some time out in Latvia until they got the band back on track.

Caro headed towards the group with Poppy in it, eyeing her friend's glass suspiciously. "That doesn't look like champagne to me," she said.

Poppy grinned. "Nope, it's grapefruit juice. If I've been reading the books and magazines correctly, the advice is not to drink while you're pregnant…"

She threw her arms around Poppy. "That's amazing news! But should you really be travelling either?"

Poppy made a face. "I don't really fancy the idea of a long haul flight with morning sickness. But as I didn't see my mum on my wedding day, I think she'd probably kill me if I told her I was pregnant over the phone."

"I guess I'm organising the baby shower?"

"Too right!"

"I think this calls for a few words." Caro tapped the side of her glass and turned to the assembled group. "Ladies and gentlemen," she said. "Thank you for coming along this evening. We've been through a lot together." She glanced towards Poppy and Olivia. "But now it's time to look to the future and everything that brings." Her eyes fell on Alik and she held up her flute of champagne. "It's time for new beginnings. Cheers!"

Cocktails, Rock Tales & Betrayals

If you'd like to get an email when I release a new book or run offers or giveaways, please sign up to my newsletter http://eepurl.com/caBvF9.
I promise not to spam your inbox!

ABOUT THE AUTHOR

Julie Archer grew up in Hampshire and lived in Reading before moving to the beautiful riverside town of Dartmouth in Devon. She still feels like she's on holiday.

Julie trained as a journalist, then went into teaching (kept meeting the sixth form students in the pub, awkward!). After that she 'fell' into recruitment, spending more years there than she cares to mention, where the most creative thing she did was to create a sexy top line for job adverts! Since moving to Devon, she set up her own business offering virtual administration and recruitment services, worked for an accommodation company and is currently moonlighting in the local bookshop…

Also, COYS, Cats, Metal. Underneath this preppy exterior beats the heart of a rock chick.

https://juliearcherwrites.wordpress.com/
www.facebook.com/juliearcherwrites
www.twitter.com/julieoceanuk
juliearcherwrites@gmail.com

Julie Archer

ACKNOWLEDGEMENTS

I'm not quite sure where to begin here, this could be longer than the book!

Firstly, thanks to Charlie and Amie. Without the Six Month Novel and their help and cheerleading you wouldn't be reading this book today. If you want to write a book and don't know where to start, I highly recommend this: http://sixmonthnovel.com/

And without the Six Month Novel, I would not have got to know my wonderful chums in the Writers Playground. Thank you to Jeannie, Janet, Sarah, Yvonne and Shanthi for sharing this journey and providing lots of virtual support and advice.

Thanks to Amie McCracken and Paul Anthony Shortt for their editorial help and kicking this book into shape.

A massive thank you to the lovely Carrie Elks who has certainly paid it forward with all the invaluable advice about this whole writing and self-publishing marlarkey.

Thank you to Jennie Rawlings at Serafim for the gorgeous cover and art work, even if it did make me cry happy tears!

Finally, to my real guitar hero, aka my husband Peter, thank you for always being there.

Julie Archer

Made in the USA
Charleston, SC
12 October 2016